THE PROTECTOR
BOOK 1

EXILED

M.R. Merrick

The Protector - Book 1 - Exiled
By M.R.Merrick
© 2011 M.R. Merrick
All Rights Reserved
Copyright © 2011 – M.R. Merrick
ISBN:978-0-9877262-1-6

Cover design by M.R. Merrick

Cover artwork by Julija Lichman © 2011

For my wife,

You and me, always.

Acknowledgments

I would like to thank everyone who played a part in making this happen. First to my wife, *Cherry*, this book would not be what it is today without you. You read the story in its roughest form, and a dozen times after that. I drove you crazy with my constant revisions and late night talks of how to improve the story. You were there to help me break down the road blocks as the story progressed, and Exiled has become something so much more because of your love and support. My daughter *Peyton*, telling you bedtime stories started this entire process and I have you to thank for all of this. Without you, I never could have realized my passion for storytelling. Thanks to *Jason Pitt* at Critical-Film for his support and for writing the back cover copy for this book. Thomas Amo, you're a fabulous writer and you've been so incredible this entire process. You read my book, you supported me, and you referred me to a wonderful artist. Thank you for all your kindness. Julija Lichman, you gave my book a face. Your wonderful artwork inspired me to write better, and deliver a story worthy of such art, and for that, I am grateful.

To all of you, from the bottom of my heart, thank you.

Chapter 1

I dodged the razor sharp claws coming towards me and turned to face the demon. I'd hurt him enough to force him to shift, but now I had to fight a bear, literally.

He stood on his hind legs with his back to me and I took the opportunity presented, unsure if I'd get another. I leapt onto his back and stuck one silver dagger into each shoulder. He roared in pain and anger as the blades pierced his furry flesh, and reacted with a flurry of quick movements that threw me from his back. I fought to keep hold of one dagger as I hit the pavement, while the other remained stuck in his shoulder.

The pitted asphalt burned and tore at my skin as I slid across it. The ground rumbled as the black bear stormed towards me. I jumped to my feet, but not in time to get out of the way. Its head collided with my stomach at full speed and smashed me into the crumbling brick building behind me.

Black dots filled my vision as the wall broke at my impact, showering me with loose bricks and pieces of mortar. I shook my head to clear my vision and wrapped my scarred fingers around the blade jutting from his shoulder. As I twisted my wrist, there came a bone-chilling screech from his toothy snout. Roaring in agony, the demon stood and hauled my body from the ground, leaving me flailing over his head as I struggled to hold on to the dagger.

I wrapped my legs around its neck while it shook from side to side with an unnatural speed, trying to dislodge me. The world blurred around me, but from behind his head, I forced the blade to his throat and pulled. The demon grunted as the blade split skin. Hot blood pumped over my hand but I didn't hesitate. The violent movements slowed and a deep gurgling sound escaped from the bear's throat. The smell of burning meat started to fill the air, and I pulled until I hit the spine. I'd sliced through the flesh; next came the hard part.

I planted both feet against the bear's back and pushed hard to help pull the blade through its spine. The bone gave under the pressure and I tumbled to the pavement as the dagger went all the way through. The creature stumbled forward, the grotesque head rolling off the shoulders. Its body started falling, and soon both it and the head were engulfed in flames and burned to ash.

I stayed on the ground as the air my lungs craved rushed into them in waves. This had been the third attempt on my life in two weeks, and I couldn't count how many there had been in the last three years. No matter how many times I survived, there was always another danger around the corner, and I still wasn't used to being the victim. I was Chase Williams, a demon hunter. I wasn't supposed to be the one looking over my shoulder; I was supposed to be stalking the prey.

I winced in pain as I lifted myself from the pavement, and brushed ash off my clothes and skin. I had to find a new way home; the demons had gotten all too familiar with this one.

The usual disappointment filled me as I approached my apartment. Broken windows and trash-littered patios were a sad sight to come home to. The broken hand rail shook and the stairs squeaked with each step. Fresh graffiti decorated the landing and I had to use my finger to open the door, which lacked a knob. All that aside, I was relieved to have made it home in one piece. Even if it required standing in the discolored, low pressure water from my shower for an hour, this blood would wash off, and I'd live to see another day.

I stood in the shower until the water turned cold before I gave in to my body's demand for rest and went to my bedroom. I took in the mattress on the floor, the scratched and faded dresser, and the wobbly lamp with a sigh. It wasn't much, but it was mine.

I fell onto the bed and relief washed over me. My body was consumed by pain that for anyone else would be even worse the next day, but not for me. I knew the scratches would fade, the scabs would heal, and the throbbing ache of having been thrown into a brick wall would be gone. By tomorrow I'd be good as new: one of the few perks to being a hunter.

I stared up at the cracked ceiling as muffled angry voices leaked through the wall. The sound of breaking glass and swearing followed as the neighbors started their nightly routine, which had become my lullaby. Their screaming pushed my body towards sleep, and as sleep approached the screaming faded. Darkness tugged at my eyes and I couldn't fight it. I gave into my body's urge for rest and fell into the dreamscape.

Chapter 2

"Happy birthday Chase! Ready for your big day?" my mom said.

"Of course I'm ready," I replied, the excited smile fixed on my face. This was the day I'd been awaiting for so many years. All the training, books and lectures were done. Today I was going to become one of them: a hunter.

"I'm so proud of you. No matter what happens today, I want you to know that." My mom's eyes were welling up with tears; she was always emotional with me.

"I know."

"Chase, the ceremony starts in a few hours. Why aren't you training?" my dad said. I hadn't heard him walk into the room. *"Dammit, Tessa stop babying him! He needs to concentrate. It's an important day."*

My mom held back the tears that wanted to fall. *"Of course, Riley. You're right,"* she said and slipped out of the room.

My stomach clenched as my father came closer. *"You should be training Chase. Just because it's your birthday doesn't mean you can be slacking off. I don't want you embarrassing me out there."*

"Yeah, Dad, I know."

"Excuse me?" He glared at me with the severe expression that dominated his face so often.

I cleared my throat and stood up straight. *"I mean, yes sir,"* I said. His pale blue eyes regarded me and he nodded. He left the room and I released the breath I was holding.

Everything around me faded, and I was standing at the entryway of the ceremony hall. The room looked bigger than I remembered. I entered slowly and my steps echoed around me.

Six whitewashed stone pillars held up the ceiling and matched the walls, making them seem to fade in and out of view.

I moved past the faces I'd trained with for years, getting closer to the altar. The muscles in my abdomen tightened with nervousness and the sweat on my palms threatened to drip. At first I feared I'd trip on the first step and embarrass myself, but as I conquered it, the fear changed its focus to the ceremony. What if I don't get a good power? If I don't get the fire element like my father, will he be disappointed? I swallowed these thoughts and ascended the last steps.

The elder members were dressed in long white robes with golden sashes. Each of their faces displayed only a neutral expression. I stepped into the center of the altar and dipped my hands into the large stone bowl. The still-warm viscous liquid coated my fingers and palms. The blood looked black sitting in the bowl, but became bright red as I pulled my hands from it.

The elders chanted in the ancient language nobody else was permitted to understand. I moved around the altar and placed a bloody handprint on each of the six pillars. Drops of blood slid down the white stone; the blood came from the demon I had killed earlier, and it was the blood I needed to spark the birth of my elemental power.

After leaving my mark on the pillars, I returned to the center. The chief elder moved towards me and dipped his fingers into the bowl. He used the blood to draw a symbol on my forehead. I couldn't see it, but I knew what it meant. "Chase Williams, you have completed the prerequisites for the ceremony. You have been anointed with the blood of your enemy. Now is the time you discover your place among us," he intoned.

Each elder brought a stone into the center and set them in a circle around me. Each stone was engraved with a glyph to represent one of the elements. I moved to the first stone and reached my bloodstained hand over it. I called to my magic and recited the phrase I'd been taught. "The blood of my enemy shall be the birth of my power. The birth of my power cements my soul to the Circle." I spoke with intensity and confidence. I waited, eyes closed, reaching deep inside myself to pull magic from within.

I repeated the phrase as I moved over each stone, letting a drop of blood stain it. One should react and reveal my element, but nothing happened each time I repeated the words.

Muffled voices reached me from the pews where other Circle members watched, but I wasn't worried. I moved my hand over the final stone, the one I'd saved for last: the stone representing the fire element. I recited the words a final time, expecting the stone to burst into flames. But there wasn't even a spark.

The voices got louder and I opened my eyes. The elders' neutral expressions had changed, some to surprise, others to disgust. I recited the phrase again but the chief elder interrupted me.

"Enough. Take him to the containment room," he commanded.

"Wait, what?" I sputtered as two hunters grabbed my arms and dragged me from the altar. "Dad, what's going on?" I shouted. My pulse jumped into my throat and panic filled my voice. "Dad?" I shrieked, before everything disappeared around me.

The containment room was bright with fluorescent lights, but the sight I wanted to avoid was my father's eyes. "I can't believe you. You're disgusting," he said. He slammed his hand on the table between us.

"Riley, that's enough," Mom said.

"You stay out of this," he replied, not turning to look at her. His gaze was locked on me, but he seemed to see me like an object. "This is impossible. My own son has no powers!" He kicked the table onto its side so there was nothing between us.

"Dad, I did everything you told me," I said. He took the final step and closed the distance. He pushed his nose against mine and his magic pulsed against my skin in a burning wave.

"Don't blame me for your failure." He poked his finger into my chest.

"Get your hands off of him," Mom said, pulling at his arm.

My father let my mother pull him back and smoke rose from the hole he'd created in my shirt, but the anger in his eyes was what burned a permanent scar. He turned in an instant and a stream of flame exploded from his hand. The flame coursed and crackled over the table, which ignited as my father stormed from the room. I winced as the door slammed and glowing embers showered from the table.

My mother stepped towards it, shaking her head. I felt her magic come to life around me as a small ball of light grew in her hands. The light disappeared and a burst of water appeared, dousing the flames. The room grew hazy as it filled with smoke and steam, and I struggled not to cough.

Her water smothered the flames and I watched as her magic faded. She approached me, not speaking, with smoke billowing around her. She wrapped her arms around me and her magic swelled again, not as a wave of water, but as a rush of calming energy that coursed through me. Maybe she could do this because she was a water elemental, but I think it was mostly because she was a mother.

"What's going to happen?" I asked.

She pulled back and cupped my face, forcing me to meet her bright hazel eyes.

"I don't know, but whatever it is, we will get through it together. You and me, always," she said.

I tried to smile but failed. Darkness engulfed me and the room also faded, but the taste of smoke was still thick and burned in my throat.

I stood before the council and the elders stared down at me from their high oak benches. Their faces were again composed with blank but somewhat disapproving expressions.

"We've taken into consideration today's events, and given your father's exceptional history within the Circle, we can only agree with his proposal," the chief elder said.

The fear and the weight I felt on my shoulders vanished. As angry as he was, he still fought for me.

"The council has discussed the situation and we are unanimous in our decision. You will be given a small amount of funds, as well as fifteen minutes at the completion of this hearing to pack your belongings. Any books or weapons in your possession will be confiscated and you will be escorted off the property. You are not to return, nor are you to have contact with anyone within this association. From this point forward, you are not to be counted among the Circle. Instead, you will continue your life outside the Circle as a mortal. Should you fail to comply with this decision, you will be dealt with accordingly." The elder's voice swirled around me and my shoulders bent as all the fear crashed back over me.

"Dad?" I said. My knees gave out and I collapsed to the floor.

He wore his proud, arrogant smirk now. "You are no son of mine," he said.

"Riley Williams," Mom demanded, firmly but with a hint of desperation. "You can't do this."

Riley shook his head. "It has been done Tessa. It's for the good of the Circle."

"Tessa Williams..." the elder continued.

"I will not stand for this!" Mom said, ignoring him.

"This is not your decision, it is the decision of the Circle and our word is final." The elder finally gave way to anger.

"Well, the Circle is making a terrible decision. How can you send him away like this? He's just a boy."

"We are not sending him alone. You, Tessa Williams, are also found guilty," the elder pronounced.

"Guilty? Guilty of what?"

"There is only one way a hunter births a child who has no powers. That is if the child has only one gifted parent, and..."

"How dare you!" Mom interrupted, but the elder raised his hand.

"You have committed the ultimate crime. You have risked exposing the Circle to the mortals and disrespected your husband in an unbecoming manner. This ruling is the will of the council, and so shall it be. This meeting is adjourned."

A film came over my vision and I couldn't see the expression on my mother's face. The tap of shoes on the marble floor moved towards me and her small hands wrapped around my waist and pulled me to my feet.

I shot up in my bed, beads of sweat falling from my face and covering my chest. I couldn't see anything until my eyes adjusted to the darkness.

The room was silent, except for my own heavy breathing. My pulse pounded in my throat as if trying to escape while I tried to shake the remnants of the dream from my mind.

The scenes were the same every time, just flashes of that day. No matter how hard I tried, I couldn't escape it. Going back to sleep wasn't an option; I knew I would fall back into the nightmare. I peeled the sweat-covered sheets off my body and headed for the shower to try to wash the dream away.

Chapter 3

I wiped a streak through the grime on the mirror. Wet blond hair stuck to my forehead and the dark blue eyes that stared back at me were different than those I remembered from my youth. It'd been almost three years since we'd been exiled from the Circle, and I wasn't sure I recognized the person in the mirror now.

I shook that thought away and pushed away from the sink. It was five in the morning; going back to bed was pointless, and I was hungry. My mom was already awake. She was a vision of beauty sitting at the kitchen table with a book in her hand. She didn't have to try to draw people to her, with those warm hazel eyes that could engulf you and somehow assure you that everything would be alright. She was petite with a slender build, but I knew the strength she carried. Her dark brown hair was shoulder length and always falling in her eyes, but there were no hints of gray yet, which was impressive given the stress of the past three years.

"You couldn't sleep either?"

"No," I admitted.

She moved towards me, reached up on her tiptoes and kissed my forehead. "Well, I guess if we're both awake we might as well have breakfast together. It's been too long." She started to gather eggs, a frying pan, and other essentials. "How about French toast?" she said. She knew it was my favorite.

"French toast sounds great, Mom."

She puttered about the kitchen. "So your birthday's coming up, the big eighteen. Do you have any idea what you want?"

I shook my head. "You shouldn't get me anything and you know that. We don't have the money anyway. I'd rather just not think about it.

She stopped and turned to me. "I'll be damned if you're going to have a birthday and not celebrate it. We'll make it work."

"You always do, but no matter how many good birthdays I have, they'll never make up for the bad one."

My mom sighed. "Chase. Riley. Williams."

"Yes?" I replied innocently.

"This is our life now. I don't regret what happened and neither should you."

"Mom, things could be better for you if I..." I loved my mother, but sometimes I hated that she couldn't admit our life was better in the Circle.

"Chase, my life in the Circle was a lifetime ago, and I don't miss it."

"Not even a little?"

"No, and you're old enough now to know that your father and I hadn't seen things the same way for a long time."

That caught me off guard and my first instinct was to defend my dad somehow, but he didn't deserve that. Mom was trying to share something with me and I didn't want to stop her from treating me like an adult.

"What do you mean?"

"You've always known your father is a fire elemental and I'm water. They're opposing forces of nature. My magic is for healing, and his element holds nothing but destructive power. Being polar opposites may be why we fell in love, but we couldn't sustain it. Your father was always a proud and arrogant man, and so hard on you. Nothing you did was ever good enough, and granted, that's part of the reason you are so good. You never stopped trying to impress him. It might be hard to believe, but once upon a time he was gentle, sweet, and kind. He wanted us to be one happy family. Then one day, something changed."

"What?"

She shrugged. "I don't know for sure. His power controlled him, and he became obsessed with you being his legacy, instead of his child. As much as you miss your old life, you need to understand exile is for the best for both of us."

"It's just hard to see that sometimes."

"I know you have to bear the burden of being Riley Williams' son, and that's not fair. You've never been able to relax since the Underworld wants to kill you just for being his son. None of this is something a normal seventeen-year-old has to deal with, but hunters are never normal," she said with a smirk.

"Yeah, try telling the Circle that," I said.

Mom shook her head. "We don't need the Circle, Chase. We don't need their help. We don't need their money and we don't need their problems."

Maybe Mom was right, but I wanted to be fighting the good fight, not fighting to survive. We could make ends meet without its help, but sometimes I missed the support the Circle could provide, and without their funding, Mom and I worked full-time just to pay the bills. Mom worked in a rehabilitation center, a worthy employer that didn't exactly make or pay a fortune. She enjoyed the work, but she couldn't use her element in the open. Mom's powers were useful, but people fear what they don't understand.

So this was our life trying to be normal. I wasn't sure why, but attacks on my mom were rare, while for me they were the most dependable thing I had in my life besides her.

"Any plans for the day?" Mom said, as the smell of French toast filled the room.

"No, I work tonight."

"I know you feel it's your responsibility, Chase, but you don't have to take so many shifts. You have enough on your plate dealing with the Underworld without worrying about paying the bills."

I grinned and gave her the reassuring words she always left with me. "Mom, we're in this together. You and me, always."

Her eyes welled up with tears and I wrapped my arms around her. She hugged me back and the calm feeling from my dream washed over me again.

"Mom?" I eyed the smoking frying pan. She didn't answer. "Mom, I think you're burning it."

She jumped up, not wiping the single tear that trailed down her face, and attacked the frying pan with the spatula. Neither of us could help but laugh.

Chapter 4

I'd had several jobs in the past year. This one I'd managed to keep for a few months. Most of my employers frowned on me coming to work with cuts and bruises all the time. It made for "poor presentation," they'd say. I was thankful it hadn't interfered with this job, yet.

I finished up my shift and had started my walk home from the burger joint when I felt it. A hunter doesn't mistake the feeling that demons are around. It moves down your spine and chills your bones. Feeling it proved I was indeed a hunter, even without an element.

The August air was warm for the late hour, and a thick layer of sweat made my white shirt cling to me. I stopped and unzipped my duffle bag, locating the silver dagger inside. Silver was great no matter what you were fighting; it could do serious damage to anything of the Underworld.

The tingle shot down my spine again. If I focused, I could feel each hair on my neck rise. I saw a blur of movement across the street and watched it disappear into a shadowy alley. I moved across the street in a low crouch, resting my weight on the balls of my feet. I slowed my breathing and pulled the dagger from my bag before I slipped around the corner.

My senses were alive and strained to see movement, or hear the sound of feet shuffling against loose rocks. As a hunter, I could see well in the dark, though the only light came from a single flickering street lamp.

I was almost to the end of the alley when it hit. I couldn't tell what "it" was, but it struck my back and launched me forward. My feet tumbled over my head and my back smashed hard into the concrete wall at the end of the alley. Hands grabbed me and lifted me to my feet, dragging me a few steps before throwing me back the other way. I flew through the air, hit the ground and rolled out into the street.

I used my momentum and came up on one knee to recover. My back burned where pavement had grated the skin off, but I pushed the pain aside as the figure stalked towards me.

"Your death will bring me great glory, hunter. Killing the son of Riley Williams will make me a legend among the Underworld," the low voice gloated.

"That's really great, good luck with that," I said.

He smiled and the fangs that slid down from his gums were long and sharp. His pale skin started to thin as the vampire changed into his demon form.

Milky skin faded into transparent flesh, revealing the moving muscles beneath. Veins ran black through the vampire's face and limbs, pushing against the thinning clear skin. Strange muscles in his hands pushed bony talons out over his finger nails, and the whites of his eyes disappeared, filling with an inky blackness. The dark orbs stared at me as his fanged mouth curled into a smile, and in a blur he sprang forward, talons swinging.

I ducked as they sliced through the air over my head. I brought the knife up into his stomach and twisted the blade before I pulled it out. Blood spilled onto the ground, but I knew the wound wasn't enough to kill him. Cut off his head or pierce his black heart – those were my options. I *could* light him on fire, but I was fresh out of matches.

I brought my foot up and kicked the vampire back to give myself some room. I steadied myself, waiting for him to charge, but his body jerked and the point of a silver blade appeared in his chest before he could move.

The vamp's body went limp and collapsed, then exploded in a flash of orange light. It burned away into a cloud of ash and littered the pavement, revealing the girl – of all things – who had beaten me to the kill.

Raven hair spilled over her pale shoulders with hints of red highlighting the occasional strand. A tight leather top revealed a sliver of toned stomach and a tease of cleavage. Black pants hugged her hips and long slender legs and met knee-high boots.

Her skin glistened in the light, but the most noticeable of her features were her eyes.

Bright green orbs sparkled with an odd glow: demon's eyes. They had the slit pupils of a cat that I'd never seen on anything other than a house pet or a shifter in animal form. I slipped back into fight mode. I'd never watched one demon kill another, but I suppose for the fame of killing me, why not?

I lunged and threw a punch at her face, but she dodged it with ease.

"You almost messed up my kill," she snarled, and I had barely enough time to dodge her powerful kick.

"Your kill? You stole it from me!" I swung my fist and hit her stomach. She bent over, winded, before she stepped back and caught her breath, regaining her stance and composure.

"Stole it? Please, I'd been tracking him for blocks." She spun and caught my chin with the heel of her boot, snapping my head to the side. I rubbed my jaw where she'd hit me and smiled.

"Well then, I guess it's a good thing I was here to slow him down. Who knows if you would have been able to catch him?"

She moved in for another kick but I was ready. I grabbed her foot and pushed her back. She fell to the ground but quickly came to her feet. "I would have gotten him just fine on my own. Hunting is an art. It would've gone on as long as I deemed necessary."

"Call it hunting if you want, but a filthy demon killing her own kind is still just that: a filthy demon." I could tell I'd offended her even before she hit me.

My eyes watered when her fist smashed into my nose and her foot connected with my stomach in quick succession. I jerked back to avoid the knee that flew towards my face and pushed it to the side, but she was already moving towards me. Her hands hit my chest hard and I soared through the air for a long moment before I hit the ground. I felt a sharp pain shoot up through my spine and I could hear her laughter as I struggled to my feet.

"I have to admit I expected more from you, Chase, being the infamous son of Riley Williams and all."

I gripped my dagger until my knuckles turned white and spoke through gritted teeth. "I'll try not to disappoint."

My fist hit her jawbone and made a loud crack. I came back with my other hand and wrapped it around her throat. I stepped into the movement and threw her forward in a burst of hunter's strength. She slammed into the ground but recovered faster than I anticipated. Before I could brace myself she was on top of me.

I pulled her body down and we rolled over each other against the cold concrete until I was on top. I kept a handful of her hair wound tight in my fist and pushed my blade against her throat.

"More what you expected?"

"Not really." She smirked.

I felt the point of a knife pushing against my stomach. Before I could react, a commanding male voice came from behind us.

"Enough!" it boomed.

I didn't take the knife or my eyes off the demon beneath me.

"But we were just starting to have fun," she complained. The smile on her face was anything but threatening. If this was her idea of fun, I didn't want to know what she considered boring.

"Rayna, enough," the man repeated.

She sighed, sticking out her bottom lip in a pout before the knife left my skin. "Truce?" she said with an innocent face.

"Not a chance," I replied, pushing the knife harder against her throat.

I was pulled away from Rayna and pressed against a wall, thick hands around my throat. I raised my blade but my opponent blocked and twisted my arm at an awkward angle. The man ripped the blade from my hand and I squirmed.

"Calm down, Chase. We are not here to hurt you," the voice said. A complete shadow hung around the figure, moving as he moved.

"So she attacked me for fun?" I snapped.

"If we wanted you dead, you would be," he said, releasing his grip, and I fell to the sidewalk. He stepped back slowly and the shadow peeled itself from his body. As it faded, it revealed a large man whose magic I'd never sensed before.

"If you don't want to kill me, what do you want?" I asked.

The man reached forward, a large dark arm holding out my dagger. I wrapped my hand around it in confusion. The contrast of our skin was drastic; my pale flesh glowed against his midnight color and the size of his hand alone made me feel small.

"What Rayna told you was true. We were tracking the vampire, not you. Although I'm happy to finally meet you, I'd imagined this moment under different circumstances," he said.

"There are ways to meet people besides attacking them."

"I agree. You must forgive us; Rayna is quick to lash out when insulted." My eyes met his and I couldn't read his expression. I knew I hadn't been polite, but I wasn't about to apologize to a demon. "You know, your father would not have hesitated to kill her, no matter his position."

"Congratulations, you've discovered I'm not my father. What the hell would you know about him anyways?"

He turned his head to the side and as the light hit his neck it revealed a tattoo. It was the one every hunter received after their ceremony. The one I never got.

The tattoo made me realize why he could bend the shadows; he was an air elemental and a powerful one at that. I had heard stories of hunters being able to work with shadows, but I'd never seen it done firsthand.

I looked him over, not sure what to think of a hunter working with a demon. He was taller than me by an inch, around six-foot three. His head was smooth shaven, though there was a small patch of hair under his lower lip. His skin seemed like a smooth dark chocolate. His body was large and square, broad shoulders making him a massive column of strength and power. He filled out a sharp black suit jacket and wore black loafers, leaving the only color on him a flash of bright blue dress shirt.

"You're a hunter."

"Once upon a time, yes I was."

He broke eye contact and cleared his throat, extending his massive hand towards me. "Look at my manners. Let me introduce myself. I am Marcus Starkraven."

My eyebrows shot up; I knew that name! "You're supposed to be dead."

"Is that what you heard?"

"You used to hunt with my father."

He nodded slightly, but otherwise ignored the comment.

"You already met Rayna," he said, taking his unshaken hand back.

I looked at Rayna and got caught in the depths of her green, slit eyes.

"What are you doing with a demon?" I said, spitting out the last word like a curse.

"How's your nose?" Rayna asked.

I touched it and looked at the blood on my fingers. "Lucky shot."

She chuckled and stepped towards me. "Care to go again?" Marcus put an arm in front of her.

"Not what we're doing right now," he said.

"You didn't answer my question."

"She is my student. And my friend."

I couldn't respond. I didn't believe it. A hunter being friends with a demon was unfathomable.

"I would have thought, being out in the real world, you'd have come to understand, Chase. Some Underworlders don't fit the Circle's black and white image of good and evil," he said.

"The only Underworlders I've come across have tried to kill me."

"Your name is feared by many in the Underworld. Your father has created quite the reputation for himself, so they fear you as well," Marcus said.

I smirked. "As they should."

He shook his head. "That wasn't a compliment. You will come to learn that the Circle is not pure good nor the Underworld all evil. There are those who belong to the Underworld, such as Rayna, who have no use for the needless killing you associate with demons. There are also those in the Circle whose intentions are not completely honorable. There is something of human frailty in all of us."

"You can't be Marcus Starkraven. He was a good man who believed in the Circle."

"Did you ever meet this Marcus?" he asked.

21

Marcus had hunted with my father when I was little, but I'd never met him. I looked back to him and shook my head.

"Then do not presume to know what I was like. Now, as always, I still believe in the cause of protecting the innocent. As for the Circle, a person in your position shouldn't be defending them after what they did to you."

"What would you know about what happened to me?"

Marcus shrugged. "I know a great deal about you, and the Circle. The Circle is not all it's made out to be, Chase. When I learned that, I found other ways of fighting the battle." He looked at Rayna.

"And what are you, anyway?" I asked her. "I've never met a shifter that could change only their eyes."

"Obviously you haven't put much time into learning anything about Underworlders, except for how to kill them," she said.

"There is more to Rayna than you see in her eyes. I wouldn't suggest you presume anything about her either."

"What..." I began, but Rayna cut me off.

"Hey boys, we'll have to save twenty questions for later. We're about to be very busy."

Before I could ask, I felt the telltale shiver move down my spine. A silhouette atop one of the buildings caught my eye. I adjusted my grip on the dagger as two more figures joined the one on the roof. Together they leapt off the building, seeming to float to the ground, landing silently and with the utmost grace. Three more vampires emerged from the shadows behind us, their clear skin and descended fangs reflecting the dim moonlight.

"You're gonna pay for that, bitch. You think you can get away with knocking us off one by one?" one of the vamps growled.

"Well, I was kinda hoping," Rayna shrugged.

"And hey, look at this. It's a three for one deal. Revenge on the demon who kills her own kind, and a side dish of hunter too."

The vampire jumped towards us and the others followed his lead, attacking from all sides. I brought my blade up and pushed it through the first vampire's chest. His skin cracked in an instant and in a flash of exploding light, his body turned to ash that disappeared in the wind.

Rayna and Marcus fended off the demons from the first group while two more jumped me, pushing me to my knees, their talons digging into my back. The pain was sharp, but their weight suddenly vanished.

Marcus stood beside me, his hand extended and the vampires floating in the air in front of him. He swung his arm and the bodies moved through the air, hitting a brick building and sliding to the ground. Marcus nodded to me and moved on to another demon.

The two vampires pulled themselves up and moved with supernatural speed. I ducked the first as his talons swung near my face. I brought my blade around and plunged it deep into his chest. As I was showered with ashes, I turned to face the second vamp, but his talons were already coming at me. They sliced my cheek, and the power in his strike forced me to the ground. Blood flowed over my lips and I sputtered as the demon fell on me.

He pinned my arms down as he leaned down and licked a stream of blood from my face with a pale pink tongue. Saliva dripped from his polished white fangs onto my skin, sliding down over my neck. I grimaced and pitted his strength against mine, but as he tried to get closer to my throat, I knew I was losing the advantage.

Suddenly, Rayna appeared above us. She landed on the vampire's back and her weight pushed him against me. I felt the tip of his fangs press into my neck, but the vampire's body lit up and a wash of heat covered me before they pierced my skin.

Rayna fell through the shower of ash and landed on top of me. She was straddling me and the stake pushed against my chest. We stared at each other for a moment. I hadn't been expecting help from a demon.

"You're welcome," she said, with an arched brow and a smile.

"I had it covered."

"Sure you did," she laughed.

"Get off me," I said, pushing her to the side.

She rolled her eyes and jumped to her feet, going to stand beside Marcus.

"Well, I think that's enough excitement for one night," Marcus announced.

"Yeah, I'd say so," I agreed, brushing the black and white ash off my clothes.

"Are you alright?" Marcus pointed to my face.

I reached up to touch the tears in my flesh. They were deep cuts, but they would heal quickly enough on their own.

"Yeah, of course," I said with all the confidence I could muster. "Now, answer my questions," I demanded.

Marcus eyed me and shook his head "It's late; there will be time for answers later. Should you be interested, I'd like a chance to talk further with you. You can find us at this address." He pulled a notepad from his pocket and scrawled something on a blank page, ripped it off, and held it out. I stared at it a moment before taking it. "I think we could help each other," he added.

"Is that so?"

"I hope you'll consider this offer. I give you my word it's a friendly one."

He and I both knew when a hunter gave his word it was his bond. You never gave your word unless you could keep it.

"We'll see."

Marcus nodded and I watched them walk away down the alley, their footsteps silent as the shadows slowly made them disappear.

I looked at the paper Marcus had given me. *2151 51st St. Suite 404*, it read. That was a few miles from my place, and in the nice part of downtown. In this city, it wasn't far from the slums I lived in to the high-class white-collar neighborhood. This address had dollar signs written all over it.

I spent the remainder of my walk trying to wrap my head around what just happened. What was Rayna, anyway? She was killing demons, which made it seem like she was one of the good guys, but I'd never had a demon help my cause before. And why was a famous hunter letting the Circle think he was dead and associating himself with Underworlders? He said the Circle wasn't everything it was made out to be, but I didn't know what that meant. Nothing he said made sense.

Exiled

When I reached the rundown building I called home, I was just thankful to have made it there alive again. My head hurt with all the new thoughts and questions I had, or maybe I had just been hurt worse than I'd thought. I needed sleep, but I smelled like blood and deep fryer oil. Although I knew what would happen when I went to sleep, I didn't care. After the night I'd just had, not thinking for a few hours would be welcome, even if it meant a nightmare.

Chapter 5

I lay awake in bed with the alarm clock showing quarter after seven – an unholy hour to be awake on a day off – when I heard the lock sliding out of place on the front door. Mom was home from work.

I sat on the edge of my bed for a few minutes and tried to decide if I should mention last night's events to her, but I couldn't make up my mind what was best, so I pushed the thought away.

Mom sat in the kitchen with a fresh cup of tea, plucking the tea bag in and out of the cup. She was staring at a stack of bills and looked as tired as always after a night shift.

"Long night?" I asked.

She looked up at me and her eyes opened wide with panic. "Oh gods, Chase! What happened?"

She rushed towards me. She gently turned my head from side to side as she looked me over. I'd forgotten I still had gashes and blood all over my face.

I forced a smile and pulled her hands away from my face. "It's okay, Mom. I'm fine. I ran into a few demons last night. It's nothing."

"You look awful!"

"I'm really fine," I assured her. I pushed away from her and went to the table and pulled two of the bills out of the pile and put the rest back. "I already paid these ones."

The look on her face was both loving and sad. "You're too young to have these troubles." She tried unsuccessfully to smile.

"We're in this together, Mom. Stop worrying so much about me."

"It's my job to worry. I'm your mother. Now, let me see these," she said, tracing her finger near the claw marks on my face.

"No Mom, they'll heal fast enough on their own," I said, but it was too late.

I felt the rush of cool water running over my wounds. It hurt for a moment before a tingle moved over my face. Her magic slid through my body and goose bumps ran up my arms. The skin pulled itself over my face, knitting itself closed over the deep wounds. The feeling of water washed over my whole body for an instant before receding.

I touched the freshly healed skin and smiled. "Thanks."

"You're welcome," she said and kissed the top of my head. "Now I need to get some sleep and you need a shower. You smell like fries." She ruffled my hair and left the room.

The smell from last night had indeed gotten worse, so I took her advice. After half an hour under the water I'd finally gotten the smell out.

There were a lot of problems with living in the slums. I could deal with the noisy neighbors. I could handle the random gunshots during the night, but the lack of water pressure was at the top of my list of complaints. This was clearly a sign my life wasn't normal.

I stopped in front of the mirror to take a look at the damage. My mother's magic had made the bruises disappear, but the dark circles around my eyes were something her magic couldn't fix. The scrape on my forehead was gone and all that remained was a light red scar. My nose was still tender from its encounter with Rayna's fist, but the claw marks along the side of my face had healed completely.

Hunters were quick healers in the first place, and all these wounds would have been gone in a few days, but Mom's magic brought it to a whole different level. I had to admit she did nice work.

I put on a pair of jeans, a long sleeved dark green shirt and a pair of black sneakers. After slipping on a holster with sheaths for my daggers around my waist, I was ready to go.

I was trying to wrap my head around the idea that there were Underworlders out there that weren't completely evil, but though Rayna had saved my life, I was still having trouble with it.

After years of being told one thing, it made it hard to believe otherwise, and the last three years of being subjected to the Underworld's attacks didn't help.

More astonishing than her saving me, Rayna hadn't tried to kill me. Now that was a twist I never saw coming. Although we fought, I couldn't help but wonder: if I hadn't jumped at the chance to attack her, would my nose still be aching?

Considering all the strange things Marcus had said, I figured it might not hurt to stop by that address. It would give me a chance to see what they were all about; plus, I had a strange urge to know more about Rayna. If there were people who could be trusted, I was interested. A hunter on my side would be great, but about the demon, I wasn't so sure. She might have been helpful once the night before, but I didn't want to get ahead of myself.

Chapter 6

The clouds were gray and gloomy, and the air was moist. I loved the scent of the air before a storm. Stonewall was famous for two things: the summer storms, and its namesake stone wall that encircled the entire city. It had been built sometime in the seventeenth century to keep out the demons of the forests, or so the legend goes. I wasn't sure how a three foot high wall was supposed to keep anything dangerous away, but who was I to judge history?

I'd lived in Stonewall all my life. With a population of a few hundred thousand, it still had a small town feel to it with all the benefits of a large city. The Circle's headquarters was just outside of town, so I'd only lived inside the wall these last few years, but I'd never been anywhere else before.

The buildings in my area were all run down, their red brick abused with graffiti. Boarded up windows and burnt out neon signs decorated the once-thriving but now forgotten landscape.

Homemade candy stores, classic barber shops, and family owned bakeries with secret recipes for funnel cake once drew people from all walks of life. Old town folklore and legends had kept tourists coming in the hope that they might see something supernatural, but interest in myths faded as years went on and the city grew larger. The remnants of what once was had faded, and all that remained were a few broken streets in the center of a thriving city.

The new sector of downtown was another world. Tall modern buildings reflected the sun all day from the bottom floor to the top. Coffee shops occupying every corner had people bustling in and out at all hours. This was the new heart of Stonewall.

The sun wasn't shining today and every other person had an umbrella in hand. They too knew a storm was coming.

I reached Marcus's just as the rain started to fall. The building was a prism of dark glass reaching into the sky and I took cover from the rain under a canopy that stretched off the entrance.

A few steps led to the buzzer panel and I searched for 404. Many of the suites had names beside them, but I wasn't surprised 404 was only labeled *occupied*.

I stared at the button. I'd walked here with every intention of pushing it, but now I was having second thoughts. I slid my hands into my pockets and tried to figure out what I would say, but my thoughts were interrupted.

"You actually have to push the button for anybody to let you in." Down the steps was Rayna, staring up at me

"I know how it works. What are you doing here?"

"Umm, I live here."

"Right." I didn't know what else to say.

Her eyes were the remarkable green I remembered. Her hair was wet and strands of black and red stuck to her pale face. She was wearing a body-hugging black t-shirt and tight dark jeans.

"Eww. Stop staring at me," she said.

"I wasn't, I was just..."

"Move it," she demanded.

She pushed past me with a bag in one hand and a coffee tray in the other. Fumbling with the keys, she tried to unlock the door. I watched her struggle until she dropped them and I couldn't help but laugh.

"Shit," she said.

"Need some help?"

"Don't look so pleased," she snarled.

I unlocked the door and opened it for her, which only earned me a glare with a side of eye rolling.

In the building's lobby, a large marble fountain spouted water into the pond that was home to several different breeds of fish. The fountain's stone matched the tiled floor, an off-white smeared with black.

I wondered how much someone had spent on the array of modern art that didn't look like anything but daubs of paint and twists of wire. Huge plants hung from the ceiling, draping themselves over each other, some long enough to meet the colorful potted flowers below. The ding of the elevator doors sounded as I admired the apparent wealth.

"You coming, or are you going to start picking flowers and singing?" Rayna asked.

I took another quick glance around the room and made my way to the elevator.

"Quite the place," I said, but Rayna's response consisted only of her rolling her eyes, again.

The fourth floor might not sound very high up, but it turned out the condos were all three stories, like houses piled on top of each other. Rayna led me to a corner suite with a huge white door, turned the handle and went in.

The far wall was nothing but windows and the room was split into two parts. The kitchen and dining area was filled with dark oak cabinets and the counter tops matched the marble in the lobby. I stared with envy at the other room, which was dominated by a black leather living room set and a large flat screen TV that hung over the fireplace.

There was one large painting in the room with a thick brown frame that wrapped around the canvas. The war scene displayed a group of dark armored warriors and an army clothed in silver. Black wings adorned the backs on the first faction, and their enemies had white ones; the wings wrapped themselves around the fighters as they battled. The picture looked antique and out of place.

I turned as Rayna reappeared at the top of the staircase with Marcus trailing behind. He moved with the grace of a man half his size and I'd underestimated just how big he was. His dark skin melted into a plain gray hoodie and black pants, both of which he filled out fully.

"I wasn't sure you'd come," Marcus said with a perfect white smile. He extended his hand towards me and although I didn't return the smile, I did shake it this time. His grip was solid and his skin calloused and rough. It was the hand of a hunter used to holding a weapon. My father's felt the same way.

"I don't know why I came…" I said. I'd come to get answers, but at the moment I couldn't think of the right questions.

"Well, I'm glad you did," he said.

He offered me a seat on the couch and I took it, the plush leather molding itself around me. Rayna was taking fast food out of the brown bag while Marcus picked up one of the coffees.

"Would you like anything?" he offered.

"No, I'm fine."

He nodded and took a sip of the coffee and made a disgusted face. "Half coffee, half sugar; that must be yours." He slid the cup to Rayna.

He reached for the other cup and Rayna laughed. Her laughter was warm and soft. I realized they really were friends, but it didn't seem right to me.

Marcus ignored the food and looked at me, spinning his coffee in both hands. "Where should I start?"

"I remember my father telling me stories about when you fought together. You could start by telling me why you stopped."

"Yes, I used to hunt with your father. As for what happened to me, well, I learned some things that changed the way I felt about the Circle. As I said last night, things are not as simple as we were taught to believe." He gestured at Rayna.

"How does she fit into all this?" I asked.

"I'm sitting right here," she said, her voice icy.

I didn't have a chance to reply before Marcus spoke "I think it would be best if, for now, I spoke with Chase alone." Marcus was calm and his voice neutral.

Rayna turned that chilly tone on him. "Don't you dare send me away because he's here; I will not be treated like a child."

"Rayna, you know that's not it. I just need a few minutes with Chase. Please."

She rolled her eyes and glared at me as she walked up the stairs. Hearing a door slam, I turned to Marcus. "She doesn't like me much." I smiled, but he didn't look impressed.

"You would be best not to taunt her Chase. We've welcomed you into our home. To treat her as less than an equal is unacceptable."

I laughed and stood from the couch. "She's a demon, the likes of which I've never seen before. I think you owe me some answers before you start demanding anything from me."

"Perhaps you're right," Marcus said. "Come with me."

Marcus went to the stairs and for a moment I thought about leaving, but I still wanted answers.

Upstairs was a long hallway lined with doors. One revealed a large bathroom, another a bedroom, and one was closed with music blaring from the other side. Another hallway branched off to the right, but Marcus continued forward up another flight of stairs.

The third floor was a massive library. Full bookshelves covered the walls, leaving just enough space for a gas fireplace. I could see over an iron railing down to the first floor living room, but the books kept my focus. All the cloth and leather covers looked well-aged. Creased spines littered the large dark table and desk, and the musky smell of old books filled the room.

"So what's the story with Rayna?" I started. "Up until yesterday, I'd never met an Underworlder who didn't want me dead, so you'll understand if I'm having difficulty accepting that she doesn't."

"Rayna is...unique, to say the least. She's part demon, but she's part hunter too."

My eyes widened. "She can't be one of us. When a hunter's blood is mixed with a shifter's, the hunter dies. Hunters' bodies can't carry the virus; we both know that."

Marcus shook his head. "Chase, the first thing you need to know is that you don't know anything. This world you're in now is not the same one you were born into. Just because the elders told you it wasn't possible doesn't mean that's the case. You are going to need to see more than what's on the surface if you want to understand."

Marcus moved to the table and slipped gracefully into a high-backed leather chair. He motioned to a seat opposite him and I found myself sitting in one of the most comfortable chairs I'd ever been in.

"You expect me to believe that everything the Circle taught me was a lie?"

"No Chase, I don't. The differences between reality and what the Circle teaches are difficult to determine. Rayna is unique because her mother was a demon and her father was a member of the Circle. She is not a hunter turned shifter."

"She was born this way?"

"When Rayna's mother got pregnant, her father disappeared. I've known Rayna her whole life and I was friends with both her parents. When the Circle found out about Rayna, they dedicated themselves to finding her. When they finally caught up with her mother, they killed her, but they never found Rayna. She didn't have anywhere to go, and after witnessing what happened to her mother, I had seen enough of what the Circle had to offer. I took her and we disappeared."

"What was her mother?" I asked, not sure I believed him yet.

"She was a witch."

"You expect me to believe that, Marcus?" I stood from my chair.

"I'm sorry?"

"It's a great story, and you almost had me believing it, but if Rayna is part hunter and part witch, how does she have the eyes of a shifter?" I said, pulling a blade from its sheath, not sure if I'd need it, but something wasn't right about this.

Marcus stood up to face me. "Please calm down, Chase. If you let me finish, I assure you we can resolve this."

"What is there to finish? More ridiculous stories?"

"He's telling you the truth, dumbass." Rayna's voice came from behind me. "Now put the knife away before I take it."

"Not a chance, demon." I spat the words at her.

Marcus had his hands on my wrists in an instant. He took the blade from my hand and slid the other from its sheath. I struggled against him, but he was too strong.

"You're a traitor to the Circle!" I shouted.

"Enough!" Marcus's voice echoed off the walls.

It was the first time I'd heard him speak above a whisper since I'd met him. I wasn't sure why, but I stopped straining instantly at the command in his voice.

As soon as I relaxed, Marcus released me. He took a deep breath and moved back to his desk with my blades in his hands.

"We don't know why she has elements of a shifter," he said.

My first instinct was to make a break for it. I didn't want to hear anything else, but Rayna was blocking the stairs, and jumping the railing was better left as a last resort.

"How can you not know?"

"We just don't. It's never happened before and we don't know how it's even possible," he said. "You're right that as far as we know, hunter blood cannot sustain the shifter or vampire viruses, but we still cannot explain Rayna,"

"After all the time you've spent with her, you still have no idea?"

"You can believe what you like Chase. I've told you what I know and I can't do better than that. And you would do well to remember that you chose to come to us, not the other way around. We are no threat to you," he said.

"So she's got it all; a hunter's speed and strength, a witch's magic, and she can shift. Am I missing anything here?"

"No, she doesn't have it all, Chase. Her magic is strong, though she is inexperienced. She cannot shift form; her eyes are permanently feline. She has a weakness against silver much worse than any demon you or I have ever faced, and it's impossible to say what else might develop over time."

I looked at Rayna in disbelief. "So what part of her is hunter?"

"She has an elemental power."

"What? A half demon has an elemental power, when I, a full blooded hunter, have nothing? Bullshit!"

"It's true, Chase." Rayna stepped into the room.

"Which element?"

"Earth," Rayna replied.

"That's not possible. You didn't go through the ceremony."

"Actually, Chase," Marcus said. "It is possible for a hunter's element to come out on its own without the ceremony. Once it was the only way. The ceremony was put into effect a few hundred years ago, as a method to bring out a hunter's power sooner."

"I can't believe this," I said, mostly to myself.

"Perhaps you have other questions, maybe some that don't focus so much on Rayna's abilities?"

I stood in silence for a moment. I didn't know what to ask and this little story seemed pretty farfetched. But I couldn't help but wonder if it was extraordinary enough to be true.

"What is it you guys do?" I asked.

"We fight. We help keep the innocent safe, whether they may be a demon, a hunter, or one of the many mortals oblivious to our world," he said.

"If you're fighting the good fight, then why don't you just go back to the Circle?"

"The Circle has lost its way. Some of its members are not as they appear. Their intentions are tainted, no matter what they'd have you believe. How can I keep my oath to keep the innocent safe when I know that innocent demons are being slaughtered every day?"

The thought of there being innocent demons was something I couldn't wrap my head around. I was still used to demons trying to kill me.

"Which members are corrupt?" I asked.

"That I will not say. I only know that the organization has been corrupted by a few," he said.

"No. I want names."

"I will not share that with you at this time, Chase," he said with finality.

"Then what do you want from me? You've got my weapons, and you tell me these outlandish stories. What use am I to you?"

"We want you to join us. You're a skilled fighter and you have great instincts," he said.

"I don't even have an elemental power – what good am I?"

I was expecting a snide comment from Rayna, but it never came. I actually looked behind me to see if she was still there. The expression on her face wasn't the scornful look I'd expected, but a compassionate one.

"I'm not asking you to join us because of the powers you have or don't. Although, I do believe there is power inside of you. We only need to find out how to release it," he said.

I laughed. "I haven't gotten my element yet and I'm almost eighteen. Face it, it's not going to show up."

Rayna stepped forward. "It's there, I can feel it." She reached towards me.

I moved away from her touch. "Look, this is a lot to take in. You're telling me pretty much everything I grew up knowing is a lie."

"Not all of it," Marcus said. "But there are things the Circle believes with an absolute conviction that we do not share. I don't believe in murdering innocent beings. We don't need to be included in the Circle to be part of what the Circle was created to be: a group of people with the skills and desire to keep this world safe from any who wished it harm. That is the cause we fight for, Chase. One we would be proud to have you be a part of."

"I need time to wrap my head around this. That is if I'm free to leave?"

Marcus nodded. "You aren't a prisoner, but please consider this a genuine offer. Perhaps speak about it with your mother. She may be able to help make things less confusing for you."

I did a double take and Marcus smiled. "Yes, I knew your mother well, and I know her well still," he said.

Once again I was at a loss. This was icing on the cake of confusion. My mother hadn't talked about Marcus in years. If she had known he was alive, she would have told me. Wouldn't she?

I stalked down the stairs and out of the condo. Something didn't feel right and I didn't know if it was what Marcus was telling me, or the thought that I might believe him. I wanted everything my father taught me to be true, but I was being pulled away from that idea.

I made it to the elevator when Rayna's voice came from behind me.

"Chase?"

I turned to face her but I didn't respond.

"Here," she said, handing me both my blades. "We're giving you an opportunity to belong to something and not fight alone for what you believe in. Believe me when I say that feels pretty good."

This wasn't sarcastic banter and there were no angry words or eye rolling. She was sincere. When the elevator doors opened, I stepped inside. We made eye contact as the doors shut and I realized I hadn't thought of what life must be like for her. If she really wasn't a full hunter or demon, she wouldn't belong to either side. I shook away the feeling of pity; I wasn't about to feel sorry for a demon.

I didn't stop to admire the foyer again. I walked into the pouring rain and listened to the thunder crashing in the clouds above. It wasn't long until I was soaked, but I didn't mind. The cool water helped bring me back to reality.

How could I believe what Marcus said about the Circle being corrupt? How could it have happened? I thought about contacting my father, but even if he would talk to me, which was doubtful, he wouldn't believe me anyway. The thought of facing my father and his disappointment again made me shudder.

The more I walked, the more questions I had. I hated not being in control, but I hated not knowing what to believe even more.

Chapter 7

I had just crossed over into my side of downtown when the tingling started. I sighed. Most days I loved a good fight to release a little aggression, but lately I hadn't been so enthusiastic.

I looked back and saw a person walking behind me. At this hour of the day that should be normal, but this part of downtown was typically deserted and my demon sense had a limit to its range.

I made a quick turn and slipped down a long alley between two older buildings that still had all their windows intact – a great feat in this part of town. I slid into an alcove by one of the buildings doors and slipped out one of my daggers.

I slowed my breathing as the sound of crunching gravel came closer. Usually I wouldn't have bothered with anything but killing him, but I wanted to know why he was following me. It wasn't normal for a demon to do anything but attack when it saw a hunter, but I didn't know what was normal anymore.

The figure passed the archway and I made my move. I shoved the demon's shoulder into the opposite brick wall and pressed my blade against his throat. As his body hit the bricks, his skin flashed from a pale white to a dirty brown, taking on the color of the stones. The brown of his eyes faded as the solid black of demon orbs flooded in.

"Who are you, and why are you following me?"

"I, wha- what? Fo- Following you? No, you got the wrong guy," he said with a heavy stutter.

I pushed the blade harder against the skin, not quite enough to break it.

"Whoa, e- e- ease up man. I wasn't following you. I sw- sw- swear," he said.

I wanted to hurt him, to cut him and watch him turn to ash, but I didn't. The honest fear that covered his face caught me off guard.

His left eye was swollen and bruised darkly. Considering how fast demons healed, I bet that it had happened in the past twenty-four hours. He had short brown hair and the stubble on his face was patchy at best. He was a few inches shorter than me, with a scrawny build, although I could guess at the demon strength of his arms. I wasn't about to loosen up my grip.

"Bullshit," I spat.

"Lo- look, I tol- told you guys everything I know, I sw- swear I don't know anything else." He cowered against the wall. "Plea- plea- please man, don't hurt me." His black orbs faded and the brown of his human-like eyes returned.

I didn't have a clue what guys he was talking about, but he thought I was one of them. I was going to use that to my advantage.

"Well, tell me again," I said.

"I, uh, like I said, I've got my ear to the gro- ground man. I've been using all my sources. Nobody knows anything about a crossbreed demon."

"If that's the best you can come up with..." I pushed the blade against his throat, nearly splitting his skin like a peel.

His eyes went wide and he gasped. "I swear, I'm wor- working on it but it ain't easy. The Underworld's on edge with you gu- guys running around. I'll find some- something. I just need more t- t- time."

I eased up on the blade. I needed a different kind of information now. "Who exactly do you think I am?"

A new fear filled his eyes. "You're not one of them?"

"One of who?"

He shook his head. "I can't tell you, they'll k- kill me." His brick colored skin was draining of all its color, getting paler by the second. I let the dagger bite into his skin again and the blood trickled onto my blade.

"And what do you think I'll do?"

"Please don't do this. Them hunters are fierce. They won't just kill me, they'll torture me. Please!" he begged. His eyes had an innocence I'd never seen in a demon before and tears started to well up in them. I couldn't do this.

I pulled the blade away from his neck, and the blood sliding down his pale flesh mixed with the rain that showered us and disappeared under his shirt.

"Alright, tell me what you know. Nobody has to know who told me," I said.

He slid down the brick wall and sat in the puddle at his feet.

"Who are you?" he asked, tears falling down his cheeks now.

"I'm the one who wants to know about the hunters," I said. I slipped the blade back into its sheath and held my empty hands out. "See, I just want answers. I'm not going to hurt you... anymore."

Guilt was tugging at me as I eyed the tears on his face and the blood on his neck. He didn't seem like a demon in this moment. He was like a human terrified of the monster in front of him: me. On any other day that would please me, but I couldn't draw any satisfaction from the fear of this helpless creature.

"It's hunters," he said. "They come around every few weeks and beat a few of us for information." His stutter faded as he calmed himself.

"Information about what?"

He shrugged. "Some demon."

"Well, what kind of demon?"

"That's just it, I don't know. They don't even know. Nobody does. Some demon that has more than one breed inside it." Now that was news. Demons could only carry one strain of virus inside them, at least as far as I knew. "But I've been asking around and looking into it. I can't find anything. It's a myth," he said.

I watched him huddle against the brick wall, wet hair dripping onto soaked clothes. I couldn't believe I was doing this, but I reached out and offered him a hand.

"I don't need your pity," he demanded, trying to sound defiant but failing.

"I'm Chase."

He pushed my hand away and got to his feet. "Everybody calls me Willy," he said, trying to wipe the dirt off his pants. "Who are you? You're not a demon, and if you're not one of the hunters, then how did you know what I was?" he asked.

"I am a hunter, or at least I was. I was exiled."

"You say that like it's a bad thing. From what I've seen you're not missing anything."

"How so?"

Willy shrugged. "That Circle is as corrupt as the vampires who run this town. The past few months they've been all over this area, not killing demons but interrogating them. They'll do whatever it takes to get what they want."

Willy hunched in his jacket and watched me. He was an awkward creature, like a timid dog waiting for you to hit him. I guessed I deserved that look after what I'd done.

"Sorry about your neck. It's been a rough day," I said. That was a big step, apologizing to a demon. I couldn't see him as an Underworlder right now though, just as somebody who was scared for his life. "That all you can tell me?"

"That's all I know. Can I go pl- please?" he said, sounding tired and beaten.

Against my better judgment, I nodded. "In case you hear anything else, where can I find you?" I asked. He pointed to the end of the alley

"You live in an alley?" I raised an eyebrow.

"Look closer."

I focused on the end of the alley, relaxing my eyes and pulling magic from within. Layers of illusion peeled off, revealing a glowing blue and red neon sign that read *Revelations*. It had been so long since I'd had to look through any type of glamour that it took some effort, but there it was.

"What's in there?"

"It's a club. A safe haven for Underworlders. Not exactly your crowd."

"True enough."

He ignored me, turned and walked to the end of the alley and disappeared through the door to the club.

I shook my head and ran a hand through my wet hair. Two demons in two days hadn't tried to kill me. Willy was a sad excuse for a demon, but a demon nonetheless. I didn't have much choice but to let him go. As for Rayna, if Marcus hadn't been there last night, who knew what the result of our fight would have been.

I believed what Willy said. Somehow I didn't think he was even capable of lying. My gut told me he was telling the truth, and with demons, my gut wasn't usually wrong.

I turned my back on the bar and started walking out of the alley. What Willy said about the Circle coincided too closely with what Marcus had been telling me. Maybe I was accepting that it might be true. I still couldn't figure out why the Circle would do these things, but maybe someone else could. Maybe these questions needed a mother's touch.

Chapter 8

The rain stopped as soon as I got home. *Figures*, I said to myself, walking up the four flights of stairs. My shoes squeaked with every step and my clothes were water-logged. I couldn't wait to change.

Mom was sitting on the couch with a book in hand. "It must be really coming down out there." She was trying – and failing – to conceal her laughter.

"Very funny," I said

A towel, a pair of gray cargo pants and a white t-shirt later, I was dry and dressed. I threw on a black hoodie to try and rid myself of the chill.

Our apartment looked even smaller than usual after being at Marcus's. An old couch, an even older chair and a coffee table filled the living area. The walls might have once been white, but they were now tinted with nicotine stains from the previous tenants, and did little to set off the decor. An ancient TV sat on the floor, but it rarely worked.

"Where've you been?" Mom asked.

There was no easy way to tell her, so I threw it all on the table. "Do you know Marcus Starkraven?"

She didn't look as shocked as I'd expected. She paused for a moment. "I do. He's a good man."

"So you know he's not dead?"

"I've known Marcus a long time, Chase. We've been in contact over the years."

"Did you know about Rayna too?"

"There are a lot of things you don't know: about the Circle, me, and your father as well."

I couldn't do anything but listen. She was about to tell me either something I wouldn't expect, or something I wouldn't like. Maybe both.

"The Circle is made up of people from all over the world, and not everybody has the same ideas as to what the Circle should be anymore. I was exiled with you not because your father suspected me of being unfaithful. I knew things about your father – and the Circle – that I wasn't supposed to. Over the years, a lot of us learned that the Underworlders weren't all soulless demons, as we were brought up to believe. A small group, including Marcus and me, came together to oppose the council. We thought we could work together to achieve a common goal. The council, as you can guess, doesn't care much for opposition and didn't think much of our plea."

"So what happened to Marcus?" I asked.

"The night that Marcus disappeared, he and your father were on a hunt, but your father wasn't hunting Underworlders. He had gotten wind of a rumor about a hunter having impregnated a demon. When he found out about Marcus having befriended a witch, Rayna's mother, he could only assume that Marcus was the 'traitor'. Riley was furious. He took Marcus out and tried to kill him. Marcus escaped, but your father had hurt him badly enough that he believed he was dead."

"What happened to Rayna's parents?" I asked.

"Rayna's mother disappeared that night, to keep herself and unborn Rayna safe. But she made the mistake of coming back, thinking that after nine years the Circle would have forgotten about her. But the Circle doesn't forget, and that was the night Rayna's mother was killed. When Marcus found Rayna, the two of them disappeared. Nobody knew where they went or what had happened, not even me. Marcus didn't know who he could trust, and his first instinct was to keep Rayna safe. As for Rayna's dad, nobody knows what happened to him."

"I can't believe you kept all this from me. You left me to think that everything the Circle taught me was right, and believe it was my fault we were exiled. I've spent all this time thinking I was a disappointment," I said.

She sighed. "You were angry at yourself and the Circle. I thought if I told you, you would turn your anger on me, and I couldn't bear to lose you too." I started to walk away, but she reached for my arm. "Chase, by the time you stopped being angry, I didn't want to tell you because I feared it would bring all the pain back."

"It's been a long day. I'm going to lie down."

"Please don't be angry with me."

"I'm not angry. I just need some time to figure things out."

"Can I just say…"

"What?" I asked, unable to veil the hostility in my voice.

"Please give Marcus's offer some consideration."

"You knew?"

She nodded. "He called after you left and told me. I'm sorry for the way this has all come out. I spent so long trying to figure out how to tell you that you found out in the worst way possible."

"You can say that again," I said, disappearing into my bedroom.

I fell into my bed and stared at the cracks in the ceiling, my mind swelling like a balloon. The old thoughts and ideas engraved in my head were some of the only constants in my life, and now they had to fight these new ones or be erased.

I was thrilled when the phone rang and it was work calling. It was supposed to be my day off, but I took the shift without a second thought. Work would distract me, and the overtime wouldn't hurt.

Chapter 9

I got off shift after midnight, and what had turned out to be a busy night was just what I needed to clear my head. The walk home on the warm summer night, however, gave all my thoughts plenty of time to rush back.

I chose a different route home than usual. It took longer to go through the park, but after running into Marcus, Rayna and the vampires last night, I was hoping that wandering off the beaten path would save me some bruises.

Halfway home, I heard strange noises and a tingle trembled down my spine. I cursed myself for taking the long way. I couldn't win.

I saw the silhouettes of people and slipped off the path to join the shadows. I thought it was demons beating the crap out of someone. Plenty of Underworlders would do that for kicks, but when I heard the voice of the victim, I knew that wasn't the case.

"I sw- sw- swear I t- told you what I know." The stutter was easily recognizable as Willy's and I got the feeling of déjà-vu. Hearing him plead with his attackers made me feel sorry for him. It was only earlier today that I had a blade to his throat, and he still had a shiner from his last run-in with hunters. This guy was having a worse week than I was.

I approached the scene and saw three men taking turns kicking Willy, who was on the ground with his back against a tree.

"Hey," I said.

All three of them turned and stared at me.

"Keep walking, buddy," the one in the middle said. "Wait a second. Chase? Chase Williams? Well, I'll be damned." It was Brock at the center of this assault.

Brock was a hunter a few years older than me, and a fire elemental. He had always been broad shouldered, but he'd bulked up since I saw him last. His red hair was trimmed into a crew cut over the familiar pale, freckled face. It had several scars, but the one across his left eye was new to me and ruined some of the effect of his bright green eyes.

Brock and I had never gotten along. We both had different ideas about how to get things done. This scene was a good example of the way he did things. The other two hunters were younger than me. I recognized their faces but I didn't know their names. When I'd been part of the Circle, I never paid much attention to the younger ones.

"Been a long time, Brock," I said.

"That it has, brother. That it has."

"I'm not your brother, not anymore."

Brock's smirk made his face scrunch up and he gave his half-snort laugh I hadn't missed.

"That's right, you're the son of Riley Williams, exiled by his own father for being a disgrace." He slugged one of the others guys in a joking way and they chuckled with him. Anger shot through me and I squeezed the blade in my hand.

"Whatcha got there, a knife?" he laughed. "What, you're saving demons now? Pathetic. You're still a hunter, Chase, even if you're not in the Circle."

"Last I checked, hunters fought evil. They don't torture the innocent," I said.

"This...thing is hardly innocent, but you're right, things have changed. You would know that if you hadn't come up short," Brock said.

I took a step towards him and looked over his shoulders at Willy.

Willy's chameleon skin cycled through different colors, trying to deflect any attention it could away from him, until it found one that let him blend in with the tree. His button-up shirt was torn and his jacket was pushed up above his shoulders. Blood ran from both nostrils, trailed down to a busted lip and dripped off his chin. His left eye was swollen shut.

"If this is what the Circle has become, then I'm happy not to be a part it."

"Bullshit! You would come back in a second if anybody wanted you," Brock retorted.

"I took an oath to protect the innocent and so did you."

"He's a demon, Chase. We kill them; it's what we do."

"Maybe, but this isn't killing, this is torture, and I won't stand by and watch it. What did he do to deserve this?"

"He didn't give me what I wanted."

I could sense Brock trying to conjure his element and I laughed. "You and I both know you aren't strong enough to create fire; you can barely control it."

"Last chance, Chase. Leave," he said.

"I'd be happy to, but I'm taking him with me."

"So, being out of the Circle, you've turned to the Underworld. That's weak, brother, but so be it." He reached behind him and came back with a Zippo. He flipped it open, and as the spark lit I could feel the oncoming heat.

I dropped to my knees and rolled to the right, taking cover behind a tree. The entire area lit up with the glow of silver and green flame.

"Things aren't the same as when you left, brother. I'm stronger now than ever before. I don't need to create fire. I just need to take it with me."

I peeked around the tree to get a feel for the battleground, but the flash of silver and green was all I saw. I slipped back behind the trunk and the fireball just brushed my skin, leaving a patch of raw flesh.

A grunt came from behind me and I risked poking my head back out. Willy had jumped onto Brock's back, wrapping both arms around his neck. He wasn't doing much but hanging on, and it occurred to me then that Willy didn't know how to fight. He was strong enough to pick up a truck, but he didn't know how to use that strength.

I took the opportunity for what it was: a distraction. I squeezed the handle of my blade and moved towards Brock. The butt of the handle made a loud crack as it hit his cheek bone and forced him down on one knee. With Willy still clinging, he lost his balance and fell.

The other two hunters sprang into action. The first wasn't as fast as me and I dodged as his knife came down near my chest. I countered with a kick. My heel hit the back of his head and sent him face-first into the dirt. The other boy was behind me before I could move and his fist hit the back of my head. I felt my skull crack and I braced myself with my arms as I hit the ground.

The pain in my head was sharp and black dots swarmed in my vision. I ignored the agony and pushed myself up. I was halfway up when the knee hit my face and pushed me into another fist. This one was covered with shining silver knuckles, and the cold metal made a spine-chilling noise as it hit my face. The momentum of the strike pushed me back and I was forced to curl up in self-defense. A flurry of fists and feet pounded my back and it took all I had to resist arching with pain and exposing the rest of my body.

It seemed like forever before the kicking stopped and hands grabbed my arms, pulling me up. They lifted me in a quick, smooth motion that made the blood rush to my head. I fought to keep from passing out as I stood in a swirl of light and dark spots. I could feel blood trickling down my cheek and nose.

Brock stood in front of me and Willy was behind him, lying motionless on the ground.

"You always have to be the hero, don't you Chase? Too bad you didn't choose a better cause. Protecting demons is unbecoming of your heritage."

"Unbecoming? You know better than to use big words like that, Brock."

He leaned back and launched his fist into my mouth. My lip exploded and more blood poured down my face.

"What are you looking for?" I said, spitting blood on the ground.

Brock leaned forward and drove his thumb into an apparent cut in my eyebrow. I ground my teeth and muffled a scream. "Blood," he said, showing me what was dripping from his finger.

The pain faded but the fresh blood ran into my eye and forced it shut.

"What does that mean?"

"Exactly that," he said. I watched him slide something onto his hand, the light it reflected glinting off the silver knuckles. "We just need to find the right blood."

All I could see with my one open eye was Brock's smile before his fist crushed the side of my face. My vision went spotty again and the pain vanished, leaving only darkness to engulf me.

Chapter 10

The moment my eyes opened the pain came back in full force. Every part of my body throbbed. Even my aches had pains. I was on my back and could see an unfamiliar ceiling above me. In a panic, I tried to sit up, but the throbbing in my head was too much and forced me back down.

I took a deep breath, and after a few mental curses and a lot of effort, I moved my head. I discovered I was on a couch, and the table beside me held old ice cream buckets full of dark liquid. I couldn't see anything else in the room other than an old armchair, covered in floral designs so faded they were colorless, with stuffing hanging out here and there.

I tried to speak but all that came out was a cough, making me nearly pass out again from the pain in my head.

"Whoa, ta- take it easy, man," a voice said.

The words echoed around my head, but once I saw Willy they made sense. He walked out of the living room and returned with something resembling water. I wasn't in a position to be picky so I drank a few gulps. It tasted terrible, but the liquid was a relief to my cracked throat.

"What happened?" I asked.

Willy smiled, but it looked like it caused him pain. His face was cut up and one eye was still swollen shut. "That was a hell of a bea- beating you took for me. Nobody's ever stood up for me before," he said.

"Yeah well, I've never stood up for an Underworlder before, so I guess it was a first for both of us." After another drink of the water, the hoarseness of my voice started to fade.

"Here," he said, reaching into one of the pails. He produced a cloth that had blotches of brownish red on it and handed it to me.

I took it, but I wasn't sure where to put it first. My whole body hurt and I didn't know what was cut, bruised, or broken. All I knew was pain. I settled for putting it above my eye, since thanks to Brock's thumb I knew about the cut there.

"Where are we?"

"This is my apartment. I know it's not much but it's the only safe place I could think of."

"Mine doesn't look much different."

A loud buzzing sounded through the room and more pain sheared through my head. Willy jumped up from the coffee table, moved to the wall and pushed one of the buttons on an old box that barely hung there.

"Hello?" Willy said.

A deep voice crackled over the speaker. I thought the guy said his name but I couldn't understand it. Willy pushed another button and went to the kitchen.

"Don't worry, it's somebody we can trust," he called.

The knock at the door came and Willy came back into the living room, followed by a giant beast of a...woman?

She looked a century old. Long white hair came down to the middle of her back and her face was aged with an impossible number of wrinkles. A white knitted sweater and green dress pants covered her frame. Her skin was pale gray, which made the blue of her eyes seem unusually bright.

Without saying anything, she reached into an enormous gray purse and took out a pack of cigarettes. She enjoyed a few puffs of one before she spoke, and her voice sounded like it belonged to a man with a crushed larynx. I'd bet she'd smoked two packs a day for each of the hundred years she looked.

"So you called me here, boy. What do you want?"

I stayed silent and averted my eyes. She stared at me when she spoke and it made me nervous. I killed some pretty nasty demons regularly, but this old lady was scaring me.

To my relief, Willy answered her. "I t- told you, I nee- need some help."

She snorted and took a drag of her cigarette. The look she gave me sent a shudder down my spine as smoke curled out of her nostrils. "He's a hunter. I'm not helping *him*," she said. She made the last word sound like something disgusting; Rayna had the same talent. So far, my batting average with new people wasn't getting any better.

"I know he's a hunter, Grams, but he saved me from the other hunters."

They went a few minutes without speaking, but from the way they stared at each other I started to think they were having a silent conversation.

"Fine," she said, taking a final puff of the cigarette before she dropped it in one of the buckets of bloody water. "Clean this up," she demanded.

Willy didn't question her and cleaned off the coffee table in a rush. Grams put her gray purse on the table and opened it. She fiddled with a few small bottles and set them out on the table. Next came some different stones, including quartz, amethyst, and tiger's eye, then jasmine, garlic, and some herbs I didn't recognize. She pulled out a knife and gestured to Willy for a clean bowl. I was surprised that she didn't have a bowl in that monster of a purse, and more so, that she thought Willy would have a clean one.

He did come back with a clean glass bowl and handed it to her. He stood awaiting more orders but only earned a glare. "Go sit down."

Willy moved to the tattered chair, watching his Grams mix ingredients. He observed closely for a few minutes before he stood up suddenly. "Grams, no! I want you to help him, not kill him," he said smoothly, with a confidence that surprised me.

She glared at Willy and grunted, but Willy didn't back down. "Grams, prom- promise me."

She gave me an evil glare before looking back to Willy and nodding grudgingly. "Oh, fine," she snarled.

We hunters had a well-deserved bad reputation among the Underworlders, so it was strange having one help me. My mother would have had me pain free in a matter of minutes, but I was in no shape to move.

Grams mumbled words I didn't understand and I couldn't help but think the voice must belong to a whole different creature. She gazed at me with a look that would make Medusa proud. "I suggest you keep thoughts like that out of your mind, boy. You'll show me some respect or I'll make sure that every day you wake up, the pain is worse than the last."

My eyes went wide and I took the cloth off my face and nodded. "Umm, yes ma'am."

I looked at Willy and he shrugged. "She's a witch," he said, like that explained it.

I tried to draw on some magic to block her from my thoughts, but I didn't have the energy, so I tried not to think.

Grams dumped bottles of liquid and oil into the bowl, then cut and mixed the herbs with them while talking to herself. She was doing a spell, and I wasn't sure what kind, but I could feel the magic against my skin.

She lifted each stone by its individual chain and hung them all over the mixture. She spoke in a hoarse whisper and the stones started to move in circles. It started slowly, at first, but within a few rotations they moved faster and swung to trace the edge of the bowl. When she stopped muttering, the chains went stiff and she lowered them into the mixture. The liquid instantly started to boil, steam rolling off it in waves as it thickened.

I waited for more special effects but none came. The liquid kept boiling and the steam got thicker until mist filled the room. The witch opened her eyes, stood up, and started packing the ingredients back into the purse.

"When it cools, drink it. It doesn't taste good but drink it all and don't be a baby," she told me before turning her gaze on Willy. "And don't miss dinner Sunday. Demons don't get sick so don't use that excuse again or I'll be banging down this door."

"Ye- yes, Grams," Willy replied.

She lit another cigarette and looked back and forth between the two of us before grunting and walking towards the door. "And clean this damn place up," she commanded, slamming the door behind her.

Willy looked at me, seeming annoyed. "I hate that she treats me like a child. I'm twenty-two and she's not my mother, she-she's just a grandma," he said.

"That thing is really your grandmother?" I asked, instantly regretting my choice of words. Thankfully, Willy didn't take offense.

"I didn't know who else to call. You lost a lot of blood. I wasn't sure if you were going to live through the night," he said.

I pointed to the mixture she'd made. "Is that safe?"

"Yeah, Grams would never break a promise. Not to me. I know she's a scary lady but she's one hell of a witch."

The disgusting mixture had gone from a clear liquid with floating herbs and oils to a dark green, nearly black syrup that was thicker than I thought I could swallow.

When it cooled, Willy poured it into a large cup and I had more to drink than I thought. I eyed the liquid as I grasped it and tried to swirl it, but the sludge had almost no movement. I didn't want to drink it, but my head was pounding and the cuts had started to bleed again.

"You're really sure this isn't going to kill me?"

Willy laughed. "Trust me."

It was one thing to let a demon walk away from me. It was another thing to take one of the worst beatings of my life – from hunters no less – to save one, but three days ago I would have sworn that trusting a demon was something I'd never do. .

After seeing what those hunters were doing, I didn't need any more convincing. Something was going on within the Circle and I wanted to know what. Marcus had given me the opportunity to join them, and now that I'd stood up to the hunters I had already dug my own grave. The only way I was going to survive was to put my trust in a few unconventional places.

"Cheers," I said, and drank the mixture.

It was harsh in my throat, like swallowing a cup of bile. It burned going down and I stopped breathing out of my nose to avoid the taste. When I'd finished the tonic, I sat in silence.

"Well, how do you feel?" Willy asked.

I started to see black dots again. "I don't know. I feel...tired."

Exiled

I could see Willy's lips moving, but I couldn't hear what he said. Before I had time to panic, the darkness gripped me and I collapsed back onto the couch.

Chapter 11

I woke to find I could open both eyes and Willy's nose was almost touching mine. I screamed, in turn scaring Willy, who fell backwards and crashed into the table.

"What the hell!" he said.

"What do you mean what the hell? You can't stand over somebody staring at them like that. That's...that's creepy, among other things," I said.

"You were making weird noises, so I came to check on you. I didn't think you would ever wake up."

"How long have I been sleeping?"

"Like two days."

"What? I've got to go!" I tried to sit up and realized the only pain I felt was in my back, and it was just the kind of pain you get from lying in one spot too long.

"I don't hurt!" I said, more to myself than anything.

"I told you Grams is good. Although, you were only supposed to sleep for an hour. I guess it works different on hunters."

I ran my hands over my face to find no scabs or scars. I had thought only powerful water elementals were capable of this kind of healing. I would have never considered a demon capable of healing magic, and even if I had, I wouldn't have expected these results.

"I've got to go. My mom is freaking out right now, I guarantee it."

"Yeah, of course. Glad you're okay."

I started to walk toward the door.

"Hey Willy I, uh..."

Willy smiled. "It was the least I could do."

I didn't reply, only nodded, knowing he would understand.

Once I got outside, I knew where I was. It should be a fifteen minute walk home, but I could do the distance in five if I ran.

To my surprise, I walked into the kitchen to find Mom being comforted in Marcus's dark arms. Both of their heads whipped around to look at the door.

Mom ran over to me, her cheeks streaked with tears and eyes swollen from lack of sleep. She reached up on tiptoe and wrapped her arms around my neck. I reached down and hugged her back, but when she pulled away, another set of emotions leapt to the surface. She slapped me so hard across the face that my head almost spun around.

"Where the hell have you been?" she sobbed. She looked furious, but her eyes betrayed fear rather than anger.

"It's a long story," I said.

"Well, I'm all ears."

I told them everything, and the anger drained from my mother's face and was replaced with fear, sadness, and then relief.

Marcus didn't say a word or change his expression throughout my tale. He was wearing dark jeans and a tight black t-shirt that looked ready to tear at any moment, and a silver chain around his neck glinted brightly, as if brand new.

Just as I finished, the door opened and Rayna strode through, wearing a bright blue tank top and low rise cargos. She looked oddly cheery wearing something other than black. Her green eyes fell upon me and her eyebrows rose. Marcus gave her a rundown of the events and Rayna was quick to comment.

"My, can it be true? One day you're putting knives to my throat and calling me a filthy demon, and the next you're having sleepovers with an Underworlder?"

"What can I say, he was prettier than you."

"That's enough, you two," my mom said.

"Have you considered my offer?" Marcus asked.

I nodded "I'm in. I want to know what the hunters are looking for."

"It could be almost anything," Marcus said. "Demon blood could be useful to anybody with a not-so-healthy agenda, but a crossbred demon is news to me. It'll require some research."

"Then let's get started," I replied.

Marcus nodded. "I'll drive."

Chapter 12

I cleaned up and changed my bloodied clothes before we left in Marcus's car, a small, black sedan with room for all of us. By the time we got to the condo, most of the day was gone, and the large bay windows let in a flood of purples, reds, and oranges from the setting sun.

Before we got to work, Mom wanted a tour. I wasn't convinced that Rayna and I should be left alone together, but I kept that to myself.

You could have swum through the thick wave of tension between us, and it was more than a few minutes before I broke the silence. "Hey I didn't mean what I said...What I mean is I shouldn't have..." Apologizing wasn't my forte.

Rayna stared at me and arched one eyebrow.

"What I'm trying to say is I'm sorry about what I said, about you being a filthy, well, you know." There, that hadn't been so hard.

The unimpressed look remained on her soft features. I stared back, not sure what my expression revealed, but anxious for a reply.

"Don't worry about it; I've gotten used to it. I'm either a filthy demon to hunters or a disgrace to most Underworlders. They know I'm a witch, but I kill demons. It doesn't bode well in the Underworld to kill your own kind, no matter how evil they are."

I nodded and the silence wrapped around us again.

"You're not wrong, you know." Rayna said.

"About what?"

"About the demons. Don't get me wrong, there are a lot of them, of us, that try to be good people, but there're a lot more that do the opposite. They're easier to spot though; none of them are as cute as me." She smirked.

I wasn't sure how to react, but before I could choose, my body decided for me. I felt a smile cross my face and we stared at each other.

"This place is amazing." The sound of my mother's voice made us jump and the smiles vanished.

"Well, if I'd known you two wouldn't be at each other's throats, we could have taken our time." Marcus's deep voice didn't match the joke he was making.

"Yeah, well, I told Chase if he didn't start being nice to me I'd kick his ass again. Now let's get to work." Rayna slipped off the couch and ran up the stairs.

"I'd like to see that," I said under my breath.

"Keep it up and you will," Rayna replied from the next floor. She turned and disappeared down the hallway, hips swaying.

Marcus spent a few minutes finding the books he wanted us to start with. By the time he was satisfied that he'd gotten everything useful off the shelves, books covered the huge table. Marcus and Mom each took a stack and moved to the desk. Rayna went to the fireplace, and I took a spot at the table.

The first few books I picked up were in languages I couldn't read. When I found one that had been translated into English, I started flipping through it. Exorcisms, communicating with the spirit world, and how to grow magical plants were all covered in this book, but there was nothing on summoning or anything related to demon blood. And so the research began.

Uncounted hours later, we took a break. We'd managed to source several books with some relevance, but had found nothing particularly helpful.

"There's plenty about summoning demons, and even more about rituals that require demon blood, but it's used in hundreds of rituals, all of which have very undesirable results. We need to find a way to narrow down what we're looking for," Marcus said.

"We could track down Brock," I said "Since he's looking for it, who better to ask?"

"No, that will draw too much attention to us, and we'd have to threaten him somehow. We don't want the hunters to know we're interested," Marcus declared.

"I can try and speak with some of the contacts I have left in the Circle," Mom said.

"That could work, but we don't know how deep this goes or who all is involved. Until we know for sure, we have to assume no one can be trusted."

Marcus paced the library and continued to decline all the solutions we came up with. I was doing my best to be patient, but I wasn't used to needing the go-ahead from someone else anymore. So far, I didn't like it.

"We'll have to start small." Marcus looked at his watch. "Rayna, you and Chase go to Revelations. Perhaps you can speak to Vincent and see if he's heard anything."

Rayna laughed. "Because bringing a hunter into an Underworld bar isn't going to draw attention to us? They'll smell him as soon as we walk in. I should go alone. Besides, you know how Vincent is."

"I do, and I don't like you being alone with him. Chase goes too," Marcus said.

Rayna rolled her eyes. "Fine. I'll need to change."

Marcus disappeared as well, leaving Mom and me alone in the library. There was some tension between us and I wasn't sure how to handle it. We had always been really comfortable with each other, but since Marcus and Rayna had come into our lives, something felt different.

"So, how are you?" Mom asked.

I shrugged. "I'm fine."

She took a seat in the chair opposite me, giving me a concerned, motherly look with her bright hazel eyes. "I meant, how are you dealing with all this?"

"I'm fine. Really."

"I know being here is a big change, but give Marcus and Rayna a chance. They're good people."

"It's pretty clear I am. I'm here, aren't I?" It sounded snippier than I intended, but I wasn't going to apologize, so I tried to change the subject. "You and Marcus seem close..." I was staring at the floor, but I looked up to try to catch her reaction to the comment.

"We've known each other a long time." It wasn't the answer I was looking for, but I hadn't exactly been direct.

"Yeah, you keep saying that."

Mom sighed. "What do you want from me, Chase? I'm really trying here."

I immediately felt guilty. She didn't deserve my resentment. "I know," I said. "It's just...this is all new to me, and it isn't easy putting my trust in strangers. You may have known Marcus for years, but I haven't, and Rayna's...a demon!" I tried to say the last quietly.

"You're right. You don't know them, and I'm not asking you to trust them right away, but I *am* asking you to trust me. I don't ask a lot of you. You do things pretty well on your own. Sometimes, I'm not even sure if you need me around, but..."

"Don't say that!" I said sternly. "We're in this together, remember? You and me, always."

Mom's eyes welled up a bit and she lowered her gaze.

I got up and wrapped my arms around her. Her small arms hugged me back with greater force than you'd expect, but she wasn't an ordinary woman; she was a hunter.

"You're right, you don't ask much of me," I said. "And I do trust you. Everything is just going to take some getting used to."

"Thank you." Mom pulled away and smiled. "And go easy on Rayna. She's a great girl and you don't know her story. Give it time and you might find you guys are more alike than you think."

"Yeah, right. I think you're pushing it now." I laughed, but Mom eyed me and I fell silent.

"I mean it. Give her a chance and I'll bet she surprises even you."

"Ready?" I hadn't heard Marcus come up the stairs. Mom turned at the sound of his voice and a smile crept over her lips. Marcus returned the smile and it seemed out of place on his face, but I realized then how little my mother smiled. She looked younger when she did. All the years of overnights and double shifts were suddenly gone, washed away by one gesture, revealing the face I remembered from my childhood.

The awkwardness I'd felt vanished, and I knew I'd do anything I could to see her smile more. If that meant putting my trust in these people, then I would. After all she'd done for me, she deserved at least that much.

"I'll be downstairs," I said.

A couple of minutes later, Marcus, Rayna and Mom all came down together. Rayna wore a black miniskirt and a tight, low-cut, red halter top that split under her breasts, flaring out to reveal a toned stomach. Her black hair was pinned up with a few red strands left to fall down her neck.

"Wow, am I underdressed?" I asked, sarcasm thick in my voice. I could feel my mom's disapproving gaze burning into me.

"You are, actually," Rayna said. "In case you hadn't noticed, the Underworld prides itself on looking good," she said.

"Should I change?"

She shook her head, sitting down to pull on knee high leather boots. "We don't have time to go back to your place and nothing of Marcus's would fit you. Besides, I doubt you own much that isn't a t-shirt."

It made me irritated that she was right. Jeans, cargos, and t-shirts pretty much made up my entire wardrobe. Some days there were even socks involved.

"Don't stay longer than you have to. Go there, talk to Vincent and don't get sidetracked. We don't need more of what happened to Chase. And no matter what happens, don't make a deal with him until we've discussed it. Understood?" Marcus said.

"Don't you think we should go with them?" Mom said.

"No, Rayna knows what she's doing and the bar is warded. Nobody can be harmed while inside."

"It's not the time they're inside that I'm worried about."

"I can take care of myself, Mom."

"Yeah, you've proven that so far," she said sarcastically.

"Rayna will be there, Tessa, and they'll get more information if it's just the two of them. As long as Chase doesn't try to kill anyone, they'll be fine," he said, looking at me pointedly.

"I'll be good," I said.

I opened the door and stepped out. "Be safe," I heard my mom say as Rayna closed the door behind us.

"Outfit's a little much, don't you think?"

"Well, at least I don't look like I just fell out of a dumpster," she replied.

I looked down at my clothes. One threadbare knee of my pants would rip soon. My shirt was clean but had holes in the cuffs; I had a habit of putting my thumbs through them. My black sneakers would have been clean if not for a few blood stains.

"What's wrong with this?"

She hit the button for the elevator and turned to face me. "Nothing in particular," she said with a half shrug.

"No, really, what's wrong with what I'm wearing?"

"Chase, you're fine; you look good."

"Really?" I said, stepping into the elevator.

"No."

Chapter 13

The alley was thick with shadows, cast by the glow of Revelations' blue and red neon sign.

"Listen, when we get in there, don't talk to anybody, okay? Let me take care of it," Rayna said.

"I can handle myself."

"Ha, I've heard how you handle yourself. This is my area, so tonight I'm taking care of things. I know how to deal with these people."

Rolling my eyes, I realized how weird it seemed to call them people, but after the last few eventful days, I couldn't argue much.

More layers of Revelations' glamour slid away the closer we got, revealing stairs that led down to the entrance.

My senses were overloaded as Rayna opened the door. Rock music blared in my ears, the scent of sweat and blood filled my nostrils, and flashing lights blurred my vision.

Once my senses adjusted, I gazed out over the crowd, absorbing everything I could. I had to push away the tingle of my demon sense as Rayna urged me towards the doorman, a creature I could only describe as both a giant and a monster.

Looking up at him made my neck hurt. He was well over seven feet tall, and what I could see of his face was covered with a thick, spiky beard. A tribal tattoo trailed down the sides of his shaved head and his eyebrows each had multiple piercings. Arms thicker than my thighs were covered in tattoos, some of which seemed to be struggling to stay on his skin. His solid black eyes made it difficult to tell where he was looking.

"No weapons." His deep voiced echoed over the music. Rayna handed two blades to him and I wondered where she had kept them. I eyed the large man and decided against any smart remarks and pulled my two daggers from their spot, handing them to him. He nodded his enormous head and let me pass, but the look he gave me wasn't friendly. "Watch your step, hunter," he said as I walked past him.

Rayna glided through the room, constantly checking to make sure I was still following. The wide space between dingy, unpainted brick walls was larger and busier than I'd expected.

Every stool at the huge square bar in the center of the room was occupied, and each patron held a strange-looking drink. Pool tables filled one corner of the room and a string of dartboards filled another. A wall-mounted jukebox near the door had a lineup, and cigarette smoke filled the air.

We moved towards one less populated corner while I ignored the intimidating looks and suspicious whispers trailing behind me. Not all of the demons could know what I was, but plenty of them could sense it from my scent or aura. It was a miracle they didn't know what Rayna was, but the demon blood must have helped mask it.

The dance floor was full of bodies meshing, all of which slowed as we walked past. We wove through a maze of tables to an area full of booths that were empty, with the exception of one.

In the middle of this booth was a man who looked to be in his mid-twenties, although considering where we were, how old somebody appeared wasn't a clear indicator of age.

His pale skin was flawless and glistened in the strobe lights. His short black hair was spiked neatly on his head and golden orbs watched us as we neared. All I could see of his clothing was a tight black dress shirt that had too many buttons undone, revealing more pale flesh.

A blonde and a brunette sat on either side of him. Both were beautiful and dressed in clothing as minimal as Rayna's. The rest of the booth held a mix of men and women, some sitting, others standing and watching as we approached.

Golden eyes watched Rayna with a strange anticipation. The man's creepy smile made me shudder as his eyes, filled with hunger, devoured her. I didn't know why, but this made me mad. I wanted shove the straw from his drink down his throat, and watch him struggle as I dripped liquid silver down it. The mental image made me crack a smile which quickly disappeared as those eyes fell on me.

"Careful of your thoughts, boy," the demon said. The accompanying gaze was very deliberately threatening, but the voice was smooth and full of seduction.

"He's a vampire. He can read your thoughts," Rayna whispered, although it didn't matter; he could hear every word.

"Thanks for the heads up," I said. The information was a little late – there went my chance at a first impression.

Contrary to popular myth, vampires aren't actually dead – at least not when they're awake. They need to drink blood, true, but as long as they consume enough, it will keep their body alive. They can reproduce, they have a pulse, and they even breathe. Not drinking blood, however, forces a vampire's body to shut down. The demon won't die, but its body will weaken until it can't operate, keeping the mind alive inside a dwindling corpse. Depriving vamps of blood is a great way to torture them, but some of them practice starvation as a form of discipline. I was really wishing we weren't dealing with vampires right now. I'd already had enough experience with them for one lifetime.

The vampire's eyes took me in and gave me the same once over he'd given Rayna. *Uncomfortable* didn't begin to describe the experience.

"I see you have a new pet." He frowned.

Rayna laughed. "Hardly, just a friend."

The vampire didn't reply and I could feel magic begin to wash over me. He tilted his head and watched me, like a dog trying to understand its owner.

His power moved over me and I put my shields up, trying to block him from my thoughts. He pushed at the edge of my shields and I pushed back with my own magic, but it only made him smile.

I'd felt a vampire's mind control before, but something was different about his. Vampires are unique among the demons. Aside from shifters, they're the only demons who can pass their heritage on to a human. But unlike shifters, they have unpredictable powers. You never knew what a particular vampire's capabilities were; they were different for each. Something felt especially strange about this one's power.

The vampire pulled his magic back from me and looked at Rayna. "He's good," he said.

"I wouldn't know," Rayna replied.

"What do you want, my sweet child? Have you come to finally accept my offer and join me?" he said.

"I need to talk... alone," Rayna said, ignoring the question and looking at the other...people...around him.

"Is it so private that you can't speak in front of my family?"

Rayna nodded and he regarded her for a moment like a predator stalking his prey. At a wave of his hand, everyone around his booth dispersed. Rayna slid into a newly available seat and I settled down beside her.

"Why you must tease me with such attire is beyond me," the vampire said in a soft, self-assured voice.

"I knew somebody would appreciate my efforts." Rayna cast a glare at me and the vampire laughed.

"What's funny?" Rayna said.

The vampire shifted in a way that was almost a shrug, and didn't reply.

"I need some inform... " The vampire raised a hand to stop her.

"Have you forgotten such basic manners as a simple introduction?"

Rayna sighed. "Of course not. Vincent, this is Chase. Chase, this is Vincent."

Vincent leaned forward in his seat, extending a pale hand. I stared at it, knowing that physical touch could increase the strength of a vampire's power, but I disregarded that and reached out my own.

His hand was smaller than mine but his grip was solid, allowing me to feel the extent of his magical strength. Vincent's fingers tightened around my hand and I let him feel my own strength as I squeezed.

I went against basic hunter wisdom and stared into his bright golden orbs. His power smashed into me immediately, and it hit my body like a truck and drove full throttle into me. I used my shields to push his power back but I'd lost my footing. His grip tightened again – any more pressure and I was going to have broken bones. His power was a wave, crashing over me again and again, each time washing more of my shields away.

"Alright boys, that's enough, before somebody gets hurt," Rayna said.

Vincent's power didn't withdraw and our eyes never broke contact. I had to reach deep within myself and push all the magic I had into my shields. I let my mind focus not on his eyes, but on the pain in my hand, letting it distract me. I was holding his strength at bay, but any more of an assault and I would be enslaved by his mind. I could see the intensity of my gaze reflected in his eyes before his power dissipated.

Vincent smiled and released my hand, leaning back in the booth.

"My gods, could you two be any more pathetic?" Rayna said.

We both looked at her questioningly.

"Vincent, everybody knows you're powerful; you're hundreds of years old, so why don't you try acting your age? And Chase, drop your macho man act. We're here to get shit done, not piss off someone who might be able to help us."

I could feel the arrogance drain from both of us and Vincent gave a simple nod. "As my lady wishes."

Rayna's glare came to rest on me. "Okay," I said.

I knew some Underworlders liked to flex their power at anybody they thought could handle it. It was partly a compliment that Vincent assumed I could hold my own, and partly his desire to be top dog. If he'd been wrong and his power overcame me, I would've been screwed.

"Now that we have the pissing contest out of the way, we need information," Rayna said.

Vincent's eyes belonged to Rayna, and with his devious smile gone, he was ready for business. "What kind of information?"

"About the hunters around town. They're looking for demon blood and I need to know what kind, and why."

"That's valuable information. Even if I was able to help, I wouldn't give that away so freely. Not even to you, my love."

"How valuable?"

Vincent smiled and gave that almost-shrug again. "That would require some thought. Besides, if I did know such things, I would not choose this place to speak of them. I will think upon your request and I'll be in touch." He flicked his wrist elegantly to wave us away.

Rayna raised a brow. "I don't have time for games. If you can't help, then I need to know that now, so I can source out other options."

"Ah, you have the patience of a human, my sweet Rayna. It never ceases to amaze me. Yes, I will be able to help. However, I will need some time to gather the information. Once I have it, I will know its price," he said.

Vincent made another motion with his hand and the group of vampires returned, surrounding the booth. "I admire you bringing him here, my sweet. He's strong, although I would have thought you too smart to bring a hunter into Revelations," he said.

The other vampires turned to me, some reacting with a hiss, while others let their faces change and fangs drop from their gums. I reached for my daggers, and then remembered I'd given up the luxury of weapons when I came in here. Before I could do anything else, Rayna's hand slipped into mine.

"Come on, Chase."

I kept my eyes on the vampires and could see Vincent's amusement.

"Chase, I said let's go." Rayna's green feline eyes were pleading with me, and I did something I never thought I'd do. I turned my back on a group of vampires and walked away.

Rayna's hand was warm and soft. The sensation was strange, but welcoming at the same time. We climbed up the stairs to the alley, where she stopped and turned to me.

"You can't be like that with these people. It's dangerous. Vincent can be an asshole, but if you're going to come to places like this, you have to control yourself. If that had gone bad, we'd be dead, or barely alive and no closer to finding what we need," she said.

"Well, it would have been helpful to know how strong he is, and that he might try that mind control crap on me. At least you could have mentioned that he's a centuries old vampire, so I could have figured out the rest," I said.

Rayna sighed. "You're right."

I was all ready to argue, but those words took the wind out of my sails. "I'm right?"

"I should have told you, but I didn't think he'd react like such a child, or that you would, for that matter. His full name is Vincent Taryk."

"Taryk? As in the most powerful vampire family in the city? Wow, yeah, that information would have been really helpful," I said. I was starting to get angry, but we were interrupted by a stuttering voice.

"Cha- Chase?" Willy stood behind us.

"Willy? I didn't even hear you coming down the alley," I said, a little disappointed in myself.

Willy shrugged. "It's what I do: try to go unnoticed. What are you doing here?"

"Seeing if we could dig anything up on the hunters, trying to find out what they're looking for," I said.

"Any luck?"

"No, but that guy Vincent is a real piece of work."

Willy shuddered at the name and held his palms up. "I'm not go- go- going in if he's in th- th- there." He turned and started back up the alley.

"Willy, wait up!" I said, jogging to catch up to him. "What's wrong?"

"That guy is insane, that's what."

I laughed. "I figured as much."

"No you don't un- un- understand Chase. He's worse than any hunter or demon I've ever met. He's dangerous."

"You know from experience?"

"All the Underworlders are afraid of him. You have no idea what he's capable of."

"I think I just got a taste of it," I said.

"Do you go around making friends everywhere? You're lucky you're not a vegetable."

"Okay, now I think you're being dramatic. I can hold my own."

"Well, I saw him shatter the mind of a warlock without breaking a sweat, and you ain't got that kind of magic," he said.

I raised an eyebrow at that. "No offense taken."

"Look, I gotta go. Good luck in your search, but I'd stay away from Vincent if I were you," Willy said and disappeared around the corner of the alley.

Rayna stared at me, a kind of smile I didn't recognize playing on her lips.

"What?"

"You made a friend. A demon friend. It's kind of cute," she laughed.

"We're not friends, we're acquaintances at best."

"Uh-huh." She let another giggle slip out but I ignored it.

"So, any truth to what Willy said? Is Vincent that powerful?" I asked.

Rayna shrugged. "I've heard the rumors, but he's never tried anything aggressive with me, so I wouldn't know."

"So you know him well?"

"Hardly. The guy's helped me out a few times, that's all."

"And what's the cost of that help, usually?"

She shrugged. "He has some strange obsession with me, so it's usually not much. If he charges me anything, it's a few hundred bucks or some blood."

I let my face show the revulsion I felt. "Yuck! You let that thing drink from you? What's the matter with you?"

Rayna rolled her eyes. "I gave him blood. I didn't say it was mine. Nothing could convince me to let him suck on me." She shivered and wrinkled her nose.

We started back as the sky was starting to show hints of pink and red. The silence between us started to get uncomfortable so I tried to make conversation.

"How did you meet Marcus?"

Rayna stayed quiet for a moment before responding. "I don't know when we actually met. He's just always been there. He knew my mother before I was born," she said.

"What happened to her?" I asked. I regretted the question the moment I said it. Rayna stared at me and I thought she might hit me again.

"She died."

It wasn't the answer I expected, but it was better than a punch in the face.

"Sorry."

"Don't be. I just don't like to think about it," she said. "What about you? What's your story?"

I didn't know where to start, but we had a long walk ahead of us, so I figured the beginning was a good place.

"Well, I started training in the Circle to be a hunter the first day I could walk. My dad wanted to get a head start. But when I didn't get an elemental power at my ceremony, the Circle didn't know what to do with me. That had never happened before, so they just exiled me. From then until I met Marcus and your fist, I've been trying to survive," I said.

Rayna smiled. "Sorry, but you kind of deserved it. My fist, that is. But why does the Underworld hate you so much? I've never known the Underworld to go after anyone the way they've gone after you."

"I don't think it's really me they hate; it's my father. He's one of the most powerful hunters the Circle has ever had. I think the demons believe that if they kill me, they'll be getting some sort of revenge against my father. Too bad none of them realize that if they did kill me it'd be a weight off my father's shoulders."

"That's not true, Chase," Rayna said.

I laughed. "You don't know my father. He thinks I'm a disgrace. He actually accused my mom of cheating on him because he couldn't believe his own son didn't have an element."

"That's terrible."

I shrugged. "You play the hand you're dealt, I guess."

Even though the topic should've had me boiling with anger, I found talking to Rayna somewhat calming. The more we talked, the more I realized we had more in common than I could have guessed. We both loved the same music and horror movies, but I couldn't help but laugh when she complained about Marcus. Considering the things he'd seen in his life, who would have thought a big bad hunter the size of a house would get scared during horror movies?

After chatting with Rayna, and having spent some time with Willy, I was starting to feel like I had more in common with the Underworld than the Circle. I wasn't anything like the hunters involved in beating up Willy, but even the Circle I remembered from growing up seemed distant and irrelevant to my current life.

I felt a little disappointment as we approached the condo. This was the first pleasant hour I'd had in a long time. Mom was right; we were more alike than I ever would've guessed. Rayna had surprised me.

Chapter 14

The sky changed from red and pink to shades of orange, with streaks of yellow that lit up the condo strikingly. The living room table was now also covered with open books, and Marcus and Mom were both asleep on the couch. Mom's head was on Marcus's shoulder, and Marcus's neck looked to be on a painful angle against the back of the sofa.

Rayna led me to the second floor to show me the room I could stay in. Oddly, I wasn't tired, so I went back up to the library. If half of what Willy said was true about Vincent, then I was praying for another source to find what the Circle was up to.

I skimmed through more books, but nothing jumped out at me. Marcus had an impressive collection, and although I couldn't help but wonder how he'd managed to get it, so far none of it was helping.

I scanned the shelves again before I ended up at Marcus's desk. The bottom drawer hung half open and I could see some books inside. I grabbed one black notebook and read the date *March/06* written on the spine. A few pages in, I found a passage about Rayna and realized it was Marcus's journal.

Rayna is showing signs of telekinetic abilities and can move small objects with her mind. The power is weak now, but it shows her progression. Although she is an earth elemental, and telepathy is a trait of air, I believe this pulls more on her abilities as a witch than a hunter.

She is developing the ability to draw power from the earth, in both a healing and destructive manner. Although inconsistent, it's piqued my interest.

Earth and air elementals are strange compared to the others; they have a wider range of abilities that can develop. *Rayna has shown signs of psychic potential* was one of the other notes written on that same page. I flipped through some more, reading a line or two on each page until one passage caught my eye.

Rayna's exhibiting more of her demonic background. There are nights I've found her screaming in her room. When I entered, she was sweating, tense, and running a blisteringly high temperature, like a shifter in the beginning stages of its first change. She has yet to exhibit any other signs of the change.

After a few days, the symptoms of the shift disappear. I haven't seen this behavior from her in many years (see entries January 5 – 10, 2001). I'd hoped they were something she'd grown out of, however, I fear their return and what it means. We still don't know where the shifter bloodline comes from. I've found nothing of it in her mother's lineage, and her father could not have carried the disease because of his hunter heritage. If her body continues to attempt a shift, I worry she will suffer permanent damage, or worse...

My pulse sped as I finished the passage and I looked back into the drawer, searching the spine of each book until I found January/01.

January 7th, 2001

The attacks started a few days ago. Her muscles have taken on an abnormal strength and tension, and her body temperature has risen to over 108 degrees. So far, the morning after the attacks she's fine, showing no signs of pain or memory of the previous night, until last night.

Rayna showed the first sign of a true change: her eyes shifted into full werecat form. I was expecting the rest of her to change, but she did not fully shift. When she awoke this morning, her eyes had not shifted back. The bright blues of her childhood are gone, and now all that remain are the bright green eyes of a cat. I fear they will not change back.

I have never heard of a shifter having experienced this phenomenon. I will have to confer with others to see if there are any other recorded cases. I have not told Rayna yet. I worked a small spell to ensure she will not notice the change, for her peace of mind. I will continue to work with her, but until puberty when her magic starts to develop, it will be unwise to assume anything.

"Anything interesting?" The deep voice cut through the silence and I jumped. I slammed the book shut and looked up to find Marcus staring down at me.

"I, uh, I'm sorry, I didn't mean to snoop, it's just, well, the drawer was open and..." I stumbled over my words. It was true I hadn't gone up to the library to snoop. Perhaps once I saw the notebook I could have resisted, but I hadn't. I had a sudden, unmistakable feeling of déjà vu which I couldn't quite place.

Marcus stepped towards me and my stomach clenched. My nerves rattled as he neared, but calmed when he extended a large dark hand towards me, palm up.

"Sorry," I repeated, handing him the book.

Marcus shook his head. "Most of what's in here isn't anything I wouldn't be willing to share, but there are some private notes I've made. I'd prefer to keep them private, for now." He slipped the book back into the bottom drawer of his desk.

"Of course. I never meant to invade your privacy."

"No harm done," he said. He turned his invariable neutral expression into a half smile that looked forced.

"You really don't know why Rayna is part shifter?" I said before realizing, given the circumstances, maybe I shouldn't have been asking. "Sorry," I added.

"Don't be. It was bound to come up again eventually, whether you read this or not. And no, I truly don't know. Her mother was a witch, as were her ancestors. Where the line of shifter DNA came from is unclear. Her father was part of the Circle, so unless he somehow, impossibly, carried the virus and lived, there is no reasonable explanation. Lately, however, it seems that's the only possible one we have."

"Did you know her father?"

"I hunted with him for many years, as did your father, but he vanished soon after Rayna was...conceived," he replied, with a hint of embarrassment.

"Rayna started showing signs of the change when she was seven, and that's early even among born shifters. I tried a spell to prevent her from seeing the change in her eyes, but I underestimated her resistance to magic. The spell should've lasted years, but it worked only days. Once a seven year old starts asking questions, you cannot stop until you've answered them all. They are most resilient opponents. But enough about this. How did things go at Revelations?"

The major subject change bothered me. Marcus was always so quick to avoid questions, but since he'd caught me snooping, I thought it best to let him guide the conversation.

"Pretty much a bust," I admitted.

"How so?"

"We met Vincent, but I'd consider him more of a last resort than a resource."

"And why's that?"

"It's Vincent *Taryk*. Need I say more?"

"Ah yes, I too have heard the rumors. But he has helped us before; he has a particular liking for Rayna."

"Yeah, I noticed that too, but it sounds like the only way we're getting anything out of him is at a price that I'm not sure I'd like."

Marcus raised his eyebrows and nodded. "I'd like to investigate further and avoid making any deals with him until we determine that's our only option."

"Why can't we go with plan "A" and track down Brock? Between him and his lackeys, we're bound to find something. It seems to be the lesser of two evils, and better than making a deal with a powerful demon. I don't want to owe anything to the Taryks."

"It's too dangerous. We'll find another way."

"You do realize we're dealing with both the Circle and the Underworld? There's nothing safe about this situation in the first place. We aren't going to find the answer in some book. We're going to have to get our hands dirty."

"I am well aware of what we're dealing with, indeed more so than you. I'm also experienced enough to weigh the danger of what you're suggesting. Neither course is worth the risk," he said firmly.

I tried to stop myself but I couldn't – my anger was already on the rise. "Is that really it, Marcus? Are you trying to keep us all safe, or are you scared of what'll happen if the Circle finds out your little secret?"

Marcus looked at me, still wearing his neutral expression. "What secret might that be?"

"Hmm, let me think. I dunno, maybe the fact that you're alive?"

"My secrets are my own, Chase, and for now I'd like to keep them that way. It's better for everybody."

I wanted to argue. I wanted to fight and provoke some emotion in him but it was no use. No matter what I said, he would have a calm response. That was more infuriating than anything.

I stared at him, defiance in my eyes, and then turned away. I didn't agree with his decision. I felt like he knew something I didn't, and I didn't like that one bit.

"Chase," Marcus said.

"What?"

"Sit down. Please," he said. I was tempted to keep walking, but turned back and slid into one of the leather chairs.

"Chase, I have no doubt in my mind you'll make a formidable leader someday. However, you're not ready yet. Your ideas aren't bad; they show how much you want to get to the bottom of things, as do I. But they're impulsive, and they put you in unnecessary danger. I can assure you, there will be some point at which the danger will be unavoidable, but throwing yourself in peril is reckless. I won't risk any of my people needlessly. I let the Circle believe in my death because it would paint a target on all of us if they knew of my continued existence," he said.

"From who, my father?"

Marcus sighed and nodded. "Yes, among others."

I felt badly now. My anger had gotten the best of me once again, probably to mask the guilt over reading the journal. "I'm still sorry about your journal."

"I'm not mad about the journal. There are many of them, all of which I will let you read, at some point. But you're not ready yet."

"What makes you think that?"

"I've seen it," he replied.

"What does that mean?"

"It means it's time for you to get some rest."

I wanted to ask more questions, but knew his lack of answers would only frustrate me further. Marcus clearly didn't tell you more than he felt he needed to. That was something I wasn't sure I'd ever be able to get used to.

I walked back to the stairs and stopped, giving in to my hunger for answers.

"Marcus, do you know what the hunters want?"

He sighed. "I have an idea, but until I know for sure, I don't want to panic anyone."

Yep, that made me even angrier.

Chapter 15

I searched the books on the lower shelves, but I knew the ones I wanted were on the top. I moved the ladder to the right spot and climbed. Dad had said I wasn't allowed to look at these books until I was eighteen. I was six years away, but too curious for my own good. I wanted to show him I was ready to know what he knew. I wanted him to be proud of me, so I was taking the initiative, just like he wanted. "You need to take the initiative to be better than the next guy, Chase. Show me you want it." I let those words propel me up the ladder.

I reached the top rung and searched for something of interest. I found a collection of small books, all the same size and color, with unmarked spines. I pulled the first one out and opened it, recognizing my father's handwriting within.

After reading a few lines I realized it was one of his journals. I always saw him writing in them, but he'd never tell me what he wrote about. I went against my better judgment and slipped the book into my pocket. It would make for some interesting reading later.

I stepped down the ladder, but when I was only halfway, the door opened. I turned to see my father's back as he closed the door. I panicked and my heart leapt in my chest. Before I could decipher my own thoughts, I slipped and started to fall.

My foot snagged a lower rung and stopped me a few feet from the floor. My body jerked violently and smashed into the ladder. I muffled a cry of pain and my father turned to face me with an unfriendly look.

"What are you doing?" he asked. His tone was one of surprise. He didn't seem as angry as I expected.

"I, uh, was just looking," I muttered, my heart pounding in my throat so hard I was sure he could hear it.

I felt the book slip from my back pocket and slide down my back, making the sound of ruffling pages as it hit the floor. I looked at my father and saw the shock on his face. All I could do was close my eyes.

I felt a hand grip my shirt and lift me up. His other hand wrenched my foot out of the rung and I cried out in pain. When my foot was free, it dropped down to meet the other, but they weren't touching the ground.

He carried me with one arm towards the door. He flung and released me, and my back cracked against the door handle.

"What did I tell you about snooping?" he screamed.

"I'm sorry! I don't know what I was thinking."

"Of course you knew what you were thinking. You didn't just accidentally climb that ladder and take one of my journals, did you? One of the very books you knew you were prohibited to touch. After all the work I've put into you, after all the training, you repay me by going through my things?"

"I'm sorry Dad. I didn't mean to make you upset; I wanted to make you proud. I was trying to take the initiative, like you said, to be better than the next guy."

"So this is my fault?" he said, his face turning red.

"No, Dad, that's not what I meant."

"Oh, I know what you meant, and you know what I think? I think it's worse than snooping. You couldn't own up and be responsible for your actions like a man. No. You had to make an excuse and blame it on someone else. Well, that's worse than snooping, that's cowardly, and I won't allow my son to grow up a coward."

Before I could brace myself the back of his hand hit my face. I fell to the floor with the heat from his knuckles burning my skin. I felt the bruise form instantly.

I hunched over on all fours, feeling the heat of his anger beat down on me.

"Get out," he said, too quietly.

I crawled to the door, moving as fast as I could, but my ankle was throbbing.

"Get out!" he yelled.

The room's temperature spiked and sweat dripped off me. He kicked me from behind, sending a sharp pain up my spine and pushing me the last few inches. I reached for the brass handle on the door, dented from my back's impact, and I wasn't sure it would work.

Relief washed over me as the handle turned, but I struggled to hold on to the near-scalding brass. I pushed through the pain and pulled the door open, using it as support to stand up. I pulled the door shut behind me and fell to the ground as the latch slid into place.

My eyes opened and drops of sweat ran down my face. My pulse spiked and panic set in until the smell of coffee and bacon washed over me. I breathed a sigh of relief as I realized it had been a dream. The scene had felt so real and I remembered it like it was yesterday. I took deep breaths to calm myself and let the scent of breakfast bring me back to reality.

It was strange to have a clean white ceiling above me. There were no cracks, no plaster crumbling on me, but most noticeably, no sounds of yelling coming through the wall. I could hear distant faint chatter laced with a bit of laughter, and it helped calm my nerves.

I opened the door and the smell of coffee and bacon grew stronger as I headed downstairs. Mom and Rayna were at the kitchen table and Rayna's laughter filled the room.

"Morning, sleepy head," Mom said.

"Morning. What time is it?"

"Almost eleven," Rayna answered in a chipper voice.

Marcus was in the kitchen moving frying pans around on the stove, cracking eggs, and creating delicious smells. I went to the coffee pot, grabbed an empty mug and filled it to the rim.

"Sleep well?" Mom asked.

I nodded, taking a sip of my coffee. "What have you two been talking about?"

The ladies looked at each other before Rayna answered. "Your mom was telling me what you were like growing up."

I choked on a mouthful of coffee and had to force it down to keep from spitting it across the table.

"Oh gods help me."

"They can't help you with this one," Rayna said. "I'm told you were quite the handful: arrogant, rude, and, well, very much like you are now."

My mom laughed. I really didn't like the way they were ganging up on me.

"I'll have you know I was a perfect child. And I'm not sure I'm pleased you two are even discussing this."

"Well, you don't have a choice. All you're doing now is interrupting," Rayna said.

"Marcus, a little help here?"

He didn't take his eyes off the cookware. "If there is one thing I've learned in all my years, it's that women will talk and you just have to live with it."

"Ha!" Rayna said.

"Great, good for us guys to stick together," I said. "Now if you'll excuse me, I'll be *living with this* in the other room."

I was still taken with the incredible view from the condo. It overlooked most of the city and I could see the edge of the forest on the other side. The main thing I loved about living in Stonewall was that once out of the city itself, there were forests full of life all around it.

I took in the scene for a few minutes before I turned on the TV, watching as it flickered to life on the news channel. The anchors talked about the weather, calling for more heavy rain and storms. They moved through a few other light topics before one caught my attention.

"Reports of kidnappings have been coming in from throughout the city. Although no names have been released, multiple calls to authorities have been reported.

There have been no missing persons reports filed as of yet, but the police are urging the public to take caution. Reports from witnesses say an unmarked van has been seen pulling up to people on the street, where a group of masked men then pull the unsuspecting citizens into the vehicle.

Again, there have been no missing persons reports filed, but the sheer number of calls placed last night and early this morning have the police on high alert."

"Breakfast is served!" Marcus announced.

I stared at the TV, wondering if the story had any correlation to the hunters. I shook the thought away and went to the table.

Plates of pancakes, sausages, bacon, eggs, and toast covered the surface and gave off warm aromas. I couldn't remember the last time I'd had a meal like this. With Mom working on rotating shifts, we almost never ate together, let alone meals like this. Mom wasn't a great cook either, so my diet consisted mostly of pizza pockets and salad bowls full of cereal.

We all dug in, loading up our plates with mountains of everything. The food was fantastic and I was grateful for it, but I was astounded by Rayna's appetite. She out-ate both Marcus and me by a plate and a half before turning in her fork.

We all helped clean up before settling down in the living room to discuss our next move. The TV was still on and everybody was enthralled by the news when it repeated what I'd seen. We were all in agreement that it could be connected to the Circle, and if it wasn't, it was a strange coincidence. The hunters were searching for someone specific, and now people were getting scooped up. That would be one hell of a coincidence.

We'd need to find out if demons were the ones being taken. The plan laid out was for Rayna and me to go back to Revelations and talk to a few people that weren't Vincent. The less we had to work with him, the better off we'd be.

Rayna changed out of her pajamas and into khakis paired with a stretchy dark blue and white striped cotton shirt. Her hair was up again, this time in a high ponytail with two black strands left loose to frame her face. When she sat down to slip brown wedges on her feet, I couldn't resist the urge to comment.

"Are you sure it's even worth going down there wearing that much clothing? Nobody is going to want to look at you, let alone talk to you," I said with a smirk.

She rolled her eyes. "Very funny, but the crowd is different during the day; I can get away with wearing this. Besides, I still look good."

I frowned, having expected a flaming response. I found myself almost disappointed not to get one.

By the time we got to Revelations, it was well into the afternoon. The club wasn't as busy as the night before, but it still held an impressive crowd. We grabbed a table near the dartboards, and I wasn't the slightest bit sad to see that Vincent wasn't there.

After we settled into our spot, we surveyed the room, trying to figure out who to talk to first. I didn't have a clue who was who or even what, so I was more or less waiting on Rayna.

"I don't see anybody who would be of any help. Actually, I don't see anyone I even recognize," she said.

I was scanning the room again when Willy came striding through the door, so I waved him over.

Wearing jeans and a white shirt with a spot of what looked like spaghetti sauce on the front, Willy looked as sloppy as usual. His shirt, which was too small, showed an inch of stomach as he moved and made his scrawny, hairy arms looked disproportionate. His brown hair was as messy as it always seemed to be, and his attempt at a beard wasn't getting much better either.

"You making yourself a regular?" he said in a surprisingly cheerful voice.

"Haven't decided," I said.

He ordered a weirdly named drink, and when it came to the table it looked as gross as it sounded, somewhere between a milkshake and the thick glop his Grams had fed me. It smelled like the inside of a gym bag.

"I don't even want to know what's in that," I said.

"Do- don't be so nervous. Try it." He slid it over to me, but I cringed. "Su- suit yourself. You don't know what you're missing. How about you?" He offered the drink to Rayna who only shook her head, looking almost as disgusted as I did.

"Willy, this is Rayna. Rayna, Willy."

"Nice to meet you," Rayna said.

"Sa- same he- here."

"Willy, have you heard anything about the kidnappings last night?" I asked, getting straight to the point.

"Heard about 'em? I saw one of 'em happen, not long after I saw you two," he said. "I thought they were coming for me at first. I was relieved to see them grab a shifter instead."

"Do you think it has something to do with the demons they're looking for?" I asked.

Willy shook his head. "Not *demons* but *demon*. I heard through a guy who knows a guy, whose sister's friend's cousin is dating a warlock, and he knows that it's just one special type of demon."

It took me a moment to catch up, but he'd answered my question.

"Do you know what kind of demon they're looking for?" Rayna asked.

Willy shook his head, sipping his drink through the straw. "Not for su- sure, but it looks like it might be som- some kind of shifter."

"Well, that's a start," I said, but Rayna shook her head.

"We need more than a start right now. If hunters are going around nabbing Underworlders, we've got to stop them. Who knows what they're going to do if they find whatever they're looking for."

I wasn't sure what to say. I couldn't believe I was worried about Underworlders to begin with, but I also knew that if the Underworld had more people in it like Rayna and Willy, I didn't want anything bad to happen to them. I was learning that bloodline doesn't determine good and evil, but people do. I had a loyalty to myself and the oath I'd made. A hunter didn't make an oath unless he intended to keep it. Elemental powers or not, I was a hunter.

"Well then, we need to figure out where Vincent is and see what he can do for us," I said.

"Marcus said it's too dangerous and I think he might be right. Vincent isn't as willing to help this time. Besides, you said yourself he was bad news. We have to find another way."

"Well, I'm changing my mind. Doing things Marcus's way isn't going to be the quickest way to get answers. Whatever the hunters want, they want it badly enough to start grabbing demons off the street and that's not their style. They thrive on being discreet. Besides, if you've gotten information from Vincent before, why should this time be different?"

"I don't know why it's different. It just is. And Marcus said..."

"Look, we tried Marcus's way and it didn't work. He sent us here to see what we could find, right?"

She nodded.

"Well, we found Vincent. Don't get me wrong, I agree with Marcus. He is dangerous and I don't want to work with him, but he's the only lead we've got right now."

Rayna took a minute to think about it. "You're right."

"Great, so where do we find him?"

"I don't have a clue. I've always met him here."

"Well, it's daytime, so we've got to figure out where his nest is."

"I know where it is," Willy said.

I smiled at Willy. He was proving to be more helpful than I'd guessed.

After listening to Willy's directions three times, I still couldn't figure out how to get to the nest. I looked to Rayna for support, pleading with my eyes in the hope that she could figure out what he meant, but she shook her head.

I interrupted Willy while he was drawing a very sad excuse for a map on a stained napkin. "Willy, I'm glad you're helping, I really am, but neither of us can make sense of what you're saying. Have you ever actually been there?"

Willy nodded, but looked haunted at the thought. I hated to put him through this, especially after seeing how scared he had been last night, but I didn't have a choice.

"Willy, you have to take us there."

Willy's face drained of all color and he shook his head firmly. "Forget it. I'm happy to help, but I'm more of a stand-on-the sidelines-and-shout sort of guy, not the get-in-the-game type. I said I'd give you directions. Look, I even have a map now." He held up the stained napkin with a sheepish grin.

"Willy, you're coming with us. Besides, it's daytime. What could possibly happen?"

Chapter 16

Willy wasn't happy and he wouldn't let us forget it for a moment, making the cab ride nearly unbearable. We passed through downtown and a few residential areas, and a ridiculous fare later we emerged from the car in Stonewall's industrial area. The sun was getting lower in the sky, but we still had a few hours before it would set.

We passed a few small buildings that looked abandoned, their windows smashed and the doors barely hanging on. Willy slowed and shook as we approached a large brick building. A chain link fence topped with barbed wire surrounded it, broken only by two giant gates in the middle. I tugged on one, but a chain and padlock held them shut.

"You sure this is the right place? It looks a little rundown to be the home of the head of a vampire family." I pulled on the gate again, but I hadn't brought anything to pick the lock, so we'd need another way in. "Willy, is this the right place or not?" I repeated. Frustrated, I turned to look him in the eye and saw a man with a gun to Willy's head.

The guy was shorter than me, but his tight black shirt showed off defined muscles. One gloved hand pushed the gun hard against Willy's temple while the other covered his mouth. Another man was holding Rayna the same way.

I stepped forward and reached for my blade, but the cold barrel of a gun against the back of my head stopped me. I closed my eyes and cursed under my breath. "I guess this is the right place."

The gunmen unlocked the gate and led us into the warehouse. We entered a large open room littered with furniture, most of it old and giving off a stale smell.

Our captors pushed us to the middle of the room, where other lackeys waited. They forced us each into old wooden chairs and tied our hands and legs with rope. I stayed silent and tried to figure out what to do. After all, these people were vamplings: humans who knew the Underworld existed and had fallen in love with their idea of it. They were unpredictable at best, and they were everywhere. Vampires, werewolves, witches, and, in fact, almost all demons had various uses for them. These ones would watch over the vampires during the day, in the hope that if they served long enough, they would be turned.

I should've known Vincent would have such minions; a vampire of his status didn't leave himself vulnerable to being staked in broad daylight. It was considered bad business to go to a vampire's nest during the day, since it signified you meant them harm.

The more I thought about it, the more I kicked myself and realized that everything was far from alright. The thought of how scared Willy had been to come here made my gut hurt. I had put everyone in danger.

"Vincent will be pleased to have such a fresh meal for breakfast," a woman said as she stepped in front of us. She was short, with a high blonde ponytail that reached her butt. Pink lips set in pale skin formed a smile that sent chills down my spine.

"Actually, we're here to see Vincent," I said.

"Isn't that what they all say?"

"I'm not sure. This is my first time."

I watched anger fill her eyes and she raised her hand to prepare a response of her own. I braced for impact, but I smiled when I felt the back of her hand on my cheek. She was a human and I was a hunter. She couldn't compete with my supernatural strength. I might not be immortal like the vampires, but I could take a hell of lot more than she could dish out. At my laugh, the self-satisfied look drained from her face.

"You're a *mortal*. You're going to have to try harder than that," I said.

A larger man moved towards me with his gun held by the barrel and smashed it against my jaw. This was more effective than the slap and it did hurt, but the pain was replaced by a burst of adrenaline. "And what exactly are you, boy?" the man said, leaning down to push his face against mine.

"He's a hunter." The voice echoed through the room. "Chase Williams, son of the infamous Riley Williams, if I'm not mistaken. Exiled by his own kind to live among the demons and the mundane."

I hated the fact everybody knew my history, but what was worse was only ever being known as the son of Riley Williams, a name not particularly welcome among current company.

I heard the soft padding of shoes on pavement and Vincent appeared in front of me. He was dressed in a dark well-tailored suit with a bright red silk shirt underneath, the kind that didn't need a tie. The simple fact that he was awake showed how powerful he was. This reaffirmed my need to be nervous and my stomach turned with more guilt.

Vincent stopped in front of us, paying particular attention to me. He smiled and crouched to look me in the eye. "I've done my research, and I expected more than this from you, Chase, considering your father..."

"Yeah, yeah, you expected better from me, being the son of the big, scary Riley Williams and all. Save it, I've heard it." My interruption didn't faze him and he turned his attention to Rayna.

"Mmm, I can't say I don't enjoy seeing you tied up, my sweet. Although I'd hoped it would be under...different circumstances," he said, with the smile I imagined he used to seduce everybody.

"How original," Rayna retorted, rolling her eyes.

In a flash Vincent moved back to me. "Ah, sweet Rayna. Such a pretty face, but she does have a venom all her own, doesn't she? You see, I am one of the few that hasn't turned his back on Rayna. While the rest of the Underworld despises her for working with a hunter and killing other demons, I have not denied her. Instead I offered her sanctuary, a home, a family, and the power that would come from being with me." He faced Rayna again. "I've offered you a place to belong," he said.

Rayna looked up and nodded. "And for that I am grateful. But I already have a home and a family." She was being polite and if we hadn't been bound, I had a feeling she would have chosen her words differently.

"Yes, the hunter. Marcus, isn't it? I never did understand how you could refuse power and acceptance among your peers to be with a hunter. I offered you a throne and still you chose our enemy."

"Marcus isn't the Underworld's enemy and you know it," Rayna replied.

"Oh yes, he's the hunter who can't decide which side he's on. And it seems you two have recruited yet another confused soul, one whose own family exiled him."

"He knows where he belongs. We don't see things as black and white. I would think you of all people would appreciate that."

He laughed and looked at me with ferocity in his eyes "Does she speak for you now, boy? Have you no voice of your own?"

I swallowed my anger and forced a smile. "No, she doesn't, but you two seem to have some personal shit going on and I am rather enjoying the show."

Instantly he was looming over me again. "Is that it? Do you get enjoyment from watching her deny me? Perhaps I should kill you and get my own pleasure from watching the pain in her eyes while I drain your blood. Come to think of it, that would bring me immense delight. If I cannot have her, perhaps I can take what she wants. We will both live unhappily ever after."

His breath on my face was warm and smelled of death. I wasn't sure why he thought killing me would cause Rayna pain, but I enjoyed that even tied up and unable to move, I could still get under his skin. I smiled and watched it infuriate him.

He stepped behind my chair and I could feel my pulse race in my neck. My arrogance had gotten in my way again, and Vincent succeeded in making me anxious as he ran his fingers down my neck. "Careful hunter, the quickening of your pulse brings my hunger, and I have yet to have my breakfast," he whispered in my ear.

I closed my eyes at the smell of old blood and shuddered as his tongue ran up the back of my ear. I tried to focus and put all my energy into calming myself.

Vincent sniffed at my neck, letting his lips graze my ear as he spoke. "It's been decades since I've had a hunter. The Circle gives off an enticing scent..."

I kept my eyes closed, trying to keep my shields up. The last thing I wanted right then was him poking around in my head.

As though at the flick of a switch, Vincent pulled away and let his calm, seductive tone return. "Well, back to business. Shall we?" The change in his demeanor startled me, but after centuries of life I could only imagine how one might get a little moody. "You want something from me and I can assume you need it rather urgently, otherwise you wouldn't have risked coming here. The information I now possess must be worth more to you than I previously perceived," he said.

Rayna jumped in. "I know the routine. What kind of blood do you want? Warlock perhaps? It's the most expensive and I know you enjoy it. Or is it cash this time around?"

"I'm afraid that won't do this time, my sweet Rayna. There is no blood that can satisfy my current craving. There's something else I need. What you've asked for brings us to a much higher pay scale."

Rayna studied him and arched a brow. "Do tell," she said.

Vincent smiled cunningly. "For years, I've kept you safe within the Underworld. I did this in somewhat of a selfish manner, hoping you'd come to your senses and accept the throne I offered. I've helped you in exchange for mere blood and pennies, and it has made me look weak among my people. I see now my good intentions will go unrewarded, so I must treat this situation as I would any business transaction. There will be no more charity from me, my sweet. If you wish to know what the hunters seek, you will do something for me first."

"What's that?"

"I want you to retrieve something, something I've been in search of for many decades. It has been brought to my attention that it's been nearby all along, and you are going to get it for me."

I looked at Willy, who had his eyes closed and whose skin had turned pale brown to match his chair. Sweat was beading on his brow and his entire body was trembling. I immediately felt more guilt, which quickly turned to anger.

"What is said item and where do we find it?" I asked impatiently.

"A scroll," Vincent said. "And outside of town, in the southern woods."

I laughed. "You expect us to find a piece of paper in a forest? It might as well be a needle in a haystack."

Vincent sighed and shook his head. "In the forest, there is a tree unlike any other. It sits in a clearing a few miles in. It holds an entrance to an underground sanctuary, and there rests the scroll I seek."

"And why do you need us to get it? Why not get it yourself?" I asked.

"Because it's guarded and I have no desire to put myself in harm's way, not when I have you, who just so happen to need something from me. It's all a matter of convenience."

"Well, we can't do much if we're tied to these chairs," I said.

Vincent nodded to one of the guards, who came and untied Rayna and me.

"I think your vampling needs some help counting. He forgot one," I said pointing at Willy.

Vincent laughed. "I'm afraid we're going to hold on to this one. Consider him an insurance policy."

"What do you mean, *insurance policy*? We do this for you and you tell us what we need to know. There isn't any need for an insurance policy. It's a fair exchange," I said.

"You don't understand. If you come back alive, there will be many others who wish to have what you possess. This will ensure you bring it directly to *me*," he replied.

I stepped forward. "No. That wasn't part of the deal."

A vampling stepped in front of Vincent before I could get closer.

"I'm afraid this is the deal, Mr. Williams. Or you can simply leave and I'll keep your little friend for my personal enjoyment. If I remember correctly, he's quite the screamer, but handles an impressive amount of pain," said the vampire, winking at Willy.

Willy's face drained of all its remaining color and his eyes pleaded with me. I balled my fists and tried to move past the guard in front of me, but his hands came up and pushed me back. I threw my fist into his face with all the force of the anger boiling inside me. I felt his jaw break and he collapsed to the ground. A look of surprise crossed Vincent's face as the body fell.

"No deal," I said and lunged towards Vincent, but he vanished.

I was thrown to the ground and vamplings piled on top of me. I struggled to push myself up, but there were too many of them.

"Enough!" Vincent's voice commanded.

The bodies and hands holding me down vanished and I jumped to my feet. Rayna had a gun against her head again, and Vincent was standing behind Willy.

"You will do what I ask or I will kill all of you, starting with him."

Willy's eyes rolled back in his head and I thought he'd pass out.

"I don't wish to harm any of you. At least not at this point in time. Do we or do we not have a deal?"

I watched Vincent; his neutral expression and disinterested tone disgusted me. He'd have no qualms about murdering Willy. Killing was at the core of his lifestyle.

"Fine," I said through gritted teeth. "But he isn't to be touched while we're gone, understand? When we get back with the scroll, you give us the information we need, we take Willy with us, and we all walk away unharmed."

Vincent's lips curled into a smile. "My, what a fine negotiator you are. Agreed. Until you return, he will not be touched."

I shook my head. "No. You're leaving out the part of us leaving safely. You'll agree to all of it or we'll take the scroll to the highest bidder and come back for him ourselves."

The smile vanished from his face. I think I had finally caught him off guard. "I agree to all of your terms on the condition that you're back in forty eight hours. My patience has its limits, hunter."

"Fine."

Vincent clapped his hands together. "I'm glad we have an arrangement."

I turned to Willy. "We'll be back as soon as we can. I promise."

He opened his eyes and looked at me. They were jet black, but I could see the fear inside them. I turned my back on him and walked away, but the sight of his terror still haunted me.

"Dammit!" I shouted as we stepped outside. I threw my fist into the side of the building and shattered several bricks.

"Chase, relax. You didn't know this would happen," Rayna said.

"But Marcus told me, told us, not to go to Vincent again, and I pushed it. I pulled you and Willy into this. I knew better."

She put a hand on my shoulder and forced me to look her in the eyes. "Forget what we should've done and think about what we're going to do. We have forty-eight hours to get to the forest and find the scroll. Don't forget that if we're not back on time, Vincent can do what he wants with Willy," she said.

I shook my head and punched the wall again. Rayna grabbed my shoulder and pulled me towards her. "Get your head straight. We need to go back to the condo, get some gear and head out." She checked her watch. "We have to hurry. Marcus will be back soon and we don't need him to know about this."

I closed my eyes and took a few deep breaths to clear my head before I nodded. We had to do this for Willy; once he was safe I could come back and deal with Vincent on my own. "Let's go."

Chapter 17

We didn't know what we were walking into, so a few daggers weren't going be enough. I slipped a sword into a sheath that fit snugly against my spine, and took the liberty of putting a few simple enchantments on our weapons. Rayna used glamour to hide them, since the last thing we needed was to be noticed walking down the street so well armed.

Watching her use magic was incredible. She had glamour on both of us in minutes, while it took me twice as long to do the enchantments. That speed was a skill few acquired, and rarely at such a young age. Being part witch must have had something to do with it; nobody I knew in the Circle could ever have pulled that off so quickly.

We took a cab to the edge of town and did our best to deflect the driver's suspicions. Two teenagers wanting to be dropped off near the woods at night would look shady, but we were paying him to drive, not ask questions.

The tops of the trees at the edge of the forest soared into the starlit sky. They were spaced out at first, but as we proceeded, the brush got thicker. Branches scraped across my skin as if they were trying to clutch at me, and I was thankful I had worn pants and a long sleeved shirt.

The further in we walked, the darker it got, and Rayna turned on a flashlight to illuminate our path. We could both see well in the dark, but a little light was to our advantage.

The woods had an eerie silence, which meant my nerves were on high alert and every sound drew my hand to my blade.

"This is ridiculous! We need to walk into the woods until we find a huge tree? There are huge trees everywhere." I wasn't speaking to Rayna as much as I was venting my frustrations, but she answered anyway.

"I know which one he's talking about."

"How?"

"Marcus took me there before, when he first started training me to use my element. It's deep in the woods and the feeling of the magic there is unmistakable. I don't remember seeing any sort of entrance though."

"Maybe that's not the place."

"I've been around these woods plenty and I don't know what else it could be. The tree there stands alone and it's the biggest one I've ever seen. It looks different from anything else in the forest. You'll be able to feel the power when we get there."

"I hope you're right. Otherwise we're wasting time."

"It's the best option we have right now. Unless you have a better idea?" she said, dodging branches and trying to avoid the increasingly aggressive bushes.

"Yeah, I say we go back and get Willy, using whatever means we have to. We'll find another way to figure out what the hunters want."

"Vincent isn't somebody you want to go to war with. His family is known for being ruthless and the two of us aren't going to bring down the Taryks. We'll only get ourselves killed and make things worse for Willy."

She was right, but it didn't change the fact that I wanted to go back and rip Vincent's throat out. I didn't handle guilt well.

It took us hours to get through the onslaught of branches, rotting logs and bushes blocking our way, before we arrived at *the* tree. One moment we were in impossibly thick undergrowth, and the next we stood in a quiet open space circled by towering trees.

A single tree stood in the middle of the clearing, wider than any I'd ever seen. Its monstrous roots coiled and twisted above the ground for several feet before plunging back beneath the earth. Swathes of huge branches reached to the moonless sky, covered in a rainbow of leaves in an array of greens, reds, yellows, and oranges, as if fall had come early. There were so many leaves littering the ground I was surprised there were any left on the tree. The tips of every branch held colorful flowers that blazed in shades from bright white, to vibrant pink, to dazzling blue. If I could freeze one single vision of beauty, this would be it.

I could feel the magic pressing against my skin, just as Rayna had said it would. She was right. This place was special and I knew in my gut we were right where we needed to be.

Rayna turned the flashlight off but the area didn't darken. A strange light hung in the air and I could see clearly in the bluish glow.

"I've never seen anything like it," I exclaimed.

"Now you know why I think this is the place."

I took a few steps forward and my feet disappeared in colorful leaves. "So now what? I can feel the power, but we need to find the entrance. I don't see anything else around here but more trees."

"I don't know. Every time I've been here I've never noticed anything but this tree."

I started searching the ground, brushing leaves away with my feet. After a few minutes of shuffling around, I'd found nothing. We'd already spent hours getting here and I didn't like how fast time was escaping us. Rayna had taken to sitting cross-legged on the ground, staring up in wonderment at the tree.

"You're being a lot of help here," I said.

She snapped out of her daze and glared at me. "I'm thinking. What if it isn't an entrance in the sense that a door is an entrance?"

My confusion was all over my face. She rolled her eyes and walked towards me.

"What if the tree is the entrance?" she said, taking my hand and putting it against the trunk. "It would explain why it looks the way it looks, why it makes you feel the way it does. It's not natural like the rest of the woods. It's made up entirely of earth magic."

I looked at the tree and back to Rayna. I knocked on the bark. "Hello?" I said, leaning in to the tree, and Rayna punched me in the arm.

I laughed and shook my head. "I don't understand how the tree could be an entrance. It looks like a tree. It feels like a tree. It's just a tree."

"What do you mean it's just a tree? How can you say that?" she said, sounding genuinely offended. "Can't you feel that?" she asked, letting hope override the irritation in her eyes.

I looked at my hand and tried to focus. "It feels like bark. What's it supposed to feel like?"

"Don't touch it like you're mortal, 'cause you're not. You have to feel it with your magic."

I raised a brow in confusion.

"Close your eyes and call your magic," she repeated.

I gave her the benefit of the doubt and closed my eyes. Reaching deep inside myself, I pulled on my magic. Just as when I'd looked through the glamour on Revelations, I let my mind grow quiet.

It was a few moments before I opened my eyes and saw Rayna staring at me. She was so close I could feel the warmth of her breath on my skin and we looked at each other for a long moment.

"Do you feel it?" she asked.

I paused, thinking for a moment. Did I feel anything? I shook my head. "It still feels like wood," I said. I wasn't sure if I was supposed to apologize but I felt like I should. "Sorry?"

"Don't be. It's not you, it's me." She thought for a moment and looked at me with new inspiration in her eyes. "It's me! It's my element, so that's why I can feel it and you can't."

Earth elementals are very much in tune with the earth, but I didn't think it changed their perception of touch. She must have seen doubt in my eyes, because she lunged at me and took my hand again. She placed it back against the tree and faced me, putting one of her hands on the tree and holding out the other. I slipped my free hand into hers and waited.

"Close your eyes." The demanding tone brought a half smile to my lips. "Close your eyes!" she repeated.

With the loss of sight, other senses change. I couldn't help but notice the warmth and softness of her skin. It wasn't rough like most hunters'; its tenderness made it feel more fragile than I knew it was.

"Relax your mind. We live in a world of magic, where the powers of the elements live inside us. Focus on that power." Her voice had lost its insistence and was now only a whisper.

I did as she asked, trying to clear my mind of anything but the tree. I imagined its bright luminous flowers, colorful leaves, and the thick strong trunk. At first, I felt only bark against my palm, firm and rough. In the other hand was the warmth of Rayna's, and I could feel her magic pulsing over my skin. The tingle started down my spine but it wasn't the same sensation I got when demons were near. I was feeding off Rayna's element.

My senses expanded and the life of the forest resonated around me in a new way. The sound of leaves rustling together carried on a soft breeze. Dried leaves tumbled at our feet. The distant chirp of birds fluttered to my ears, accompanied by the soft padding of paws on the forest floor.

The tree now felt smooth, warm and full of life. I could feel its energy beneath my skin and the sensation was unlike anything I'd ever felt. I fed off Rayna's element and it warmed me from the inside out, like my soul was emitting a gentle heat.

A smile pulled at my lips as I felt Rayna's earth magic run through me. The power that had escaped me three years ago felt so close, and it was amazing. The warmth lasted only a few moments before it vanished, like someone had blown a light out inside me. My smile faded as the power withdrew and I opened my eyes.

The brightness surrounding us made our pupils contract. When my eyes adjusted, I found myself staring into bright green cat-like orbs. Rayna stared at me and enchantment filled her face.

"That was incredible," I said.

Rayna smiled and her grip on my hand tightened. She was holding both my hands and it took a second before either of us realized that the tree was gone. We weren't in the forest anymore.

"Where are we?" I asked.

She pulled her hands from mine and stepped away. "We're where we need to be."

I couldn't tell where the light was coming from. It hung in the air on its own like the bluish glow that had surrounded the tree, but it was brighter now. I didn't know what powered it. It was magic. No matter how hard you tried, you couldn't explain magic.

I looked down at my watch, but the minute and hour hands were spinning in opposite directions. "Does your watch work?"

Rayna shook her head. "No, this place is pure magic."

"How did you do that?"

She smiled and faced me. "I'm an earth elemental."

"I know, but how did..."

"I called on my elemental power and it clung to yours, and here we are. I'm not sure how I knew what to do. It was just...magic."

I had a moment of jealousy towards Rayna for having the power I had never received. "Your element clung to mine? But I don't have an element."

Rayna laughed. "You have something. I could feel it inside you. I can still feel it." She shuddered. Her comment surprised me and I didn't know what to say, so I stayed silent.

We stood in the middle of an aisle lined by trees, warm air brushing against our skin. The glow that lit the area made it as bright as noon, though there was no sun in the sky.

We followed the path between the trees towards a hill. Despite the lack of breeze, the trees swayed with a life of their own, as if in control of their limbs.

Scattered large and small boulders created a path towards a gentle hill, and as we climbed it, the path got wider and the rocks thinned. Flowers sprouted from the ground, in the same colors that had grown on the tree that was an entrance. They moved and tried to follow Rayna as she walked by them, reaching their petals towards her.

We reached the top of the hill and the trees began to narrow our trail. At the bottom, they came together in a cluster. In the center of this area was a huge pond with a white marble statue standing high above the water. A stairway of the same marble led us down to the edge of the pond.

The figure of a man with perfect muscles carved from the flawless stone towered over us. He held a gold trident that sparkled in his white marble grip. His other arm was extended and formed into a fist. Sculpted robes adorned him from waist to sandaled feet. Water flowed over the statue's square pedestal and down into four shell-shaped bowls, which overflowed into the pond. The entire display reminded me of an ancient Greek memorial built to worship the gods.

"This is unbelievable," Rayna said over the trickle of falling water.

"You can say that again." I replied. "And that's what we came for." I pointed to the marble man holding a scroll in his white shining fist.

"That's great, but how are *we* supposed to get it?"

I took a few steps back then ran towards the statue. I pushed off the ground as hard as I could and leapt. My hands reached out to grip the stone, but just as I was about to land on the pedestal, I hit an invisible barrier and there was an explosion of white light. I felt my body moving through the air as the statue got farther away and I hit the cool, grassy earth hard.

The sting in my tailbone was sharp and I looked up to see a woman standing before me. Her entire form was wrapped by a white glow. She was illuminated with a brightness that didn't hurt my eyes, but it was impossible to perceive any of her features distinctly. She was perfect and beautiful, yet nothing about her stood out. It was remarkable on many levels, and her presence exuded comfort and warmth.

"Who might you be?" the lady said. Her lips didn't move and the sound seemed to come from the air around me. Her voice was soft, smooth, and as perfect and simple as her form. I looked up in awe and couldn't remember my name.

Rayna approached and helped me to my feet. "I'm Rayna, and this is Chase," she said.

The lady didn't look at Rayna. Her eyes stared only at me.

"We came for the scroll," I said. "Who are you?"

The lady watched me, her expressionless face glowing. "I am Elyas, the guardian of her lady, the goddess. Who are you to seek her power?" Again the voice came from all directions. It moved the blades of grass beneath my feet and echoed in the rustling of the leaves.

"We don't seek her power," I said.

Elyas laughed and it echoed around us, the warm sound flowing over me from every direction. She moved towards the statue, though her feet did not move; her body floated along, not disturbing the grass. She pointed to the scroll and her words were not as gentle and warm as they had been, imbued instead with ferocity.

"Lies. Everyone seeks my lady's power."

I shook my head helplessly. "We don't even know what your, or her, power is."

Elyas looked insulted somehow. "What do you mean you don't know?"

"We only came for the scroll to save our friend," I said.

Her head tilted to the side as a smile passed over her face.

"So you are a protector, using your powers for the good of others."

"No, I don't have any powers. I came up a little short in that department."

Elyas moved towards me and her hands moved over the air in front of me. "There is power within you; I can feel it vibrating off your vessel. You would not have been able to enter this place without it."

"But it wasn't my magic that brought us here, it was hers," I said, pointing to Rayna. "She's an earth elemental. Like I said, I don't have any powers."

She floated towards Rayna. "Hmm, strange creature. Her soul must be pure, otherwise she could not enter this place, but yet, she is a demon. A demon with a hunter's magic? Interesting." Elyas examined Rayna from every angle. "Interesting indeed."

Elyas straightened and regarded me again. "To obtain the scroll, you must pass a test."

"Okay, what kind of test?" I asked, somehow not terribly surprised.

"The challenge has never been completed. Hence, the scroll is still here. It can only be undertaken by one of you, however, and that will be you, Chase."

"Why can't I do it?" Rayna protested.

The woman smiled. "I'm sorry, child, but you have the blood of a demon, and this challenge is not for your kind." Rayna looked ready to argue, but she was cut off. "Your soul is pure, but this task must be completed by a hunter of pure blood."

Rayna didn't look pleased, but she held back whatever she was thinking.

"Are you ready?" Elyas said.

How was I supposed to be ready when I didn't even know what I had to do? "I guess I have to be," I said.

"Excellent. But to understand what you must face, first you must understand where you are from."

"Um, I'm from Stonewall, New York."

"No, where your kind truly came from." Elyas drifted effortlessly back to the statue and turned back to me. "In the beginning of time, your world was full of humans, pure and perfect in the eyes of the goddess Serephina, just as she'd made them. But the demon god Ithreal was enraged with jealousy at the goddess's power and used her world as an arena to release his anger. He released his own creations on Earth to wreak havoc on her precious humans. In retaliation, Serephina joined forces with the other gods and banished Ithreal to a demonic dimension and blessed her special soldiers with the powers of nature, giving birth to the Circle, a group of warriors bearing elemental magic. These newly anointed hunters fought long and hard before driving the demons back into their own realm. The Circle then locked the portal to their home world with magical seals, but it was too late. The worst damage had already been done. The demons had inflicted their curses upon some of the humans, and the demons you've come to know as Underworlders were born. Your world is now full of these half demons, like this one," Elyas said, pointing to Rayna.

"I never knew that was how the Circle came to be," I said.

"This scroll holds true power, hunter, and to earn such a treasure you must fight true power. Now that you know how your kind was born, I give you your challenge. Defeat three of Ithreal's pure blood demons, and the scroll and all it contains are yours." She raised her hands above her head and the tingle of magic fired up my spine.

Thunder rumbled in the cloudless sky and the ground shook. Three columns of light burst from the ground and a single demon shot into the sky from each. The ground trembled as the demons hit the earth, each like something from a nightmare.

I took a step back, studying the beasts. Three on one wasn't great odds, but with these creatures it was outrageous. I'd only heard of pure blood demons in legend, and I had never planned on seeing one. Underworld half demons were strong enough as it was, and I could only imagine what kind of power these demons possessed.

The light vanished around the smallest of the demons and it rushed towards me. The other two stayed trapped within their circles, sealed away from the fight.

The demon approaching me ran on four legs like a wolf, but instead of fur, it had scale plates covering its back, chest, and tail. Its legs and neck didn't have the same plating, but a slimy green skin, spotted with black. Horns covered the beast's long snout and three black eyes were locked on me. White fangs the length of my forearm hung from its upper jaw and bone spikes on the tip of its tail dragged on the ground.

The demon's mouth opened and a stream of bright green fluid shot towards me. I jumped out of its trajectory and watched it melt the bark off the tree behind me. The demon swung its tail around, which I dove over to end up behind the creature. It was slow to turn and I lunged onto its plated back. The beast growled, an ungodly sound, and shook from side to side. I held on with one hand and brought my dagger across its throat, much like I had done to the bear.

I pulled the silver through its flesh and it howled. Orange blood exploded from its neck and pumped out over my skin as the demon fell limp to the ground. It burned the moment it touched my skin and I leapt from the corpse to make a break for the fountain. I shoved my scorched hands in the cool water and looked back at the dead demon.

That wasn't so bad. I thought. *I can handle one at a time.* But before relief set in, a burst of light exploded behind me. The ground shook, and before I could pull my hands from the water, a larger demon hit me with a giant wooden club.

The two remaining demons were both loose, and the larger of the two towered over me. It was wearing spiked shoulder pads and a rusty steel helmet. Its skin was bright red, and full black eyes peered down at me. So many razor sharp teeth filled its mouth that it couldn't close, and drool streamed from thick black lips.

The club hit my chest and sent me tumbling backwards. The demon stomped towards me with the other following more slowly.

The second demon had a very human looking shell. He walked on two feet, but was hairless. His arms were gorilla-like and hung down past his knees, and although he didn't carry any weapons, on the end of long fingers were fierce looking talons. He opened his mouth to reveal chiseled teeth made for tearing flesh, or steel, or anything it decided to chew.

I stood and slipped my sword from its sheath, taking a ready stance as the demons neared. The red-skinned demon brought his club up and swung. I had plenty of time to react, so I ducked and brought my sword up, slicing at his wrist. He let out a thundering moan as my sword went halfway through his forearm.

He pulled away and ripped the sword from my grip with the blade still stuck in his flesh. He gave the sword a tug and pulled it free, throwing it to the ground. He released another ghastly roar and I found myself armed only with my daggers, which seemed rather inadequate, considering my opponents.

The red skin reached down and grabbed me by the neck with one hand and dangled me over his head. I struggled to suck air into my lungs but the red fingers squeezed too tight.

The other demon watched as this one started to crush my throat. He could've done it in a single motion, but he enjoyed seeing me struggle.

All I could think was *this is it*. I thought of Willy, Rayna, and my mother. If I died right then, I would let them all down. I could picture my father, but the disappointment I wanted to see on his face wasn't there, replaced by laughter: laughter at how weak his son was, and happiness to be rid of me at last. That image filled me with anger so fierce it pushed the fear away.

The other demon roared with envy and the red one looked at him before what I took for a laugh escaped his thick black lips. He released his grip and tossed me towards the ground. Black dots filled my vision when I hit the earth and I sucked the sweet air into my lungs, but as the dots faded the red demon's foot connected with my ribs. He kicked me towards the other one and the impact expelled what air I had left.

I blacked out for a few seconds but when the darkness receded the hairless demon was grinning down at me with yellow stained teeth. It raised both razor-tipped hands and brought them down towards me. The claws hit my chest and face at the same time and I immediately felt warm blood pump from the wounds. I knew the cuts were bad because I didn't feel the pain at first, only a soft burning sensation.

I winced and covered my face as I waited for another blow, but it never came. I moved my hands away and the demon stared down at me, licking the blood off his talons. I tried to squeeze the daggers in my hands, but I realized I wasn't holding them anymore. Somewhere between where I'd been kicked and here, I'd lost them.

I cringed as the demon raised his hand again and prepared for the blow. The talons came down quickly, but stopped as a blade shot through the creature's chest. The arm fell limp and I had enough time to put my hands up before he fell on top of me.

I rolled the demon to the side and saw Rayna standing above me, my bloodied sword in her hand. Her mouth moved but I couldn't hear her words. "What?" I said, but she didn't have time to repeat herself.

She rolled to the side as she swung the sword above me. The red demon loomed behind me, a fresh cut across his chest. It wasn't as deep as I might have hoped, but it was start. His club came down and smashed my face in response, foiling my attempt to get up.

When my head cleared enough that I could stand, I could see Rayna dodging strikes – first from his club, then his fist, and back and forth. She wasn't making any more progress injuring him, but at least she wasn't getting hurt.

I tried to run towards her, but something grabbed me and I couldn't move. There were no hands holding me, but Elyas was beside me and her magic squeezed me.

"I cannot allow you to assist her. She entered this battle of her own will and against my warnings. She will now suffer the consequences."

"But she saved my life," I said through gritted teeth, trying to fight the magic.

"She was not to interfere."

"I won't watch this. Let me go!"

"I cannot. She knew this battle was for you, and you alone. She has chosen her own fate."

My guilt and anger filled me so quickly I burned, and I put all the strength they gave me into pushing away the magic holding me. I used my power, both physical and magical, to push at what held me. The squeezing lessened briefly before reclaiming its hold and clutching me again. I screamed in pain as the magic squeezed the air from my lungs. I wouldn't let Rayna die for my failure – I couldn't! I made one final push.

Power exploded from my body in a wave of heat and Elyas's spell broke around me. I fell to the ground and collapsed to my knees. Breaths came in heavy gasps as I struggled to fill my lungs with the oxygen they craved.

Rayna was still dodging the red demon's attacks and the first one I thought I'd killed was making its way towards her. The gash around its throat had healed and its slimy legs were covered in dried blood. I looked at Elyas, who was rubbing red and blistered hands, before I ran to Rayna.

She had a demon on either side of her and I watched as the red demon raised his club and brought it down across her back.

The sensation of magic surrounded me as I got closer and I prayed it wasn't Elyas's. The magic was stronger the closer I moved. I could feel it build up until it exploded.

The force pushed me to the ground and burst around Rayna. Shards of stone and dirt shot up from beneath her. Jagged rocks emerged from the ground and drove the demons back. They were forced to the ground and Rayna stood surrounded by massive stones that stuck motionless in the earth. The focus on her face was fierce and I could feel the magic pouring off her.

The demons crawled to their feet and ran towards her again. I made a break for the red one and jumped on his back, letting fury fill my core. I wrapped my legs as far around him as I could and put my hands around his thick throat. I didn't know how I knew what to do, but the knowledge was suddenly there.

I pushed my anger into my arms and out of my hands, feeling warmth pulsating in my fingers. The demon snarled, trying to reach me with his free hand, his bulging muscles not allowing him the flexibility to grab me. I thrust power through my body and reached down into my soul with an invisible hand and suddenly my own palms were ablaze.

The muscles in the demon's neck tensed and the cold, rough skin grew warm. My hands were a ring of fire, and flames caught his skin and spread up his face. The skin softened beneath my fingers and I reached for the front of his throat. I dug my fingers in and tore the flesh away.

Black blood exploded from the wound and the demon dropped to one knee. I took this chance to leap from his back. His screams had become a deep gurgling sound as blood oozed out of his throat. He dropped the wooden club and clutched at his neck before collapsing to the ground.

I reached down and picked up my bloodied sword, swinging it above my head. I brought it down on his neck and watched as his head rolled away. I wanted to make sure this one was dead.

I turned to Rayna, who had blood dripping from her face and saw the smallest of the demon's head roll away from its body.

"Look out!" Rayna shouted, pointing behind me.

The talons cut into my back before I could move, but I didn't fall. I absorbed the pain, and in a single motion, I turned and grabbed the demon by the neck and lifted it off its feet. I took a step forward and threw him, driving my magic into him.

The flame exploded from my hand as I released my grip and followed the demon as it flailed in the air. Another flame, this one bright blue, arced in a stream towards him and engulfed his body until it exploded. Black blood erupted from the charred flesh before evaporating among the ash that rained from the sky.

Rayna stood beside me and we stared at the mess of bodies around us as they blazed red and orange and crumbled. Rayna's bright green cat eyes gazed at me. Her skin looked paler when accented by splashes of bright red blood.

"I could have handled it," I said.

"You're welcome."

A bright light shone behind us and we turned to Elyas.

"You are just as I'd hoped," she laughed.

"What?" Rayna and I said in unison.

Her warm laughter faded into a glowing smile. "I've waited millennia for a warrior worthy of this," she said, extending her hand, into which the scroll materialized. "It was worth the wait. I found not only one, but two champions."

I hesitated before I reached out and grasped the scroll. A tremor of power moved through me as my fingers wrapped around the parchment and I nearly dropped it.

"But you tried to stop me. You almost got us both killed!" I said.

"I needed to know you were worthy of the mark."

"What mark?"

"The mark of the gods," she said, pointing to the scroll. "After all, you didn't come here for just a piece of paper, did you?"

The scroll was made of parchment that looked older than anything I'd ever seen, filled with creases and cracks. As I unrolled it, black ink filled the roll of paper in a language I didn't recognize, and a ring slid down from the top. It was a plain silver ring with a small red gem. I picked it up and realized it was the source of that vibrating power.

"Put it on and claim your prize, warrior," Elyas said. I looked up at her and she nodded. "Go ahead," she added, gently and encouragingly. I slipped the ring on my index finger and felt power course through my body. "Read," she instructed.

I shook my head. "I don't understand this."

Elyas smiled. "It does not matter if you understand. The power is in the words themselves."

I looked at the scroll and tried to sound out the syllables as best I could. "Ariaca, tracious, ona-forle, ma-tre-meendo, straticalla," I said.

Nothing happened. *Déjà vu.* I thought.

I looked at Rayna, who shrugged, before a sudden flood of light consumed us and forced my eyes closed.

Thunder roared and the light faded. The statue behind us began to move with a strange grace, as if not made of stone. The man twirled his trident and pointed it towards me. Different colors of light shot from each of the three points and I turned away to shield myself.

The energy hit my back and I collapsed from the searing pain. I couldn't keep the scream from escaping my lips as heat washed over me. Then, as fast as it had come, the pain was gone and Rayna was kneeling next to me. She stood and helped me to my feet.

"Oh my God," Rayna said.

"Oh my Goddess, actually," Elyas said. "It was after all, a goddess, not a god, who created your world. And it is from that goddess this gift comes." Rayna's hand touched my cheek and our eyes met.

"They're healing! All your wounds are healing themselves," she said.

I touched my face and felt the skin moving back over my exposed flesh. My fingers came back with blood, but the skin was knitting itself back together.

"How did you..." I said, looking at Elyas.

"The mark of the gods comes with many gifts, but this is not one of them. This healing is your own power. What you thought did not exist was inside you all along." Elyas said.

"What are you?" I asked.

"I am a piece of the goddess's soul. Each time a god or goddess creates a world, they are forced to give that world a piece of themselves. I belong to Earth."

"What is this?" I pointed to the ring on my finger.

"It is Serephina's ring. It will help you on your journey, as your elements will," she said.

"But I don't have an element."

Elyas chuckled and displayed her palms and the red blisters upon them. "How do you explain how you wielded the flames, or used the healing power of water to close your wounds?"

"But I went through the ceremony; I wasn't blessed with any elemental powers," I protested.

Elyas sighed. "A hunter's power is not meant to be forced out. It is raw magic that emerges on its own. It matters not when you get your powers, hunter, but that you get them when you're ready. You have always had both the damaging blaze of fire and the healing calm of water. It seems, however, both blessings have chosen to reveal themselves to you only now. There is more power inside you than you know, my dear boy, and in time it all shall reveal itself."

"How do you know all this?" Rayna asked.

"I am a piece of the goddess's soul. As with any soul piece, I know what she knows," she said.

My eyes widened. "There are multiple pieces?"

Elyas nodded. "Every world has one."

"But the vampire who sent us here wanted the scroll. He never said anything about a goddess's soul piece," I said.

A cold expression washed over Elyas's face. "Under no circumstances are you to give him this ring or the scroll. Although the scroll's magic has been released, the object itself can still be used to lead him to other pieces. You do not want those in the hands of the wrong person."

"What are the other pieces, and where?" I asked.

She sighed. "They are everywhere, in every dimension, and they take on many forms."

"You said something about a mark?" Rayna said.

"Your hunter has a destiny to bear the mark of the gods. Only one true warrior receives such an honor – one who will lay down his own life for another's."

"What does it do?" I asked.

"It's the mark of the gods. It does what it does."

I raised my eyebrows and looked at Rayna, who only shrugged.

"That's it?" I said.

"You are the protector. It is not a duty you should take lightly."

"But I don't know what that means!"

"You will. I wish you well on your journey."

She turned and began floating away from us.

"No, wait!" I called out after her.

But there was no answer. She raised her arms and her form shifted into a ball of light that grew larger before dissolving into a blinding white radiance that forced my arm up to shield my eyes. When it faded, I pulled my arm away to find we stood back in the forest in front of the giant tree.

"I'm not sure what just happened," I said.

Rayna eyed me. "I thought it made perfect sense," she replied, walking past me towards the woods.

"Really?"

"Are you kidding me? I have no idea."

Chapter 18

Night had swallowed the sky and the street lamps were buzzing as we walked through the industrial park.

"How's it feel?" Rayna said.

"What?"

"Does it feel strange to suddenly have elemental powers, and two of them at that? That's pretty rare."

"I know, but I don't feel any different. Besides, we were in a place of magic. Everything was different there, so who knows what I can actually do."

Rayna stopped and turned to me. "Try."

"I don't know how."

She smiled and stepped closer. "What do you mean you don't know how? You already did it. Reach down into the same place you get all your magic. Like when you focus on breaking down glamours, you have to focus on the element you're calling."

I closed my eyes and focused on drowning out everything around me. Sweat formed on my hands, mostly from the fear that nothing would happen.

I opened that magical place inside and let the magic pour out. I felt it warm me as I thought of fire, heat, and burning. The heat moved outward through me until I thought my insides would ignite. It hurt as I focused that power into one hand, imagining a fireball growing in my palm. I pushed at my magic and felt a flicker of warmth. I pushed a second time and the burst of warmth turned into a small ball of blue flame. I pushed harder and watched it grow, filling the palm of my hand with a tingle.

"Not so tough, is it?" Rayna remarked.

I laughed with excitement. "I guess not," I said, but speaking made me lose focus and the tingle turned into a burning sensation. Panic replaced my excitement and I shook my arm furiously, the flame swaying with the movement. The heat blistered my skin and Rayna's eyes went wide.

"Think about water, or something about smothering the flames out!" she yelled in a panic.

I did as she said, but it was hard to focus on anything through the pain. I gritted my teeth and pictured the flame being snuffed out and the smoke that would rise. The pain seared through me for one more moment before vanishing. I breathed heavily, feeling my pulse in my throat.

My hand smoked and I caught sight of the large blister seeping clear fluid. The pain had been mild until I looked at it. I tried to move my fingers but a cry of pain escaped my lips.

Rayna took hold of my arm. "I should have known better than to push you before you knew how to control the effects of your magic."

She was right. This sort of thing is what happened when elementals tried to use their powers without knowing what they were doing. "This is going to take a long time to heal. Unless..." She looked up at me.

"Unless what?" I said, wincing in pain.

"Elyas said you were both a fire and water elemental. Maybe you can heal it like you did your wounds in the sanctuary."

After how this first experiment had gone, I was nervous to try. Water might seem like a harmless element, but I'd seen what it could do. "Did you not see what just happened? I might try to heal it and end up drowning myself."

Rayna nodded. "You're right. You probably couldn't do it on purpose anyway." She shrugged. "Let's go, then."

I watched Rayna take a few steps and my arrogance got the best of me. I closed my eyes and thought of a creek with clear water moving over smooth stones, cool to the touch and pure. I pulled my magic up through me again. It came faster this time, but with an icy sensation. I pictured my wound wrapped in that cold, healing water and washed clean, the water flowing over it, pulling the skin back together.

"Wow..." Rayna said.

I opened my eyes and the searing pain had been replaced with a cool tingle. The blisters on my hand vanished before my eyes and new skin crept from my wrist over my palm. It didn't stretch my existing skin, but the new skin grew at an alarming rate. I'd always healed faster than most, but this was remarkable. The skin knitted itself inch by inch over my palm and fingers. After a few minutes, my hand was covered in fresh skin without a trace of a wound.

"I guess that answers your questions," Rayna said.

"What questions?" I asked.

Her warm cat eyes met mine. "First, your power is strong. I mean, insanely so for someone who just received it. Second, it wasn't just the magic in the sanctuary; you really are a fire and water elemental."

"Well what about you? What you did back there with the rocks was amazing."

She smiled and inclined her head slightly. "I've done things like that before, mostly by accident, but it's never been quite that impressive. Marcus thinks the mixture of the demon and hunter powers within me must complement each other somehow. It's hard to say what's what when it comes to my magic."

We stared at each other a moment and for the first time I could see Rayna not as a demon, but as a person. I didn't know exactly what I felt, but it was good, and that scared me.

"We should get Willy," I said, shaking the feeling away.

Rayna stared at me a moment longer before she nodded. "What's the plan?"

"What do you mean? We give Vincent the scroll and get Willy back."

"You can't be serious. We're not giving Vincent the scroll."

"That was the deal. We get the scroll so we can get Willy back safely."

"You can't honestly give the scroll to an evil demon after what just happened down there. We don't want it in the hands of someone like him."

I sighed. "We made a deal."

"So what? You were intended to have it, not him."

"I gave my word and I intend to keep it. The magic of the scroll is gone. The worst that could happen is it leads him to another soul piece, and they're all in other dimensions. The portals to them have been sealed for thousands of years. I don't care how powerful he is, he's not strong enough to break the seals. Besides, the two of us can't take on an entire nest of vampires. You said so yourself."

"I know what I said, but…"

"Look, if all Vincent can get from the scroll is a clue to another soul piece, if he's even smart enough to figure that out, then so be it. The power of the scroll is inside me now, whatever that means."

"You're right. We'll get Willy back and worry about the scroll later."

I think Rayna realized I wasn't willing to negotiate, but I also knew she was right. Vincent shouldn't get the scroll, but I couldn't think about that now. First, I needed to save Willy.

Three vampires stood outside the gate as we approached and one stepped forward. He had bleached blond wavy hair and light purple eyes set in his pale skin. His body was skinny and he looked like a teenager. The poor kid hadn't had time for his body to fill out before he was turned.

"You have the scroll?" he said. His voice was still a kid's too, not given time to deepen.

"Where's Willy?" I demanded.

The vampire smiled, letting his fangs drop from his gums. His skin became a transparent film, his veins ran black against his flesh and talons extended over his nails. I knew he wasn't very old as a vampire, as the younger ones always thought that was impressive. All it did for me was give away that he was, at best, a few decades old.

"I'm Max and I'll be handling the exchange. Give me the scroll and you can have your friend," he said. His fangs gave him a lisp.

Rayna laughed and it surprised me. "No, that's not going to work for us. We'll deal with Vincent directly."

Max returned the laugh. "You're not in a position to be bargaining, little girl."

I couldn't resist cringing at those words. I didn't think being called a little girl would go over well with Rayna.

Her fist flew towards him and her knuckles cracked against his face. The crunch of his nose breaking made me grimace. He hunched over and brought his hands to his face as blood poured from his nose.

"Dammit," he swore loudly.

I patted his back as he hunched over. "I know, I've been there."

"Get 'em!" he yelled. His voice was muffled through his hands and fangs as blood seeped through his fingers.

The other two vampires shifted in response, fangs dropping and razor talons extending. In a flash, they rushed towards us.

Rayna and I both fell into fight mode. Rayna unlatched the whip from her hip and pulled it back. It cracked as the silver tip snapped against one vampire's skin, splitting it open. A fierce roar escaped his transparent lips as he touched the gash across his face.

The other vampire stopped and looked at his buddy. I took that moment to slide a dagger from its sheath. When he turned back to face me, the blade was already screaming through the air. It finished its last rotation and slid deep into his chest. His skin crackled with a faint orange glow and his body lit up as though a star exploded inside him before it shattered into ash. The dagger made a soft *tink* as it hit the pavement.

I did a dive roll to pick up the blade and the other vampire attacked. I had the dagger in hand, ready to push through his chest, but before he got close enough, the silver-tipped whip coiled around his neck. Rayna pulled back on the whip and he went flying. His back hit the pavement and Rayna was already plunging her blade deep into his heart. His ash swirled in the air before settling over the ground.

We turned to Max, the fury of battle painted on our faces. He watched us from between his fingertips, hands still cupping his face. "I'll get Vincent," he said in a defeated voice. His face changed back to its more mortal appearance and he ran back to the warehouse, a puddle of blood pooling on the ground where he had stood.

Rayna still had her battle-ready look on her face. She nodded to me and I nodded back gravely, as a sign between soldiers to acknowledge we had each other's backs. If a warrior could have one thing that was irreplaceable, it was a good partner. I'd never had one before and Rayna had proved to be not only capable of covering my ass, but willing to. Somewhere along the way I had begun to trust her, and I think I had even started to need her, which was probably a mixed blessing.

Max returned with a dirty rag covering his nose. He beckoned to us and we followed him into another part of the warehouse.

A mix of vamplings and vampires stood in a circle and parted as we came towards them. Hissing followed us as we walked through the opening, but neither of us acknowledged it.

A large area rug covered a piece of the concrete floor in the middle of the room and was covered in standard, if old, living room furniture. Considering that Vincent's family was the most powerful in the city, I wasn't sure why he stayed in such a slummy building.

Willy sat on the smaller of two couches with Vincent in a single chair opposite him. We took our seat on the unoccupied sofa and Willy sighed in relief.

A smile pulled at Vincent's dark red lips. "I must say, I'm surprised to see you," he said. "You've been gone but a few hours."

His flawless skin seemed to glow as the moonlight flooded the room. I could feel more vampires staring down at us hungrily from the second level. I felt like I was sitting in a bucket of fried chicken in the middle of a dinner table.

"We hurried," I said.

His eyes fell on me and I could feel the press of his power against my shields, faint but present. He was trying to be inconspicuous this time, but my shields were up. I wouldn't make the same mistake twice.

"Hmm, you look different, hunter. You feel different."

I tried not to let my surprise show. Was it that obvious? "I'm the same as when I left."

He watched me for a moment before turning his golden gaze on Rayna. "And you look tired, my sweet."

"Thanks for pointing that out."

He shook his head. "My dear Rayna, I must apologize for my outburst earlier. I have since regained my composure and I offer you an honest apology for my words and actions. I was brash." His words and eyes displayed every ounce of sincerity he intended us to see, but I wasn't buying it.

"Of course," Rayna said, smiling.

"I am thankful for your warm, forgiving heart, my sweet Rayna. You have an understanding of me like no other. That is what I find so irresistible about you. You have the compassion that so many have lost during their long years."

Rayna kept the smile on her face. "Does this change of heart mean we can have Willy and the information for the usual price?" Rayna said with a flirtatious stare.

Vincent's reply began with warm laughter, but he shook his head. "I'm afraid a deal is a deal, my sweet. Your dear friend returned to you, unharmed, and you will have the information you requested in exchange for the scroll. Now, I have held up my end of the bargain, and as much as I'd love to give you everything you ask for, this is one thing I cannot compromise. I assume since you're here that you've fulfilled your end of the bargain."

Rayna's smile faded and she looked at me, her eyes begging me not to give the scroll to him.

"We have," I said, and disappointment washed over Rayna's face.

Vincent's yellow eyes flickered with excitement and his attention turned to me.

"But..." I added with a smile. "...you have not completed your end of the bargain."

Vincent's eyes went cold again. "Whatever do you mean? I have your little friend right here. Ask him yourself if he's been harmed."

I looked at Willy and he shook his head. A portion of my tension escaped me.

"I can see he hasn't been harmed, however, our deal was for us to be allowed to leave unharmed as well."

Vincent smiled with only his lips. "I have a level of appreciation for your thoroughness, hunter, but you have killed two members of my family and injured several others in your two short visits here. Surely you do not expect this offense to go unanswered."

"It will go unanswered, that is, if you ever want to see what's on this." I pulled the scroll out of my pocket and his eyes glowed with excitement.

"Is that it? Let me see it!" he said in a rush.

I shook my head. "We'll need to arrange another way to make the exchange that ensures safety for me and my friends."

Vincent stroked his chin and watched me. "As you can see, you are quite outnumbered. I could simply take it." His straight tone implied that he didn't offer this idea only to tease us, but had considered it seriously.

I tried to think of another way out and I did the only thing I could think of, something I knew I shouldn't have. I gripped the scroll tightly in one hand and opened my free hand below it. I focused as quickly as I could and opened the fiery part of my soul. I pushed that warm magic through my body and into my hand. I felt the heat pour out and a ball of bright blue fire ignited in my palm.

Rayna's eyes opened wide with panic and the circle of vampires stepped back. They knew it didn't take more than a spark to make them to go up in flames. It was one of the more painful ways for them to die.

Vincent's expression had changed from arrogant glee to panic.

"Or I could burn the scroll as well as any of you who come closer," I said.

"W-wait, wait, wait!" Vincent stuttered, losing his verbal grace. "Don't do anything out of haste, n-now. Surely we can come to an...agreement." The fear was plain on his face and it wasn't fear for his life, but for the destruction of the scroll.

It brought me satisfaction to see Vincent fumbling over his words. All his confidence flew out the window at a spark of magic. I was in the driver's seat and now, all I had to do was figure out which way I was going.

Rayna knew I wouldn't light the scroll on fire. Her fear was that I would lose control and burn myself, not an unreasonable one. If the vampires saw I couldn't control my own element, things would get bad really fast, but I didn't see any other options.

I put my focus back into the fire and thought of the cool rush of water moving over it. The flame snuffed itself out and smoke billowed from my hand, leaving no damage this time.

"Now, let's talk about this in a civil manner," I said.

Vincent relaxed in his seat and nodded. "Yes of course. But do tell, hunter. Were you not exiled from your little hunter club for having no powers, no element?" The coolness had returned to Vincent's voice, as he presented himself as in control of the situation once more.

"That's the story," I said. I locked my gaze with his, not giving any hint of deception.

Vincent watched me with careful eyes before responding. "So, what will you have of me?"

I smiled and leaned back in my seat. "Well, since I don't trust you and we're on your turf, I would like a change of location. We'll take Willy with us now and meet you at Revelations tomorrow night, and then we'll make the exchange."

Vincent shook his head. "Absolutely not. That was not the deal."

I arched a brow and smiled. "I'm afraid this is the deal," I said, feeding him back his own words.

"Touché, hunter, but how do I know you'll show?"

I shrugged. "You don't give us the information we need until you have the scroll. We meet at Revelations, you give us what we want and you get what you want. Agreed?"

Vincent thought about it for a moment. "Agreed. Midnight tomorrow then."

I nodded and Vincent rose from his chair. "Don't even think about trying anything clever, hunter." I took it as a compliment that he thought I could be capable of tricking him. "Maxwell, show them out," Vincent ordered.

Max came up, the bloody rag gone from his nose and the bleeding stopped, but dry blood covered his face. Willy rose from his chair, nervously looking about as if not sure it was safe to move. He took one step, then two, before rushing over towards us.

We all followed Max to the door and once we were outside, he slammed it behind us, clicking the locks into place.

The cool air caressed my skin as I breathed in the fresh air outside. As I exhaled, Willy stormed off towards the street.

"Willy," I said. "Willy," I repeated, but he didn't respond, only sped up. "Willy!" I said a final time, jogging to catch up to him. When I did, I kept his pace, which took some effort, despite my longer legs. "I'm sorry, Willy."

He stopped abruptly and stared at me. "You're so- so- sorry? Sorry? That's great, but apology not ac- accepted." He pushed me away and I struggled to keep my balance. I'd forgotten that he was demon-strong.

"Willy, look, you have every right to be angry. I know that. I didn't know what would happen. I thought we'd go in, talk to him and everything would be fine. I never even planned on you coming in with us."

"Yeah, well, everything was not fine."

"Believe me, if I had known what would happen, I would never have made you come."

"That's not the po- point, Chase. The point is you knew I di- didn't want to go. You knew I was scared of him. But you pushed and pushed and dragged me here, and look what hap- happened."

"I know, and I promise you I feel terrible about it."

"Good, I hope you feel bad. And what was that crap you pulled? I thought you didn't have any magic mojo."

"I don't, I mean I didn't. It's...a long story."

"Are you kidding me? You put me through that kind of severe mental distress and you're not even going to tell me what happened?"

I turned back to Rayna and her look clearly said *he has a point*. I decided that if catching him up would help him forgive me, I'd be okay with it. Plus, Willy had proven I could trust him, so I owed it to him to at least be honest.

I explained everything as we walked him home, and he eventually realized that we went through a lot to make sure we got him back safely. After much pleading, he accepted my apology.

"You know, you're like a walking magnet for weird shit, Chase. I've only known you a few weeks and I've been in more b- bad sit- situations with you than I have in my entire life. Next time I see you, I hope it's under more normal circumstances."

I couldn't help but laugh. There wasn't anything normal about any of our lives. "I hope so too."

Willy disappeared into his building and Rayna and I were left alone. We stayed silent most of our trip home and it wasn't until we stopped outside the condo door that Rayna turned to me.

"We need to figure out what to tell Marcus," she said. Her green feline eyes peered up at me and I realized that Vincent was right; she did look tired.

"Well, I don't know what to tell him. You've known him for years. How pissed will he be if we tell him what happened?"

The door opened and we both jumped. "Less pissed than if I find out you lied," said Marcus's deep voice from the doorway.

Chapter 19

With no time to prepare an excuse, we were forced to tell Marcus everything. To say he was unhappy was an understatement, but Marcus wasn't the type to yell or remind you how you screwed up. He said what nobody wants to hear.

"I'm very disappointed in the two of you." Shafts of sunlight pierced the sky, silhouetting him in front of the windows as he paced the living room. "You went behind my back and against my instructions and put yourselves in an excessively dangerous situation neither of you were ready for. You're lucky you're alive."

He stopped pacing and I could feel his stare. Rayna and I kept our heads down to avoid eye contact. In a week I'd be eighteen, an adult, and I felt like a ten-year-old being scolded for playing in the mud.

"We said we're sorry, Marcus. There's nothing else we can do," I said.

"You're both almost adults and I'm well aware you can handle yourselves, but I would've liked to be included in the decision making. We could have made arrangements to go to Vincent's together. Going there alone was not a wise choice."

Rayna rolled her eyes. "Well, we got the information we needed, didn't we? At the very least, we're one step closer to it. What would you have had us do? Keep flipping through pages in the library?"

Marcus shrugged and fell into one of the chairs. "Let's look at the other side of things for a moment. Chase has developed his elemental powers. That's interesting," he said. "What have you discovered about your newfound abilities?"

"Well, in the fight with the pure blood demons, I melted the skin off one, and forced another to burst into flame. But after the fight, I tried to conjure the power again, and that time it didn't go so well."

"And the next?" Marcus inquired.

"At Vincent's it went better."

"What about the water?"

"After I burnt my hand, I healed it in a matter of minutes."

Marcus's eyebrows rose. "That's a unique amount of power to have right away. Having two elements is impressive on its own, but to have them appear with such intensity is uncommon. We'll have to start training you as soon as possible. That level of power is dangerous if you cannot control it."

"You're telling me," I said, looking at my hand.

"I wouldn't have thought it wise to use your powers in front of the vampires, though. You've been known for years to the Underworld and the Circle to be powerless. I'd say it's best to let them continue to think that. Underestimating one's opponent is the very worst mistake. I'd suggest keeping your powers to the confines of this room unless absolutely necessary."

"Why did my powers come out now and not in the ceremony?"

"The elders use the ceremony as a means to bring young hunters' elemental powers out sooner, but before that, they always came out on their own – usually, as I believe is the case with you, in a moment of extreme emotion. But I think the ceremony has prevented many hunters from reaching the full potential their power might have reached had it come out on its own."

"What do you think about this?" I said, holding up the ring.

Marcus shrugged. "I have heard prophecies about the Protector and the soul pieces before, but they have been passed on for so many centuries that it's become difficult to separate truth from legend."

"Great, so now we don't know what I am, or what this is."

"For now, I think you two should get some rest. We've got less than twenty-four hours before you meet with Vincent. I will try to learn as much as I can before then, but neither of you will be of any use if you don't rest."

Rayna and I both stood up and made our way to the stairs.

"Chase," Marcus said. I sighed in disappointment. I should have known I wouldn't get off that easy. I sat back down and dared to look at Marcus as Rayna escaped to her room.

"What's happened to you is rare, and you need to take caution. I don't want these new abilities to cloud your judgment."

"You don't have to worry about me."

Marcus looked to the stairs and back to me. "I'm not worried about you, Chase, but Rayna is important to me. I can't protect her if I'm not there. Such powers as yours are addictive; they bring on a new wave of confidence that can, at times, lead to poor judgments. I'm asking you to take care in your actions, not for you or me, but for Rayna. She is special in many ways and I don't want the two of you involved in something you can't handle."

"Rayna can handle herself, more than you know."

"I'm aware of what she can do. I hope to have answers to share soon, but until I know some things for sure, I'm asking you to be careful."

I watched Marcus's eyes as he fought to keep composure. It wasn't often he let any emotion show, but in this moment he was almost tender.

"More secrets, surprise surprise," I said.

"I'm doing what I think is best." I sighed and stood up. I didn't want to play the question game with Marcus again. "And Chase, I think it would be best if I was the one to speak to your mother about this."

"You're probably right." I said, relieved I wouldn't have to tell her myself.

I walked up the stairs and into the room I'd claimed as my own. Both my mom and I were going to stay here at least until Marcus felt it was safe to go back to our apartment. After my run-in with the hunters, it was best if we all stuck together until we figured out what was going on.

As soon as I saw the bed, my eyelids drooped. I hadn't felt tired until that moment, and it all hit me at once. I threw my shirt and pants on the floor and crawled onto the bed. As soon as I moved into a comfortable position, sleep took hold and the world slipped away.

Chapter 20

I woke to sunlight pouring in through my window and relief washed over me. It was the first time in as long as I could remember I hadn't woken up in a nervous sweat from a nightmare. I'd had a great sleep and hadn't awoken with the aches and pains I'd expected. I felt great.

I lay there, enjoying the moment. If I never got a good night's sleep again, I didn't want to forget this feeling.

A soft tapping came from the other side of the door and I rolled out of bed. "Come in."

The door creaked open and Rayna came in. "Marcus wants...Oh gods, sorry," she said, closing her eyes and turning away.

Confused, I looked down to see I was wearing boxers; I wasn't naked! "What's wrong?"

"Umm, how about putting some clothes on?"

"They're boxers. They cover the same as a bathing suit. I don't see the big deal." She turned to face me, but her eyes were still closed. "If you can't handle it I'll change," I said with a chuckle.

She opened her eyes, one at a time. "Oh, I can handle it."

"Alright," I said, crossing my arms. Her green eyes moved over my body and my smirk turned into a smile. "Did you have something to tell me or did you just come to check out what you were working with?"

She looked up and struggled to meet my eyes, her cheeks flushed. "Don't flatter yourself. I'm here to tell you Marcus wants to see you."

"Alright, I'll be right down."

"Okay," she said. Her hands started to fidget and her eyes drifted down my body again.

"Was that it?"

"Yeah, that's it. Come downstairs when you're ready."

"I got that much."

"Good, then I'm going to go," she said.

I turned to pick up my pants. A gasp escaped her lips and I turned back. "You really are enjoying this aren't you?" I said, but her face said something different. "What?"

"Your back," she said. "Follow me." She disappeared from the room. I had spent another minute trying to look over my shoulder when Rayna called me again. "Get in here!" she demanded.

I followed her voice into her room. "Okay, what?"

She walked past me and closed the door. "Look for yourself."

I looked over my shoulder into the full-length mirror hanging on the door. My entire back looked tattooed in dark ink. The hilt of a sword started at the base of my neck and the blade went down my spine all the way to my lower back. Along the center of the blade were two glyphs, one representing the fire element, and the other water. On either side of the sword extended a large pair of dark feathered wings. They reached across my shoulders and down to my waist in intricate detail.

"What the hell!" I said.

"I guess we know what the mark is."

"I think I better go see Marcus now."

I threw on my pants and a shirt and went downstairs. Rayna was already sitting at the kitchen table with a bowl of cereal, but she averted her eyes as I came down the stairs, her cheeks reddening. It felt good to know I could fluster her.

"Come in here, you two." Marcus said, poking his head out of one of the doors near the stairs.

The room within was huge, and blue exercise mats lined the floor. Exercise equipment filled each corner, from punching bags to free weights. Marcus stood in the center.

"You weren't kidding when you said we'd start training right away," I said.

"I'm afraid your training will have to wait. There's a group of hunters from our territory and the surrounding area who have either been exiled or are rogues who chose to leave. I've been in touch with most of them and we've decided to meet."

"That's great! The more people on our side, the better. When do we leave?"

"*We* don't leave; your mother and I will be going alone."

"Why can't we come?"

"Firstly, because you aren't yet eighteen. Secondly, you've got a meeting with Vincent tonight, one that I regret to say I cannot attend."

"Wow, and you're going to let us go on our own?"

"I have no choice. If we try to cancel, or reschedule, Vincent will be far from pleased, and we don't want him as our enemy."

"Fair enough."

"I've made a copy of the scroll and hope to gain insight into its meaning at the meeting," he said.

"Any luck regarding the ring, or anything about the mark?"

"None of my material makes reference to them, but everybody will be looking into it. It's piqued many of the hunters' interest, but without knowing what the mark is, it's a difficult search."

"Maybe this will help." I turned my back to him and lifted up my shirt. "Any ideas?"

"I... no," he replied. "Strange. And this just appeared?"

"I woke up and there it was."

Marcus stared at the tattoo, seemingly lost in his own thoughts. He cleared his throat. "I'll take a picture of this and bring it with me. We should be back in a day or two, and hopefully by then we'll have some answers. Until then, you two are going to go to your rendezvous, make the trade and return here. Do not leave this condo otherwise. Is that understood?"

"Yes, sir," I said.

"I mean it, Chase. It's not safe in this city for either of you right now, and I don't want anything to happen while I'm gone." he said with his neutral, disinterested expression.

"What do you mean it's not safe?"

Marcus shook his head and ignored the question.

"You know, I'm getting a little tired of secrets, Marcus."

"I don't have any answers yet."

"Yeah, well, it would be nice to be included in what you do know, or even what you think."

"Chase, we've been over this. I need you to be patient and trust me. Rayna will be working with you while I'm away. She can teach you the basic exercises to help you control your element."

I was tired of him changing topics and tired of trusting him. He had yet to do anything but add to the mysteries that seemed to fill my life, but before I could respond the door opened and Mom entered.

"Marcus we need to get going if we're going to...." she stopped and gasped. "Chase, what is that on your back?"

"Umm, surprise! I got a tattoo." I smirked.

My mom rushed over but Marcus quickly interjected. "Tessa, he's kidding. I believe this is the mark."

Mom looked at Marcus and then back at me. "Oh, Chase," she said, shaking her head, but there was a worried tone in her voice. "I know Marcus has told you the rules, and I expect you to follow them." She gave me the no-nonsense look that all mothers have.

"I know, I know. Don't leave the condo."

"I mean it. It's important you listen to Marcus on this one. It's for your own good."

"Don't worry so much."

"I'm your mother. That's what I do."

"I know."

"Alright, well you two be good," she said, wrapping Rayna and me in a hug.

"Mom, relax. Everything will be fine. It's just a couple of days. How much trouble could we get into?"

Mom pulled away and glared at me. "Rayna, don't be afraid to keep him in line."

"No worries, Tessa. If he gets out of line, it'll only take a few smacks to straighten him out." She smiled.

"Good girl," Mom replied.

We walked her and Marcus to the door with their overnight bags in hand. When they had gone, I turned to Rayna. "A few smacks, hey?"

"If necessary."

"Well if it comes to that, I'll just take my shirt off. You won't be able to do anything but stare."

She brought her fist around and hit me in the arm. "Ouch," I said, rubbing the sore spot, but she just rolled her eyes and went back to her breakfast.

Chapter 21

Rayna and I spent the few hours before our meeting working on exercises to improve my control. They were boring, to say the least, but anything that would help was a worthwhile. Still, I was more than happy when the clock showed that it was time to go. Rayna was a miniature Marcus in training, and I'd had enough for one day.

We armed ourselves lightly; we both knew whatever weapons we took would be confiscated at the door.

Rayna dressed herself to the nines again, in tight black pants and a green tank top that made her eyes look extra fierce. Black boots with four inch heels brought her to my eye level. She had her hair half up, the dark pieces all held together in a silver clip with the red strands falling down around her shoulders. Her pale skin showed how little she got to be out during the day. In our line of work, there wasn't much time to get a tan. Our quarry tended to avoid the light.

We left the condo and caught a cab. Even after hundreds of years of life, I doubted Vincent had much patience for tardiness. Rayna and I hadn't talked about what we would do once we got there. I think we were both hoping to make the exchange as quick and painless as possible, although I had a feeling that Vincent did very few things in a quick and painless manner.

He sat in the same booth as before, surrounded by beautiful girls. The vampires standing around him pretended not to notice us as we approached. Vincent whispered into one girl's ear, then made her giggle with a kiss on the neck. Rayna had to clear her throat to get his attention as we approached the table. Vincent turned to us, wearing a smile that chilled my bones.

"My sweet Rayna, I thought you might change your mind, so I took the opportunity to... entertain myself."

"I'm glad you were able to occupy yourself while you waited," Rayna replied. She faked a smile, but she wasn't as talented as Vincent when it came to feigning pleasantries. Then again, who was?

"My dear, I do love your ferocity. It's always a breath of fresh air."

"Shall we?"

Vincent inclined his head. "Shall we what, my dear? I could take that offer to mean so many different things." His smile changed into something different, more primal. I thought for a minute that he might try to swallow Rayna whole. The innuendo gave me a mental picture I'd need to scrub out of my mind with steel wool.

"Shall we do the exchange we came here for?" she asked, displaying a flash of the scroll. I thought Vincent's eyes would pop out of his head at the sight, and he pushed Rayna's hand under the table with lightning speed.

"Put that away!" he demanded, scanning the room.

Rayna smiled and I looked over the crowd, in search of anything that might be a threat. Tonight, I trusted Vincent even less than usual.

"You're a little on edge this evening, Vince," Rayna said.

Vincent shuddered. "Please, it's Vincent." He waved everyone around him away and invited us to sit down. "What you're holding is not something to be flaunted. You never know who could be watching." Vincent's eyes met mine and his power pushed against me, but I had my shields up. I wasn't playing that game again. "There are eyes and ears everywhere," he continued in a whisper. "I would prefer to complete our arrangement at a different location."

I laughed and shook my head. "Forget it, Vincent, we're not giving you the chance to blindside us. Right here is fine. There are plenty of eyes around in case you try anything."

Vincent shrugged. "There is much going on in the Underworld of which you are unaware, hunter. The sudden disappearance of Underworlders has left many among us with an uneasy feeling. It's been rumored vampires may be responsible, that we're working with the hunters. This is something I know nothing about, but the rivers of information that flow my way are running dry. People are distancing themselves from my family, and that is bad for business. So as you can guess, doing any sort of business with the likes of you is criticized."

I watched Vincent, but his tone and expression gave no hint as to whether he was telling the truth or not. Five hundred years of life – if you could call it that – could teach a person a few things about lying. Vincent's magic pushed at the edge of my shields again and I put my focus into pushing them away.

"Not this time," I said.

"This will be much easier if you cooperate, hunter."

"You're not getting in my head."

His magic let up and he leaned towards me. "Let me make one thing clear, Mr. Williams. You are not welcome here, and Rayna is a disgrace to this world. Nobody else will be willing to help you, given the current state of affairs, so you should feel lucky I am being so generous with my time."

"That's exactly why we shouldn't trust you. You've got it in your head that we need you. Well I'll tell you something: we don't need you. We can take this fancy piece of paper elsewhere if you think you're above working with us."

"Chase..." Rayna interrupted, but I put up my hand.

"We're doing the exchange we agreed upon, here and now. Unless you don't have the information we need, in which case we'll be holding on to the scroll."

"Chase, will you stop and listen..." Rayna began, but I interrupted her.

"Now, do you have what we need or not?" I said, my blue eyes gazing intently into his yellow orbs.

Vincent gave a dramatic sigh before turning to Rayna. "Really, Rayna, why must you involve yourself with the socially inept? He's like a caveman. He has no appreciation for politics whatsoever."

Rayna smirked. "But he's so cute when he gets all determined and commanding, isn't he?"

Vincent looked at me a moment and nodded. "Yes, I suppose you're right."

I raised my eyebrows. Were they really talking about how cute I was when I got mad? Talk about taking the wind out of my sail! I wanted to say *'It's not cute, it's very manly!'* but I didn't think either of them would appreciate that.

"Are we going to do this or not?" I asked impatiently.

"No, I'm sorry. With the Underworld fearing that vampires are involved in the abductions, just being seen with the two of you is a mark against me. If I'm seen doing business of any sort with you, it will damage the reputation of my family. I know you can't understand the politics, so I won't bother to explain."

"Fine," Rayna said, and pushed me out of the booth.

I shot Rayna a look, but she ignored it.

Vincent smiled. "Thank you, Rayna. I knew I could count on you to understand."

"Oh, I understand. You're a vampire – a soulless creature with his own agenda," she said.

"Now, now, that isn't fair. You know as well as I do that I have a soul."

"No, Rayna, we're doing this now!" I said.

Rayna looked at me. "Relax. We'll find another way. Trust me."

I didn't want to trust her. I wanted to reach across the table and beat the information out of Vincent, but I didn't. We had something Vincent wanted, and I didn't want him or his family coming after us for it. But at some point, I was going to have to put my faith in something, and putting it in Rayna seemed as good a plan as any.

"Okay," I said.

Rayna turned and leaned over the table. "Thanks for nothing."

"You're welcome, my sweet Rayna. I'm sorry we could not come to an agreement."

I caught a strange movement out of the corner of my eye, but before I could interpret it, Rayna picked up Vincent's drink and threw it at him. The thick red liquid slid down his face, but he didn't react.

"Well played, my sweet. A little over the top if I do say so, but well played nonetheless."

Vincent's family rushed back over, but Vincent's hand shot up to stop them.

Rayna pushed away from the table. "Let's go, Chase." she said, walking past me.

"Rayna, my dear!" Vincent called, the dark liquid running down his pale flesh and his pink tongue slipping out to catch drops of it.

"What?" She scowled.

"I truly am sorry," he added, looking sincere in a way I couldn't quite place.

Rayna's unimpressed expression changed to one of confusion. She nodded hesitantly and continued to the door.

"Rayna, what the hell?" I said, coming up the stairs into the alley. Rayna ignored me and continued walking. "Rayna!" I called again and ran down half the alley to catch up to her. Her head was down as she read a piece of paper.

"What's that?" I asked. She didn't answer me, and she wore a sad expression. I felt comfortable enough with Rayna to know she had my back. She'd proven worthy of my trust more than once, but I still didn't know her well enough to read her moods. "Rayna?"

"It's an address."

"Okay…" She stopped walking and looked at me, her eyes glazed with tears. "Rayna, what is it?" I reached over and slid the paper from her fingers as a single tear trickled down her cheek. I looked at the address. I had never been near there, but I knew it was outside of town. "I don't understand. You've got to give me something here," I said.

Rayna closed her eyes and took a deep breath. The single tear had run down her face and clung to her jawbone, but as she exhaled it shook loose and fell to the ground. "It's where I used to live," she said. Rayna reached out for the paper in my hand. "This is the place Marcus found me. It's where they killed my mother." I could hear her choking back more tears. She took another deep breath and a new determination filled her eyes and replaced the sorrow. "We need to make a stop before we go."

"I'm so lost right now," I said.

"It's done. The trade is done. Vincent has the scroll and this address is where we're going to find the answers we need," she said.

"Wait, what?"

"Vincent was talking to us, only it wasn't with his lips, but with his mind."

"Why didn't I hear anything?"

"Because you wouldn't drop your shields. We were both trying to explain, but you weren't listening. You were too busy *being in control.*"

I wanted to react with anger, but she was right. "Why couldn't we make the trade as planned?"

"Because of what Vincent told us. The Underworld is watching him right now, with the demons being kidnapped. The victims aren't low level players in the Underworld – they're powerful. They think the Taryk family is trying to make a big move. Everybody's on edge and Vincent doesn't want to attract unnecessary attention."

"So you two made the trade while acting like he was breaking the deal. Nicely done." I couldn't help but admit it was well played, even if I was embarrassed about missing it.

"Shouldn't we wait for Marcus?" I asked. Rayna shot me a hostile look. "I'll take that as a no."

"If Marcus knew the information was there, he wouldn't let me go. This is something I have to do."

"Okay."

I couldn't argue with her. If it were me, there would be nothing that could stop me. All I could do was support her decision. Whatever was at that address was a different kind of demon for Rayna, one I was betting she hadn't thought she'd ever have to face. I knew there was no weapon or magic that would help her defeat it.

Chapter 22

Back at the condo, Rayna took a set of keys from the kitchen and led me to the underground parking area.

"You have a car and we've been taking cabs and walking everywhere?"

Rayna gave a half smile, which was the most I'd seen since we left the club. "It's Marcus's other car, and I'm allowed to use it in case of an emergency. It's not what you'd expect."

"Well, I think this qualifies as an emergency, and I've come to learn that very little is ever what I'd expect," I replied.

Rayna led the way as we passed vehicles worth more money than I'd probably see in my lifetime. We passed classy car after classy car before we came to a stop in front of an older model Jeep with a customized lift kit and large mud tires.

"You're kidding me," I said, eyeing the blacked out Jeep with tinted windows.

"I told you it's not what you'd expect."

I watched her struggle to pull herself into the Jeep and I came around to the passenger door. "You sure you don't want me to drive? It's a pretty big truck for a girl." I smiled.

Rayna gave me her unimpressed glare. "I can handle it. Besides, it's a little too much machine for you." She winked, turned the key and made the engine roar to life.

Aside from the rumble of the engine, the ride out of town was quiet. Once we got onto the freeway, Rayna turned on the high beams and settled back in her seat. I could see her body relax as she started taking deep breaths.

"You sure you're up for this? We don't have to do this now. We can wait until Marcus and my mom get back, and let them do it."

Rayna shook her head. "I'm fine. Is it difficult? Absolutely, but I can handle it."

"Are you sure?"

"I need to do this. You can understand that, can't you?"

"Of course I do. I didn't mean you couldn't handle it. I just didn't want to push you into it. Not like I did with Willy. That didn't turn out well."

Rayna laughed. It sounded forced, but it was a laugh nonetheless. "*Not well* is an understatement. But on the plus side, you discovered a few tricks, didn't you?"

I nodded, but I didn't think I'd come to accept my powers yet. After all these years of feeling like less than a hunter, I suddenly had not one, but two elements. I should've been excited and eager to use them, but I wasn't. I was nervous. I wasn't sure if I was scared because the magic had just appeared, or that it might disappear just as quickly.

The more I thought about my powers, the soul piece, and the mark, the more on edge I was. There were too many unknowns in this equation. My thoughts were interrupted by the crescendo of the engine as Rayna passed the only car we'd seen since we'd gotten out of the city.

"So what do you think we can expect when we get there? I mean, we asked Vincent for information and all he gave us was an address."

"I don't know what to expect," Rayna said. I could hear the nervousness in her soft voice. At least I wasn't alone in that particular emotion.

"I guess the real question is: if there are people there, are they going to be willing to help?" I said, but this time I didn't get a response.

Rayna turned off the freeway and a few miles later we coasted onto a gravel road. Tall stalks filled the fields to either side of us and dust blew up around us, limiting our vision. At the moment I saw the bright yellow sign signaling a dead end, Rayna jerked the Jeep to the right and drove off the road.

"Where are we?" I asked, my voice wobbling as we went over endless bumps. Rayna jerked the wheel again without answering. The car slid down into a ditch and started to push through the field. I gripped the dashboard and door as the Jeep rocked back and forth.

I watched the vegetation fold under us as we moved forward. The Jeep made a final push forward and we plunged out into a rocky clearing. I could see another source of light in the distance.

As we neared, I could tell it was a house, but it was still too far away to make out any details. We drove down another ditch and back up the other side before we were back on a dirt road. Rayna slowed down and pulled to the side of the road, turning off the lights and killing the engine.

We got out of the Jeep and walked down the road before jumping back down the ditch and into the field. The house was still a mile away, but we wanted the element of surprise on our side.

A barbed wire fence surrounded the property, but we both leapt it with ease. We were a few hundred yards from the house when Rayna's voice came in a loud whisper. "Stop."

I froze in confusion. The heavy silence around us was eerie, and my senses strained to detect whatever had spooked her. It hadn't been a sound.

A wall of magic hung in front of me. I didn't know where it had come from, but there it was. I put my hands out and crept forward, stopping when I felt the edge of it. I closed my eyes and pushed against it.

"Can you feel it?" Rayna asked.

"What is it?"

"It's a threshold. If we cross it, it alerts whoever is working the spell, a sort of an early warning system for the magically proficient."

"Do you want to go through it?"

"No." I waited for her to say more as she stared at the invisible wall, concentration painted on her face. "I think I can get us through," she said, finally.

I gave a quiet chuckle. "Well that would be both impressive and convenient. How do you plan on doing that?"

"You forget I'm a witch. I have more than just rocks available at my beck and call." She was right. I was used to her eyes now, and had almost forgotten she was part demon.

I felt her magic come alive around me. She spoke in an unfamiliar language and after a few words, her magic overwhelmed me and I felt the wall in front of us break. She stepped forward and held her hands out, repeating the words as she moved over the threshold. She waved me over.

"What did you do?"

"I made us a doorway." The feeling of magic became strong again and I turned back to face the wall. "It's only temporary," she said, as the magic closed behind us.

"So whoever put the spell around this place doesn't know we're here now?"

She looked at the house. The lights were on, but we had yet to see any movement in any of the windows. "They shouldn't. The spell only works if someone crosses the threshold. It shouldn't react now that we're inside."

"Here's hoping," I said.

We walked towards the house, taking care with each step as we neared. The lamp on the front patio was lit, casting a glow in front and to one side of the house. The place looked weathered from the outside, its white wooden siding chipped and faded. Some shingles curled while some areas of roof had no shingles at all. Enough light came through the windows that we had to hug the shadows as we neared. We crouched in the darkness, hearing no sound from within and seeing no cars in the driveway.

"I'm not sure anyone's here," I whispered.

Rayna strained to listen. "Doesn't seem like it."

Creeping forward, I leaned against the cracked siding and sidled along to the front window. It was grimy and I had to wipe a corner to peer into the living room, which was empty aside from a single couch covered with a stained white sheet. I could see into the kitchen and partway up the stairs, but there was no one there.

I jumped as Rayna slid up beside me. "What do you see?" she whispered.

"Nothing. There's nobody in there as far as I can tell." I ducked down below the window and crept up the porch.

"Chase, what are you doing?"

"I'm going in. That's why we're here, isn't it?"

Before she could respond, I turned the door handle and pushed. I cringed uselessly as the hinges shrieked, and the quieter I tried to be, the more noise there was.

Once I stepped inside, the scent of death hit my nostrils. I pulled a dagger from its sheath and walked further into the house. The carpet was stained, tattered and pulled up in the corners, revealing worn wooden floorboards. The walls looked like they'd once been white, but now they'd taken on a darker shade of yellow. I whirled at a sudden creak behind me to find Rayna.

Her mouth opened slightly as she cast her eyes over the room. I couldn't tell if the expression was of shock or sadness, or maybe both.

"Rayna..." I trailed off. I didn't know what to say. She had watched her mother's murder in this house, and as far as I knew, this was the first time she'd been back here since. I couldn't imagine what she was feeling. "Are you sure you want to do this?"

She took a deep breath and looked up at me through a film of unshed tears. "I need to do this."

The main floor held nothing other than the couch and empty kitchen cabinets. The stairs squeaked as loudly as the door, but we found nothing on the second floor but more empty rooms.

Rayna kept her composure as we scanned her old room, but when we entered the master bedroom, I noticed a single tear slide down her cheek. The floor was stained brown with old blood and the room stank of death. I had no words of comfort, so I pretended not to notice and ushered her back downstairs. All that was left to check was the basement, but it was locked.

"That's strange. We never had a lock on this door," Rayna said, her voice sounding hollow and distant.

I felt stupid for not bringing anything to pick a lock with. Rayna stepped forward and mouthed a few words. She put her hand over the lock and it clicked.

"Wow, you really do have a few tricks up your sleeve," I said. Rayna tried to smile but failed.

I turned the handle and opened the door. The smell of blood and death came in a potent wave as air from the basement rose from the darkness. Rayna gagged and her skin turned a pale shade of gray. I knew she'd been around death before, but something told me the smell wasn't what was getting to her. I tried to give her a look of warmth and concern. She was breathing heavily and her eyes welled up with tears again. I reached for her but she stepped away.

"No. No, I can do this," she repeated.

"I know you *can*, but it doesn't mean you have to. Not every demon needs to be conquered."

She took a deep breath and spoke with a steadier voice. "This one does."

Bright lights suddenly shone through the window.

"Shit!" I shouted as panic raced through my bones. "Is there a back door?"

"No, go downstairs!"

I leapt down the first steps to the landing then turned and barreled down the rest. The railing had fallen across the stairs and I almost lost my footing.

Rayna bumped into me as she reached the bottom. We stood in darkness in a room with no windows, and disappointment set in.

I heard the sound of a light switch being flicked up and down. "It must be burnt out," Rayna whispered.

I closed my eyes and focused my energy as best I could through the adrenaline. I took deep breaths to calm myself and I pulled at my magic. I managed to generate a flame in my hand in record time. It took a moment for my eyes to adjust to the light, and the panic I'd calmed returned with vengeance.

The basement was one open room with concrete floors and walls. Old plumbing and wiring were visible above us, and in the middle of the floor was a symbol painted in what I had no doubt was blood. The smell of it hit me again, hard enough that I almost gagged.

The streaks of blood formed a large pentagram with various glyphs around the outside. Chains were mounted into the concrete, three sets dangling loose against bloodstained walls. The fourth set held a man's naked body, filthy and covered in wounds. From his appearance and the stench, I was sure he was dead.

Rayna gasped and covered her mouth. Two large steel cages sat on the far side of the room, neither of which was empty. I could see the glow of eyes staring at me from within and chills spilled down my spine as the creatures inside let out a low growl.

"Werecats," I said.

The stomping of feet echoed through the basement and dust showered us as multiple people came through the front door of the house. My pulse pounded as though my veins might rip themselves from my neck, and I cased the room looking for a place to hide. Before I could decide which way to run, Rayna took my hand and pulled me towards the stairs.

Under them was a small wooden enclosure made of poorly nailed together plywood. Rayna pulled at one panel to reveal a narrow doorway. We squeezed through, one after the other, into the small space and pulled the panel door shut behind us. My back pushed against Rayna's body as we hugged the staircase. I focused my magic and snuffed out the fire, covering us in darkness again. The voices upstairs were quiet at first, but even as the volume rose, I still couldn't understand the muffled words.

The door to the basement creaked open. "Hey Brock, did you lock the basement?" a man's voice said.

"Of course I did." Brock said.

"Then we have a problem."

Dust rained down on us as footsteps shook the stairs. My pulse pounded in my ears as flashlight beams slipped underneath the wooden panels and the hunters scoured the room. Rayna's hand squeezed my shoulder and I could feel her breath, trembling and warm, on the back of my neck as she edged closer to me. This had to be traumatic for her.

"This one's almost dead. He's no use to us," the male voice said, and the chains rattled. I heard the sound of soft flesh being beaten and a flash of orange and red light exploded and vanished in seconds.

"These two are still alive," a female voice said. I couldn't quite place it, but it was familiar to me. "Kitties are tougher than I expected."

"Well, somebody opened the lock without a key. I can smell their magic," the other male voice said.

"Maybe they left already. We'll need to find them before the boss gets here. If he finds out someone knows what the hell we're doing out here, he'll have a fit," the woman replied.

I breathed a sigh of relief as the footsteps moved up the stairs. I could feel the tension leaving Rayna's body and her head fell against my back. My own pulse slowed, but my breath caught when a loud crash echoed around us and a hand shot through the panels.

"Gotcha!" the man said, as he grabbed Rayna's arm.

Her scream cut through the small room and my heart rate skyrocketed. Her nails gripped my shoulder as the man tried to tear her through the wall. I pulled in the other direction, aided by my adrenaline, and broke the man's grip.

Rayna fell on top of me, and when our eyes met, I could see her terror. The hand shot back through the wood and Rayna was pulled from my grasp. The panels shattered then and splinters of wood fell over me.

I crawled through the new hole in the makeshift wall after her, but when I emerged, a blade pushed against my throat. The man held the knife and the girl had Rayna. I could finally put a name to her voice then.

Lena was a lethal blonde I'd grown up with, and was as crazy as they come. Her blue eyes pierced me like daggers, and her smile made me more than a little uncomfortable.

"Chase? What a pleasant surprise." She and I both knew it was anything but pleasant, but she maintained her typical seductive tone.

Rayna struggled against Lena's grip, so Lena pulled a small blade from the waist of her tight jeans and pressed it against her throat. Rayna stilled.

"Good girl. We wouldn't want to have an accident now, would we?" Lena giggled and it reminded me of how much I had always disliked her. She wore a tight black tank top that accented her milky white shoulders and flawless skin. Bright red lipstick adorned her pouty lips and smoky makeup made her eyes stand out. Long platinum hair was tied tight against her head. As crazy as she was, it was impossible to deny that she was beautiful.

Brock's footsteps were quick and heavy on the stairs. He came to stand in front of me. "I told you to leave it well enough alone, Chase. I gave you a chance to walk away, but you had to stick your nose where it doesn't belong," he said, poking me hard in the chest. It didn't hurt, but it succeeded in pissing me off. "And you've brought us another one of your mutts. You can't get enough of these things, can you?"

"What can I say? I prefer their company to yours."

Brock answered with a fist to the side of my face and the sting resonated through my head. "How dare you insult your noble heritage? How can you turn your back on what you are?"

"The Circle turned its back on me, remember? It abandoned me and I adjusted to the life I was forced into. It just so happens that I like it better." I spat my words at him, letting him feel my magic push against his.

He looked eager to respond, but his expression changed as my power pulsed. I thought for a moment I could see fear on his face, but he disguised it as surprise.

"What's this? Little Chase has some magic of his own?" Brock's freckled face scrunched up in a laugh. Bright green eyes looked for a reason to hurt me, maybe even kill me. "A parlor trick, or another one of your enchantments? We all know you don't have any *real* power."

I kept my expression as neutral as possible and bit my tongue. I didn't want to give anything away, not yet.

The man behind me spoke. "You want to sit here all night and chat or what? There are still some open graves in the back. We could kill 'em and toss 'em in." His tone was cool, as if killing was something he did every day.

Brock shook his head. "Not him. We can't kill him."

151

The man's grip loosened a bit and a confused voice rolled out. "Why not?"

Brock shook his head. "Because I said so. Kill the girl and chain him up," he ordered. He moved up the stairs and slammed the basement door behind him.

Rayna was motionless, trying not to get her throat slit. The man's grip on my arms was loose and I thought to take advantage of it, but the moment didn't feel right. "You heard him, Lena. Get rid of her," he said.

Lena's voice purred through red lips. "Oh Hal, you're too nonchalant. It's killing; you can't just *get it over with*. It's an art, something to be cherished. You have to take your time and enjoy its beauty." She pushed Rayna into a chair between the two cages in which the werecats were lying motionless. Lena pulled a strip of leather off one of the cages and tied her captive's arms and feet to the chair.

Hal didn't chain me up. He kept his blade on my throat and watched. His interest in what was about to happen told me one of two things. Either he didn't know Lena's style, or he enjoyed what was about to happen as much as she did. The latter idea gave me chills.

Lena kicked the cages "Get up kitties. Time to play." Her voice was smooth, sultry, and dangerous. The cats started to stir and she kicked their prisons again. "Hurry up now," she said. The creatures rose: two black panthers.

The cats roared as they stretched and the sound made my stomach flip. The kennels were large enough that they were able to reach their paws through the bars. They sniffed the air and clawed out in Rayna's direction, then roared in frustration as Lena slapped at their paws.

"Now, now, you have to wait. It's my turn first."

The cats hissed, batting at their prisons. Rayna turned her green feline eyes on them. The panthers' gold ones gleamed in the darkness and stared into hers. Rayna's body relaxed somewhat and one panther lay down, watching her, emitting a low rumble. It took me a moment to realize that it was purring, like a pet.

Lena kicked the cage. "Making friends will not be tolerated," she said, the poise gone from her voice. Her face flushed and she slapped Rayna. The cats roared and Rayna's eyes glowed in anger. "Don't make this harder on yourself," Lena snapped. She drew a long, thin, silver knife from a sheath strapped to her hip.

Rayna kept a neutral expression as her eyes met mine. I tried to somehow convey that it would be okay, but Lena hit her across the face again. Rayna whimpered and the cats hissed. "Shut up, you filthy creatures." Lena kicked at the cage. "And you. Pay attention to me," she said. She took a breath, brushed her blonde curls behind her ears and stepped back, eyeballing Rayna from head to toe. "So many juicy parts...where should we start?" Rayna remained silent and Lena crouched in front of her, blue eyes meeting green. "Tsk tsk, not answering my questions will only make this worse."

In a blur, the blade sliced across Rayna's arm. She screamed and Lena's face lit up with excitement. She brought the blade down across the other arm and reveled in Rayna's next cry.

Lena turned to me, her bright red lips curled into a smile. "Ooh, a screamer. You're a lucky boy, Chase." She winked and turned back to face Rayna.

The moment I thought to move, Hal's knife pushed at me. "Down, boy," he said.

I had thought that if I waited it out, Lena would talk until she was in a vulnerable position, but so far she'd been careful. I hadn't counted on that. We needed to do something before Rayna got hurt any worse. The silver knife was extremely unhealthy for an Underworlder, and even worse for Rayna. Blood flowed down Rayna's arms and her breath was heavy. Her eyes met mine and the sheer panic in them made me turn away. Lena's hand connected with Rayna's face again.

"My, you're a terrible listener, girl." Rayna's panic turned to anger and it made Lena laugh with glee. She twirled the blade in her fingers before striking Rayna's arms again, in a different place this time, but the wounds were deeper. Rayna screamed and Lena's eyes danced with pleasure. She turned her back on Rayna and walked to the center of the room. Rayna looked at me again, the anger now filling her eyes, and I nodded.

I snapped my head back as fast and hard as I could, smashing Hal's nose with the back of my skull. I heard the instant crunch and knew I'd broken it. I swung my elbow back, and with tears filling his eyes, his perception was off. He tried to block it and missed, and my elbow hit his temple. I used the momentum to follow through, forcing his head against the concrete wall. Hal fell to the ground and Lena came at me swiftly, but I was ready. I brought my foot up into her stomach and kicked her to the ground.

Rayna couldn't free herself, and she hobbled on the chair towards one of the cages. The panther stretched out a thick, powerful paw out and snapped the tie on her legs with a single claw. My jaw dropped, but I hadn't had time to process my surprise when hands grabbed me and tossed me backwards.

My back hit the floor and I rolled. Hal ran towards me, blade in hand and blood staining his face. I grabbed his wrist as he brought his dagger down and smashed his hand against the wall repeatedly until he dropped it. I wrapped my arm around his body and spun, throwing him hard against the wall. His head hit the concrete again and this time his body went limp.

Rayna ran at Lena, hands still tied behind her back. She jumped and kicked but Lena ducked and Rayna soared over her, landing on her feet. Lena threw a punch that met Rayna's jaw, and with her arms tied behind her back, she lost her balance and fell to the ground.

Lena was immediately on top of her and the cats roared in the background. I was there in an instant and used both hands to push the bitch sideways. She flew towards the stairs, cracking the bottom step as she hit the ground.

I dropped down beside Rayna and slipped a blade from my sheath. Footsteps came clattering down the steps as I cut through the leather binding and suddenly Lena was beside me. Her foot met my face before I had a chance do anything but cut the ties.

Brock had reached the bottom of the steps. Head down, he rushed towards me and knocked the wind out of me with his shoulder. Pushing me back like a linesman, he slammed me into the wall. He kicked me in the face and I slid to the ground, my head snapping against the concrete. Everything went black.

I came to after a few seconds, my face against the cold floor. Brock had Rayna by the hair and flung her off Lena, who looked the worse for wear. The parts of her face that weren't covered in blood were swollen with bruises.

Rayna hit the ground on the blood-smeared symbol and leapt quickly to her feet. Brock and Lena moved to either side of her and began circling. The wounds on Rayna's arms still bled steadily. Blood trickled down off her elbows and splattered on the cold gray floor. The painted symbol reacted.

It started to glow, no longer a dark smear of dry blood but a bright red light. The symbol wavered and rose off the concrete floor. It floated around Rayna's waist and Lena's eyes opened wide.

"You're the one?" Lena exclaimed.

"The one?" Rayna eyed the symbol that moved around her.

"The one we've been looking for! You're the key," Brock said with excitement.

Rayna backed up out of the pentagram but the symbol remained alight. "I don't know what you're talking about."

Brock and Lena closed in on her with a new hunger in their eyes. "Not you, your blood. Your blood is the key." Lena's voice rolled out in a seductive purr that didn't match her bloodied face.

I silently got to my feet and stepped towards them. Brock had his back to me and Lena's focus was all on Rayna. Rayna shook her head and opened her mouth to argue, but she'd seen what had happened and didn't know what to say.

Lena lunged to grab her and Brock moved in after her. I ran forward and slammed the butt of my blade against the back of Brock's head. He crumpled to the ground.

Lena got Rayna in a tight hold and they rolled end over end, each trying to gain the dominant position. The werecats roared in the background and slammed themselves against the cage doors.

I waited for Lena to be on top of the scuffle before I reached down and grabbed her by the throat. I felt my magic flare up within me, and with that additional power I took a few steps and threw her. Her skull crunched against the wall and I was sure I'd knocked her unconscious.

The concrete broke at her impact and rained down on top of her. Her limp form crashed onto the top of one of the cages. Her body weight and the chunks of cement crushed the bars, and with the structure compromised, its door broke off its hinges.

The panther crept out of the cage, its golden orbs observing me. It growled deep in its throat as it stalked towards us. I reached down and helped Rayna to her feet as the panther turned its attention to the second cage.

With a single graceful stride, it reached its companion's prison and swiped at the door with long claws, fully extended from thick black paws. It hit the door several times to no avail before looking back at us and growling.

Rayna moved towards the cat and reached for the door. She pulled the pin and backed away from the huge cat baring long white teeth. The panther pushed its nose against the door and emerged with supernatural grace. The pair rubbed against each other before turning their attention back to us.

I reached for Rayna as she backed up and our fingers interlocked. We froze as they approached. They pressed against Rayna, brushing against her legs and pushing themselves between us. They circled her, keeping one between her and me. At the instruction of a deep growl, I stepped away.

One of the cats reached above her knees, while the other was as high as her hips. Seeing a house cat doing something like this would have been cute, but watching two werecats molesting her legs was less than comforting.

Rayna didn't look panicked – she seemed to be enjoying this, and I wasn't about to interfere. The felines circled and purred deeply before they turned and disappeared up the stairs in a few strides. Paws thumped above us before a loud crash reached our ears.

All our assailants were unconscious – for the moment – and we took that as our cue to leave. The bay window in the living room had been smashed out and shards were scattered over the floor. Doorknobs must be tricky for cats.

We slipped out the front door and let the darkness shroud us while adrenaline drove us forward. The moon and the receding glow of the lights from the house lit our way, and we ran with all the speed we could muster.

When we got to the Jeep, Rayna got in the passenger side and I drove. The roaring of the engine grounded me, comforting after the strangeness of caged werecats, magic symbols and Rayna's blood doing who knows what in that basement. Right then, normal was good.

I pushed the pedal to the floor. Whatever the hunters had been looking for, they seemed to think they found it in Rayna. That could only mean things were going to be even less normal from this point on, and I wanted to get far away, fast.

Chapter 23

The rear-view mirror was my best friend the whole drive home. I waited for bright lights to appear and run us off the road, but they never came. I exceeded the speed limit for most of the drive, just praying not to get pulled over. How would I explain a bleeding girl with possibly fatal wounds inside a vehicle neither of us owned?

Rayna hadn't stopped bleeding and I had started to worry. Her wounds weren't closing like they should've. It hadn't occurred to me before that she would react *this* badly to the silver. We didn't have a first aid kit in the car, so we used my shirt. I'd taken it off sometime after we hit the freeway and ripped it into strips. Rayna had managed to tie them around her wounds, and although the blood was soaking through, they would have to do until we got back to the condo.

"What the hell happened in there?" Rayna's voice was strained, frightened, and exhausted. I kept my eyes on the road and stared into the darkness ahead while I tried to come up with an answer. "Chase?"

My words came out in a whisper. "I don't know."

The silence that followed was not the uncomfortable kind, but a silent understanding. For the past few weeks, demons had been snatched up for reasons unknown to us – at least until thirty minutes ago – and now we'd painted a target on Rayna's back.

I tried to imagine what was racing through her mind right then, but I couldn't wrap my head around it. A few hours before, we thought we were going to talk to somebody, maybe get answers to our questions. Despite knowing *who* the hunters had been looking for, we were still left wondering *why*.

I took my eyes off the road and glanced over at Rayna. The reflection of her face as she stared out the window revealed how worried she was. "We'll figure it out," I said. I wanted to reassure her, but I didn't know what else to say.

"I know." She pulled her gaze from the darkness and looked at me. "I know," she repeated. She tried to seem confident, but sounded distant and afraid, and her effort just made me feel worse.

The rest of the drive home was quiet. I regretted not having waited for Marcus since we had no idea what Rayna's blood had done to that symbol. Now there was a whole new set of issues to deal with, topped with keeping Rayna safe.

Once home, I directed Rayna to the kitchen table and grabbed the first aid kit. The strips of shirt she'd wrapped around her arms were blood-soaked and dripping. She winced as I pulled them from her skin and started cleaning the wounds. The cuts were deeper than I'd thought and hadn't even started to heal. Multiple gashes on each arm were still full of blood that ran down her arms and off her wrists. I had to grab towels to protect the floor, and though I tried several bandages, I still couldn't slow the bleeding.

"It's the silver," she said. "It's stopping my blood from clotting."

I tried wrapping the wounds again, putting plenty of pressure on them, but it was useless. The bleeding wouldn't stop.

"I don't know what else to do. What do you usually do when you get hurt like this?" I asked.

Rayna's eyes glazed over and her breathing slowed. "I've never been hurt like this." I applied more pressure but nothing was working. "Chase," she said, her voice weak. "You're going to have to use your magic."

I froze as she said it. It was one thing to make light in a dark room, and another to try and heal myself, but to use it on somebody else, most of all Rayna...that I wasn't sure of. Water was a powerful element. One minute it can heal and the next drown, crashing over its victim. I wasn't comfortable with that possibility.

"It's not safe, Rayna. I could do more damage than good."

"You have to. Please," she said. She was losing consciousness. "There's...nothing else."

Marcus had said that without proper training, my elements were unstable and I could end up doing more harm than aid, and I knew he was right. Every time I'd gone against his advice, something bad had happened, but as I watched Rayna's body slowly go limp, I knew we were out of options.

I was preparing to call upon my element when Rayna collapsed and fell off the chair. I dropped to my knees to check her pulse. It was there, but weak. I closed my eyes and reached for my magic.

I thought of rain coming down from the sky, warm drops hitting my skin, and a lake on a windless day, like a mirror reflecting the sky. The magic filled me, very different from the fire. The power was cool and calm, rather than hot and unstable. The water flowed inside of me, smooth and slow.

I put my hands over Rayna's wounds. Even though some powerful water elementals could heal others simply by focusing on the necessary healing mentally, I couldn't risk it. This wasn't the time to be experimenting, and magic is always more powerful with touch. I pictured her blood clotting and no longer dripping from her arms. I imagined her wounds closing, the skin knitting itself shut, then water running over the lacerations, washing the blood away. I focused those thoughts and let the images cycle through my mind. I put all my energy into willing them to become truth.

I pushed the magic from my core into my arms, and I felt it in my veins, moving down into my wrists and through my hands, until it left through my fingertips. The cool, tingling sensation almost broke my focus, but I strained to hold on to the power, letting it move through my palms and into her body. The magic seemed to take on a will of its own, until I was no longer pushing it, but letting it pour out of me. Rayna lay motionless on the floor, but the wounds had stopped bleeding. New skin grew until the cuts were nothing but tiny scars in her pale flesh, then they disappeared completely .

I sat back on the floor and stared at my blood-soaked hands. The towels littering the floor were now all dark red. I moved my fingers over Rayna's neck and felt her pulse pounding harder against her skin. Though her arms were still bloody, the wounds had disappeared, but I didn't feel the satisfaction I should have. Instead I felt anger, anger that Rayna had almost died, anger that the answers we searched for nearly cost us our lives. Now that the hunters knew who they were looking for, all their energy would be focused on Rayna. We had been lucky, but our troubles had just begun. Only answers would rid me of my anger and guilt, and only one person could provide them.

Chapter 24

I couldn't leave Rayna alone while the hunters were after us, and she couldn't come with me. Her wounds were healed, but I couldn't put the blood she'd lost back in her body. She needed to rest. I refused to call Marcus, so I called the only other person I could trust.

Willy said he would help, his only condition being that he didn't have to see, talk to, or be anywhere near Vincent.

Before he came over, I threw the soaked red towels into the laundry room and closed the door. I had a feeling Willy wouldn't react well to large quantities of blood. I'd moved Rayna to the couch, cleaned her up the best I could and tucked a blanket underneath her. I didn't want to explain to Marcus why his couch was covered in blood, and I wasn't going to try to change her clothes.

The buzzer sounded and I let Willy up, but his barrage of questions upon seeing Rayna forced me to tell him what had happened. I tried to be vague, but there was no way to keep out all the details. After the update, he looked like he wished he had never agreed to come.

"Is she in danger here?" he asked, on the verge of panic.

"I don't think so, not yet anyways. They don't know who she is, only what she looks like, and they don't know where she lives. I just need you to watch her for a while. I won't be gone long." Willy nodded and looked over at the couch awkwardly. "You can watch TV or something, okay? I just don't want her to be alone when she wakes up."

"I can do that," Willy replied.

"I'm taking Rayna's cell phone with me. The number's on the table. If she wakes up, call me right away."

"Okay."

"Thank you Willy. I owe you one."

Willy laughed "With all the ones you owe me, I should be living in a place like this."

"Yeah, I know it."

I had taken the time to change my clothes and shower, since the last thing I wanted to do was walk into a vampire nest covered in fresh hunter's blood. I checked to make sure I'd wiped all the blood off my shoes and slipped out the door.

Chapter 25

The sun was still low in sky and I took the Jeep to save time. Vincent's warehouse looked worse for wear in the daytime. The windows on the upper floor were boarded up and the chain link fence surrounding the building was falling over. I wondered again why he lived in such a ramshackle place. For someone from a family so rich and powerful I'd expect a mansion of some sort, but who was I to question the living habits of the sunlight deprived?

I slipped inside the grounds through a hole in the fence, and my anger grew the closer I got to the building. I could feel the blood coursing through my veins and it felt like it was boiling under my skin.

The doors we'd gone through before were locked, but this time I'd come prepared. It took me a few minutes but I was successful with my lock picks. I didn't have the same kind of magic as Rayna, so I had to resort to more mundane methods.

The warehouse was empty, which made me nervous, and the air smelled of stale blood. I knew the majority of the vampires would be sleeping, but the vamplings should've been watching the doors. I made it to the middle of the open space. Though it seemed eerily quiet, my anger fueled me onwards.

There was a balcony above the main floor, and multiple stairwells all led to metal doors with no handles. The only way up was an elevator, but it was key-operated and my lock picking skills wouldn't help me override that.

My anger swelled and I let out a scream without fear of waking the dead. Vampires were strange compared to other demons. They drank blood to keep their bodies alive. They could reproduce, they had a pulse, and they breathed, but every sunrise their body died. Their eyes sunk into their heads, their skin sagged and decayed, and occasionally even their hair would fall out. It was one of the less glamorous things about being a vampire. But still, every night their bodies reformed anew.

The scream echoed through the open room and finally I got the attention I sought. The sound of multiple guns being cocked back made me to turn to face the five vamplings who stood behind me.

"Well, well, well, I didn't think you'd be quite stupid enough to come back," the blonde said, with a rather disturbing smile. She and her companions formed a circle around me.

"What can I say? I'm a sucker for blondes."

"Cute, but you're not my type."

"It's the teeth, isn't it?"

She lowered her gun slightly. "Because you kill our kind."

I couldn't contain my laughter. "Your kind? You realize you're a human, right? I know some of you have this misconception that you're one of them, but you're not. Do you know how often one of you gets your wish to be turned? You're an emergency snack, nothing more."

"Shut your mouth," she snapped.

I smiled. She did all the talking, which meant she was my ticket to the second floor. I scanned her body and saw the short chain with a single key around her neck.

"You and your group here are a snack. If the vamps were to turn you, they'd have to find new lackeys to watch over them, and that'd be too much work. If they were going to turn you, they'd have done it already. The fact that you don't see that confirms that you're frigging insane," I said.

"You know, I'm going to enjoy this. It'd be too easy to shoot you, so I think I'll hurt you first," she said. She put the gun back into its holster and lunged at me.

I fell with her on top of me and she grabbed my neck, nails digging into my flesh. I held her hands with one arm and gripped her against me with the other, to shield me from the others' guns. I rolled on top of her and let her roll back over me until we'd gained some distance from the rest, breaking up the circle.

I tore her fingers off my neck and forced one more roll so I was on top. I pulled her up with me as I stood. I kept one hand on her throat, pulled her gun from its holster with the other, and held it against the side of her head. A whine of pain escaped her lips and the other vamplings were on their guard. I kept my body behind hers and walked us back to where we'd started.

"Tell them to stand down," I said. She struggled at first, but I pushed the barrel harder against her temple, cocking back the hammer. She stopped squirming at the sound and I loosened my grip on her throat.

"Stand down," she said. The group watched her, but didn't react. "I said stand down!" They lowered their weapons. We backed up to the elevator and I grabbed the key from around her neck.

"Open it," I ordered. I had my eyes on the others as she turned the key. The elevator dinged and the doors opened. We both walked backwards inside and I took the key from her hand. I pushed the number two and waited. As the doors started to shut, I dropped the gun and shoved her through. They closed as she hit the cement floor and the elevator jolted upwards.

It rose slowly before the doors slid open again. To the right, the balcony wrapped around and overlooked the main floor. There was single metal door with a chain and padlock on that side. To the left was another metal door with a lock and handle. I slid the elevator key into that door and turned, and to my surprise it opened.

The room was pitch black and I felt along the wall until I found a switch. As the lights overhead sparked to life, they revealed a long room full of coffins and a single wooden door at the far end. Each coffin was a different size and style. Some had designs engraved into them while others were covered with stickers, and some were plain wood. Hundreds of coffins filled the room and at first I thought I'd never be able to tell which one was Vincent's.

I made an effort to be silent as I walked through the room, even though I knew none of the demons would wake. I turned the brass handle of the wooden door and opened it into a separate room.

Inside were three coffins, lit only by the dim light from the larger room. Two made of a solid, dark wood matched, and between them rested a single pearly coffin. It seemed like Vincent's style to have such a standout coffin. I was betting those to the left and right contained either his lovers, or his bodyguards. Maybe both.

I stared at the pearl coffin. In a moment, my bubbling anger would have the chance to escape. I closed my eyes and took a breath. Dagger in hand, I raised the lid. I started to bring my blade down, but the coffin was empty.

Smooth, soft, white satin lined the interior and a small white pillow with ruffled trim rested at the head. The light from behind me darkened and a chill went down my spine.

"You didn't honestly think it would be that easy, did you?" Vincent's voice echoed in the dark room. He stood shirtless in the doorway, arms crossed, his body so pale it almost glowed. He had a more muscular build than I'd expected. His golden eyes looked at me with curiosity, and the oddest smile tugged at his lips.

I focused all my anger into my stare, imagining the release I would have if I pulled my blade across his neck. I pictured the blood flowing over the milky white flesh whose perfection I would mar and watch explode into ashes.

"Really, hunter, I'm not that easy to kill. You don't survive for centuries being this easily found. You thought I would sleep in a stale dungeon like this? Tsk, tsk, I expected more from you." Vincent's eyes flickered as he stepped into the darkness and ran his hands along the white satin lining of the coffin. His golden orbs glowed in the light and I followed him with my eyes, my knuckles turning white as I clenched my blade.

"The hate in your eyes is great. What have I done to deserve such attention? I gave you what you requested, so have you come here to thank me?"

He acted like he hadn't set us up, and the smile that crossed his lips was the final straw. I twirled the blade in my hand until I held it by the tip and put all my effort into being faster than him. I moved my arm in an arc and released the dagger at the perfect point.

The blade spun end over end as it shot towards him, and I was close behind. I had almost closed the distance before Vincent's expression changed to shock – I'd succeeded in catching him off guard. The blade finished its last rotation and slid into his chest above his heart. I wrapped my hand around the handle and twisted the blade.

Vincent screamed in pain as his yellow orbs lit up with fear. His pupils expanded as his eyes turned to straight black. His skin went translucent, the red veins coming to the surface and running black as his inner demon came out. He fell onto his back with a muffled scream and pulled me down with him. I could see all the veins, bones, and muscles of the hand wrapped around my wrist. He squeezed hard to stop the dagger and cut off his own scream with gritted teeth as fangs dropped from his gums. His free hand reached for my throat but I pushed it away and pinned it to the floor.

"You set us up," I screamed in his face.

Vincent was strong and his hand squeezed my wrist so hard I should've been writhing in pain, but my anger overrode everything in that moment. "I should've done what you did to us, and put this blade in your back. But I'd much rather look you in the eye while I kill you," I said.

Vincent stared at me, more shock than anger showing on his clear veiny flesh. "If you plan on killing me…next time, go for the heart," he said, wrenching himself away from me. He brought his knee up hard into my gut and pushed. I lost my grip on the dagger and tried to turn as I rolled onto one knee.

Vincent stood, and the blood dripping from the blade looked black and silver as it ran over his veiny chest. I could see his heart beating through his skin and his muscles twitching and contracting. His body was working overtime to fight the silver that poisoned it. He didn't take his eyes off me as he pulled the blade from his chest, maintaining a neutral expression.

"How dare you accuse me of such treachery. We had a deal and I kept it. I gave you the location where you could find your answer."

"Oh, we got the information alright, after Rayna almost got killed by hunters. All thanks to you holding up your *part of the deal*. Sending us into mortal danger was not part of the agreement."

Vincent shook his head, the wound on his chest closing rapidly. I'd used a silver blade, stuck it deep, and twisted it to make the wound larger; he shouldn't be healing like this.

"I did no such thing. If I had thought you were going alone...Well, it would've been tempting, but I would never put Rayna in danger. If what you say is true, perhaps there was a problem with my source. For it seems I've been, how do you say..." With lightning speed, he moved and stood nose to nose with me, his bare chest inches from mine. "...duped, I think is the word," he finished.

"No, somebody like you doesn't get duped."

"Perhaps, but I had it on good account I was giving you the location of someone who would help." Vincent smiled.

I shot my hand forward and wrapped it around his throat, squeezing tight. Vincent looked unfazed and it only fueled my anger. "You lie," I said through gritted teeth.

"You're fast, hunter, faster than most, but I do not lie, this I swear. Besides, your threats are better left for when you have the advantage. Take your hand off of me, now."

"It's just you and me, Vince. What better advantage is there?"

Vincent smiled and it sent a chill down my spine. I turned to find a gang of vampires and vamplings behind me. Perhaps it hadn't been the smile. The vamplings had their guns aimed, while the vampires were baring fangs and showing off their full demon forms.

"Death would be worth it to know that you, a traitor and deceiver, died at my hands," I said.

I could see the fury even in Vincent's pure black eyes. He pushed at me with superior strength and I stumbled back. He simply stood and stared at me. All that remained of the wound on his chest was the stain of blood.

"I've been many things, hunter. I'm a vampire who was once mortal, I'm a killer, and I'm an Underworlder. I play tricks with words to bend the world to my will, but a man who breaks his word I am not, nor will I ever be," he stated.

It was the first time I'd ever seen him offended, and I didn't know why, but I believed him. My gut told me he was telling the truth, despite my rage.

"Well, if you didn't lie to us, somebody lied to you. Where did you get your information?"

Vincent shook his head, the black in his eyes receding and the gold shining through. His clear skin mutated back to milky white and the dark veins faded beneath it.

"My channels of information are my own. I can assure you, the one who gave me false information will be dealt with in time," he said. "Will Rayna be alright?"

His change of tone caught me off guard and I couldn't deliver the witty response I'd have liked. "She'll be fine, no thanks to you. I still want to know where you got your information."

"Everyone, leave us!" he commanded. His family and minions responded immediately and flooded out of the room. Their obedience was impressive. "Come, let us talk civilly, if you will?"

My anger was fading. "Fine," I said.

Vincent twirled my bloodied blade in his hands across from me and inspected it intently. "You didn't mean to stab my heart with this, did you?" he asked. I didn't respond. I maintained eye contact and a blank expression. "Of course you didn't. Someone like you doesn't miss by accident, do you?"

"Not typically," I said, and that was the truth, although after seeing him heal the wound I'd made, I wasn't sure even a stab to the heart would have killed him.

"Now, why don't you tell me what happened?" Vincent said.

I explained what had gone on at Rayna's old house. I didn't need to sugarcoat anything, like with Willy. I told him everything I knew, and he listened as though in a trance.

"So it's true?" It sounded like both a question and an answer.

"What's true?"

"The prophecy." He stared at me but looked right through me at the same time.

"I don't follow," I said.

"There is a prophecy, one that is millennia old, that many have spent lifetimes trying to decipher. Others have searched for the original documents in the hope that they may contain a key that would help interpret it."

"What does it say?" I asked.

"And so shall the one of both bloodlines be the key to opening that which has been denied."

I shook my head. "What does it mean?"

"It means Rayna's blood is the key, Chase. I can't believe I couldn't place it before. She was always different from the rest of the Underworld, an outcast for killing her own kind and interfering with Underworld matters. I thought that hunter friend of hers had her confused about her heritage, but I never thought she herself might be part hunter."

"You said her blood is the key, but the key to what?"

"Many interpret it to mean the key to the other dimensions. *That which has been denied* is the portal to the Underworlds. She is of both bloodlines. She has the blood of the demons denied entrance to our world and the blood of the hunters who closed the portal to begin with. It only makes sense that she be the one to open it."

"The hunters closed the portal and dedicated their lives to trying to destroy the demons, so why would they want to open the doorway again? It doesn't make any sense."

"Think of the great powers of this world Chase, the power that the Underworlders hold and the power of the Circle. They have been diluted over time and aren't what they once were. What if you could get hold of that magic in its purest form? There would be nothing that would stand in your way."

"That's why you wanted the scroll," I said.

"Of course, should more power be offered to me I would be foolish to decline it, but I'm more interested in the power that keeps the seal in place, and the power inside Rayna. Before I was changed, I was a scholar of prophecies and legends. Becoming a vampire never took away my lust for answers to the puzzles that surround us. Searching for things that are said to exist but have not been seen for thousands of years has always thrilled me. If even one person had the knowledge of how that magic works, we would be one step closer to harnessing it. That could be most profitable. Hypothetically speaking, of course." He smiled.

"You stay away from Rayna."

"I could never harm my sweet Rayna, but it doesn't make her ability any less intriguing."

Before I could respond, I was interrupted by a cell phone ringing. It was a girlie ringtone and Vincent raised an eyebrow as the song chimed from inside my pocket.

"Hello?" I answered.

"Cha- Cha- Chase. Ray- Rayna's awake and..." The rest of Willy's words were muffled.

"Willy, relax, it's good that she's awake."

I heard a loud bang through the phone.

"Willy? Hello? Willy, are you there?" The phone rustled loudly before Willy's voice came through again.

"They're here!" Willy yelled, sounding distant and full of panic.

"Who? Who's there?" I heard Rayna scream.

"Hunters!" Willy's voice echoed through the phone before a loud crash came and the line went dead.

"Hello? Willy?" It was no use. The phone displayed "Call ended."

"What is it?" asked Vincent.

"The hunters have Rayna."

I ran to the door and pulled it open. I didn't stop for the elevator and hopped the railing without thinking. I soared down until my feet hit the concrete, which made a loud crack as my body made impact. The floor sank lower and the cement cracked in different directions. Dust and small rocks whirled around me and I hadn't realized how high the second floor was until that moment. It surprised even me that I wasn't hurt.

I ran towards the exit and Vincent called for me to stop but I ignored him. As I neared the door, a blur passed me and Vincent stood in my way.

"I'm coming with you," he stated.

"Absolutely not. You're the last person I'd want fighting beside me. I'd rather take my chances alone than with someone who's just as likely to eat me as help me."

"Whether you trust me or not, I've cared for Rayna for many years. You've known her only weeks. I am coming."

"I know why you're interested in Rayna, and I'm not letting you anywhere near her."

"I am coming with you," he demanded, and I felt a wave of his power wash over me. It pushed against my shields and I pushed back, not letting his will override my own.

"Fine. I don't have time for your games," I said. I pushed past him, opened the door, and stepped outside.

The sun beat down on my face and I looked at Vincent. "Come on, let's go," I said. Vincent backed away from the doorway as he covered his eyes. I shrugged and walked away.

"Chase, please."

I stopped, hearing the plea in Vincent's voice. "Wait here," I said. After all, I didn't *want* to be going into this fight alone, and his power would be useful. I'd deal with anything to help keep Rayna alive.

I ran to the Jeep and jumped in, pushed the pedal to the floor and took off with a jolt. Jerking the wheel towards the building, I crashed through the chain link fence, driving over it with ease. My foot slammed the brakes as I pulled the wheel hard again and skidded alongside the building. I dropped into reverse and stopped outside the door, popping the hatch open.

"Get in."

Vincent disappeared and returned with a blanket, wrapped it around himself and jumped into the back. I shifted into drive and let the gas pedal hit the floor again, the tires squealing as we pulled away.

At the speed I drove, it took no time to get to the condo. I flew through the underground lot and sparks flew as the top of the Jeep grazed the concrete roof.

We both moved with supernatural speed to the elevator and it couldn't move fast enough. I squeezed through the doors as they started to open and pulled my blades from their sheaths, sprinting for the condo. The door was off its hinges and I burst through the opening, ready for a fight.

The kitchen table was destroyed and the TV was shattered in pieces on the floor. The blood spatter was minor, but easy to spot on the white walls around the picture hanging askew.

"We're too late." Vincent pointed from under the blanket to the corner of the room where Willy lay slumped, blood dripping from his mouth.

I sheathed the daggers and fell to my knees in front of him. His eye was swollen shut. I put my fingers to his neck to find a pulse; it was there and steady.

"Willy," I whispered. "Willy!" I said again louder, but he didn't respond. I slapped his cheek. "Come on man, I need you to wake up." Willy's head shook back and forth a few times before he leaned over and spit blood onto the floor.

"I don't think we can see each other anymore, Chase," Willy said.

"I'm sorry, Willy. I'm so sorry. I don't know how they found us."

Willy opened his one good eye and looked at me. It also took in Vincent and he screamed, panicking and pressing back into the wall. His skin flashed different shades of white. "What's he doing here?" he screeched.

"He's here to help, not harm, I swear." Willy stared at Vincent a moment longer before letting his eye fall on me again.

"It was magic. They used ma- magic to find you. I heard them talk- talking about it. They traced Rayna's magic here. I told them she wasn't here, but they didn't be- believe me; they said a spell had led them here. They beat me with a silver chain until they found her in one of the bedrooms. I tried, I did, but I couldn't keep her safe. I didn't tell them anything, I sw- swear," Willy pleaded.

"You did great." I sighed. "On the phone you said hunters took her. Hunters can't do that kind of magic."

"There weren't just hunters. There were warlocks too."

My eyes widened and I could feel the blood drain from my face. "Are you sure?"

Willy made an attempt at a shrug, but it looked like it hurt. "I recognized them from Revelations: Drake and Darius Sellowind."

Vincent made a strangled sound before stepping forward. "Are you sure?" he asked.

"Of course I'm sure. You don't mistake somebody else for the Dark Bro- Brothers. I'm not an idiot."

Vincent looked like he was going to say something, but I put a hand up before he could respond. "Who are the Dark Brothers?" I asked.

"A pair of rather loathsome and overly powerful warlocks," Vincent said. "Most of the Underworld steers clear of them just for the sake of staying out of their way, my family included. They practice dark magic beyond what most in the Underworld consider safe, and few can rival their power."

"Chase, it's bad enough that the Circle is getting help from the Underworld, but these two are a pair you do not want to cross paths with," Willy said.

"Great, what's one more thing to worry about?" I reached down and pulled Willy to his feet. He winced, clearly hurting more than he was trying to let on.

"We need to go get Rayna back. You sure you're okay?" I asked.

Willy brushed some debris from his pants and nodded. "I'll be fine. I've had worse beatings than this."

That thought made me sad, but I didn't have time for pity.

I went to the armory and took a sword and two strings of throwing knives to add to my daggers. If I needed more than that, it was a lost cause.

"Pick whatever you need," I said.

Vincent pulled down a long sword. "This will be fine."

Willy looked up at the weapons rack, a thoughtful look on his face, and I placed a hand on his shoulder. "You're not coming, Willy."

He flinched and turned to me. The look on his face wavered between sadness and relief. "Chase, I have to come. If I was stronger, Rayna would still be here. It's my fa- fault they took her."

"That's for certain," Vincent added.

"Will you shut up!" I snapped at Vincent. "Willy, there was nothing you could've done. Even a skilled fighter would have been useless against the hunters, especially if they had warlocks with them. You're lucky to be alive."

"What am I supposed to do, sit here and wait?"

"No. I need you to call Marcus. He and my mother are out of town and need to know what's happening." Willy gave me a look of displeasure. "Willy, I appreciate everything you've done for me, but somebody needs to tell them what's happened, and I need to get to Rayna before it's too late.

"Okay," he replied grudgingly.

"Thank you. Marcus's cell number is on the fridge."

Willy nodded. "Be safe."

Vincent and I headed to the garage. I hoped Willy could reach Marcus soon. If the hunters were working with warlocks, we needed all the help we could get. I didn't know the Dark Brothers, but I did know warlocks were tricky. They weren't stronger than the average demon, but their speed was unparalleled. Unless you were a lightning elemental – one of which the Circle hadn't seen in centuries – cutting off their heads with a silver blade was the only way to kill them. The silver blade I could manage, but getting close enough to cut off their heads might be a problem.

Chapter 26

I knew we couldn't be far behind the hunters and I hoped we'd arrive before they did anything drastic.

The girlie ringtone sounded through my pocket and I fumbled to answer it in time.

"Hello?"

"Chase? Why do you have Rayna's phone?" Marcus said in a panic.

"It's a long story."

"It's not important. What's important is that you get somewhere safe. You two are in terrible danger, Rayna especially," he said in a rush.

I didn't respond. I was trying to focus on the road and think of what to say.

"Chase, are you there?"

"Yeah, I'm here."

"What's going on?"

"Rayna's already in trouble. The hunters have her."

"What?"

I took a breath. "Go back to the condo. There's a demon there named Willy; he can fill you in."

"Chase, what..." I heard Marcus say as I flipped the phone closed. I turned it off and threw it on the passenger seat. I didn't have time to explain. I didn't want to be the one to tell him, and I didn't care if that was cowardly or not.

As the sun made its final descent and darkness fell around us, we drove up to the driveway of Rayna's old house. We didn't have Rayna's magic with us, so sneaking in wasn't an option. This was a *bust down the door and hope you don't get killed* kind of situation.

I would go in first and Vincent would follow. If he'd been Rayna, I'd have been comfortable with the plan, but having

Vincent at my back made me uneasy. I knew he was here to help Rayna, but he wouldn't go out of his way for me.

Each step creaked as I walked up the porch. The door handle turned with ease and sent a loud squeak through the house as I pushed through. The moment I was over the threshold, I saw the hands coming at me.

I threw up an arm to block the rain of fists and ducked down to pull out a dagger. I slid the blade across the attacker's stomach and blood spilled on the floor. The demon doubled over and I stepped forward to bring my knife down through his back. The dagger pierced his heart and the scream only stopped when he exploded into ash.

I could hear footsteps storming up from the basement. The basement door broke off its hinges and crashed to floor as three demons came through. I pulled out three throwing knives and hurled them at the oncoming trio.

Each knife hit a separate attacker, not killing any but slowing them down. I couldn't help but wonder where the hell Vincent was, but that moment of lost focus was a mistake. An elbow slammed into my forehead and my ears rang. I ducked to avoid the next blow and brought my dagger up under the demon's chin. It hit the soft spot behind his chin and slid up through his mouth and into his brain. I pushed him away and watched him explode.

Another demon leapt towards me and I pulled my sword from its sheath in time to force her to the ground.

There was a loud crash as Vincent jumped through the boarded-up back window. He stood in the kitchen with splinters of wood falling around him and his less-than-subtle entrance distracted me from the third attacker.

The demon pulled the throwing knife out of her chest and dragged it across my back. I gasped in pain and Vincent reacted. His demon form emerged and he grabbed her by the throat and pulled her away from me. The inhuman muscles moved under his skin and pushed his bone-like talons out over his fingernails. They pierced the demon's neck and blood exploded over her body.

Vincent's fangs dropped as he leaned into her. His golden eyes turned black and I expected him to bite her, but he pulled her head down and snapped her neck instead. He sank his fangs into the next thing through the door, ripping its throat out while I pushed my sword through its heart, leaving nothing but an eruption of light and ashes.

Blood trickled down my back from my cut, and I dodged left and right trying to avoid getting hit again. I moved around the next demon and swung my blade through his leg. He dropped to the floor and tried to block as my sword went in for another strike. The blade cut through his wrist, and I cut off his scream with a final blow to his neck. His hand and leg were ash before they hit the floor.

My pulse raced as adrenaline pumped through my veins. Vincent's black eyes turned back to golden and his skin to pale. The sharp bones receded into his fingers and he looked at me, the smile on his face revealing the joy he took from killing. That only succeeded in making me more nervous to be fighting alongside him.

My thoughts were interrupted as I heard Brock and Lena's voices float up from the basement. Two other voices I didn't recognize chanted with them in a language I couldn't place.

"They've already started," Vincent whispered.

I breathed deeply and closed my eyes, thinking of Rayna: her dark hair that fell past her shoulders, with its undertone of red that accented her pale skin, her bright green feline eyes I'd somehow grown to appreciate, and the verbal banter we had with each other. Images of what they might do to her flashed through my mind and I shook them away.

A new determination filled me as I took each step down the basement stairs with the utmost silence, moving closer to the soft glow that lit the room.

Candles burned throughout the basement. The heat washed over me and the fresh scent of death hit my nostrils. Brock and Lena stood only steps away from me while two men circled the symbol, chanting in an ancient tongue. One of them had short, spiked black hair while the other's hair hung down to his lower back in frayed black dreadlocks. They looked like twins; their skin was smooth and flawless, and the color of a pale moon in contrast to their midnight hair.

The short-haired Brother wore an ankle-length leather trench coat, a blood red dress shirt and smooth black dress pants. The other wore a biker jacket, a similar red shirt, and well-worn black bondage pants.

Their deep voices echoed off the concrete walls and their magic filled the room as they moved around the pentagram in opposite directions. Rayna lay in the center, unconscious. She still had her pants on, but her feet were bare and her top half had been stripped down to her black bra. Small symbols were drawn over her stomach and chest, and strange glyphs covered her ankles and wrists. I couldn't see if she'd been hurt, but as far as I could tell, the blood on and around her was painted on.

Brock and Lena turned as Vincent touched down on the concrete floor behind me, and neither hesitated to attack. Vincent and I moved in opposite directions: I took the far side of the basement and he stayed near the stairs, both of us hoping to keep the fight away from Rayna.

Brock swung his sword at me but I blocked it with my own. Sparks flew and Brock stepped back. He placed the tip of his sword in the flame of one of the candles and I felt his magic flow through the room. "I'm going to enjoy this," he said. Silver and green flames ran down his blade as he channeled his element.

He swung at me again and I ducked, a trail of green flame streaming over my head. I swung my sword at his ankles, hoping to catch him off guard, but he jumped over it and stepped back. He pointed his blade at me and magic exploded from the tip. The flames came towards me like a flamethrower stream. I wanted to turn his own power against him and push those flames back over his body, but I needed to hold on to my magical reserves for as long as I could. It was the only ace up my sleeve, and I still couldn't control it very well.

Balls of silver and green fire followed me as I ran partway up the wall and pushed off. I dove to the ground and flames crashed over the concrete in a colorful explosion. The heat made my skin tingle and I jumped to my feet, meeting his flaming blade with mine. I parried his weapon and smashed my elbow across his face. He stumbled back and I sliced down his arm from elbow to wrist. He stifled a scream as blood gushed from the wound and I pressed the tip of my sword against his throat. Brock dropped his weapon and fell to his knees, eyes pleading with me to spare him.

Vincent and Lena were behind me, their swords clanging together. I turned to see Vincent smile at me and it sent chills down my spine. Brock took that moment as his opportunity. Before I could react, silver knuckles hit the back of my head. The wave of pain pushed me into darkness as I collapsed to the floor.

When my eyes opened, everything was a blur and my skull pounded. Ropes around my wrists held me to a chair. As my vision cleared, I could see I was closer to the circle now. Rayna was still unconscious, and I could see swelling and bruises along her cheek bone. Dry blood covered her chin under a split and swollen lip.

The Dark Brothers still chanted and circled the symbol, and Vincent was tied to the chair next to me. He looked to be in good condition aside from his being held by a silver chain.

Brock and Lena stood guard on either side of us. Brock's left eye had swollen half shut, and that side of his face had already started to bruise. He had a bandage wrapped around his arm and the blood had already started to seep through.

Lena's lips were both swollen, one cheekbone had a deep cut, and there was a vicious looking bite mark on her neck. Still, she was smiling as she watched the Dark Brothers. Neither she nor Brock acknowledged me.

The warlocks were throwing the final ingredients into the symbol, covering Rayna in green and yellow flakes. A few drops of oil hit her stomach and slid down to the floor before the Brothers stopped, bowed to each other, and moved off to the side of the room.

"Excellent." A man's voice sounded through the room, familiar to me, but I couldn't quite place it. "It's almost midnight. When the clock strikes twelve, we will start the bloodletting, the portal will open, and it will be the beginning of a new era." The last piece of the puzzle fell into place when I realized whose deep voice it was.

"Dad?" I said.

I could hear the smile in his voice before I saw him. "Yes, son?"

I tilted my head to look at him and my heart felt as though it was being ripped from my chest. I hated him for causing my exile, but I'd always looked up to what he was: the best hunter the Circle had seen in centuries. He was well-respected in the worldwide hunter community and highly feared in the Underworld.

I opened my mouth to speak, but nothing came out. I choked on my own breath and stared at him with wide eyes. I hadn't seen him in three years and to see him now, here, gave me feelings I couldn't describe. The man of honor who taught me all I knew was behind all this?

"I know, I'm probably not who you expected," he said.

"I don't understand."

He looked out of place between the warlocks, dressed all in black with his sandy blond hair neatly cut. He wasn't any taller than me, but had a thicker build. The skin I remembered as smooth and flush now looked pale and weathered. The dark blue eyes that matched mine dominated his face, but were framed by dark circles.

"Control, power, heroism...pick one. Once I've achieved what others have only dreamed of, there will no longer be different territories within the Circle, no more separate districts. They will all be united under one banner. There will be no council, Chase, just me, a single ruler. I will decide what's best for the Circle. There will be no more waiting on the word of the council to take action."

"The council is there to make decisions that benefit the Circle, not hold it back. All you're going to accomplish is opening the doors to the other dimensions, letting pure blood demons in. We'll be overrun, Dad. Things will be worse than ever."

Riley laughed. "You don't understand, and how could you? This is for the greater good. I won't just be opening the doors; I will be one step closer to having control over the demons." My confused expression made him smile. "You're so naïve, so young.

182

This isn't about unlocking the Underworld, Chase. It's about power, control, and invoking Ithreal."

My eyes widened in disbelief. "Ithreal? Like the demon god, banished-to-the-Underworld Ithreal?"

"Once the demon god's power runs in my veins, the demons will not dare to challenge me. They'll bow to me! The very power that created them will be part of me, don't you see? I'll rule the Underworlders too."

"Why would you want the blood of something you've dedicated your life to destroying? The purest form of that evil will be inside you! You won't be able to control it."

Riley walked away, stopping at the edge of the Circle to look over Rayna.

"It's a shame you've been reduced to such companions," he said, ignoring my comment.

The fire was building inside me and my rage showed on my face. "That's ironic, you've got demons all around you as your lackeys."

"They obey me! These *lackeys* believe in my cause and I can use them. If their lives are lost in the struggle, then so be it. Better they lose their lives rather than my hunters."

"You're a hypocrite. You're going against everything you believe in to gain control of what you're supposed to hate."

The back of his hand connected with my face. Blood welled up in my mouth and I leaned over and spat it at his feet. The bloody saliva found his shoe and I looked at him with loathing.

"You always needed to be difficult. You're just like your mother, trying to challenge my authority when I know what's best."

"Don't you talk about her like that!"

"I will talk about her any way I wish. If you persist in your disrespect, you will only gain a new enemy. Trust me, you don't want that. One day you will understand that what I'm doing is best for everyone. The hunters will no longer be fighting for their lives to defeat the Underworld, and the Underworld will belong to us and do our bidding. The war will be over. The sooner you understand that, the better off you'll be."

"They're people, Dad. They can't be owned."

My father looked at me with revulsion, not for the first time. "Now I know you're not my son. Listen to those filthy words! You speak as though they're our equals. That mother of yours has filled your head with poison. I'd hoped we could put the past behind us and work towards this great cause together. Either I was naïve, or I have my work cut out for me. Once I show you what I'm doing is for a valiant cause, not an evil one, you will understand." He looked at his watch. "But there is no time now. Today I will go into another world and complete the first step towards invoking Ithreal's power. Once you understand the potential, you will change your mind, I promise you."

"I won't let that happen," I said, but Riley ignored me.

He turned to the long haired brother. "Darius, is everything ready?"

The warlock stepped forward and his long dreadlocks swayed as he moved. "Everything is prepared," he said. He bowed his head and stepped back.

This mighty Dark Brother bowed to Riley Williams? I understood that the Underworld feared my father, but to see they were obeying him, treating him as their ruler, surprised me. Why would they support his cause when his success would cost them their freedom?

"Excellent. Prepare the girl for the bloodletting, and remember, be careful with your blades. We need her alive," Riley said. He reached into his jacket, pulling out a vicious-looking knife. He wore a smile I didn't recognize as my father's.

The Brothers stood at the border of the pentagram, near Rayna, and drew their own blades. They each took one of her wrists while Riley moved to her feet and gripped both of them together.

They all chanted in unison and I pulled at my bonds, trying to free even one hand. The ropes weren't as tight as they should've been and I knew then that Brock had tied them – he always did things half-assed, and this time it would cost him. I pulled a hand free and the rope relaxed around the other. Brock had been foolish enough not to tie my body and feet to the chair, and I saw the panicked look on his face as he realized that.

The Dark Brothers looked ready to do something about my escape, but Riley's voice boomed through the room. "Leave them. The ritual cannot wait!" he commanded.

Brock pulled out his blade but I didn't give him the chance to use it. In any other situation, I would've disarmed him, but I didn't have time. I slipped my knife out of its sheath and drove the pommel into the side of his face. I felt his cheekbone shatter under his skin and pushed him sideways so I could hit him again on the back of his head. His head hit the concrete as he collapsed and lay limp in a pool of blood.

I turned at Lena's footsteps in time to see her blade. I brought my dagger up to block it, but missed and caught her arm. I felt it slice through the flesh and muscles of her wrist. The tendons snapped and rolled up her arm like water rippling under her skin. She fell to the ground, shaking, but didn't scream. She was going into shock.

Her undamaged hand groped at the limp appendage hanging from her right wrist. I hadn't meant to hurt her like that, but I shook the guilt away and drove my foot into her face. Blood burst from her nose and she fell unconscious. I unlatched the chain holding Vincent and went to face the others.

Blood seeped out of Rayna's wrists and ankles; each glyph had been slashed. The Brothers and Riley stood at their respective places, blood dripping off their blades. I tried to lunge towards them but I was frozen in place.

Vincent was motionless in his chair, and I could see the fight going on in his eyes as he struggled to move. Darius stared at us, his eyes fully black and his magic wrapping itself around me.

Rayna's blood rolled down her skin and onto the concrete floor. Once it hit the ground, it moved on its own to outline her body. The circle lit up and glowed red, moving up over her. The light got brighter and changed from red to blue to white, forcing my eyes closed against its brilliance. Light erupted from each symbol and beamed towards the center, where all the rays met. A rainbow of colors exploded and swirled to expand over one wall.

Riley's face was lit with excitement as wind rushed through the portal. A wide open space full of strange plants and trees showed beyond the wall. Warm air rushed into the basement, smelling of rain and something sweet I couldn't place.

The short-haired Brother, Drake, picked up Rayna and slung her over his shoulder. I tried to scream for them to stop, but no sound came from my lips. I pushed against the spell, but despite my full effort, I couldn't move. I reached inside to call my magic and felt the fire move through my body and come to my fingertips, but it wouldn't ignite.

Riley and the warlocks moved towards the portal. My father turned and smirked at me with a smile that wasn't his own before he disappeared through it.

Once they were gone, the spell broke and I tried to follow. The portal was spiraling inward, consuming itself, and I ran at full speed and jumped towards it. It was shrinking fast, and I thought for an instant I would hit the concrete wall, but as I prepared for the impact, warmth and sweet air surrounded me. Bright colors blinded me and everything went black. I floated in that darkness for a long moment until a warm glow sucked me in.

Chapter 27

The colors closed in tight around me and I was engulfed by a steady pressure. The pain was excruciating, and if the air hadn't been sucked from my lungs I'd have screamed. My body spun as the pressure increased and I thought I might implode.

When I stopped spinning, I slammed into something hard, and a different pain washed over me. I opened my eyes and squinted as they adjusted. I was moving towards a bright white light and a rush of warm air swept over my skin as the ground came into view. I was falling at an incredible speed as the pressure of the portal released me and sent me spiraling towards stony ground.

I hit the slate surface and my back arched in more pain. The portal that hung in the air above me swallowed itself, leaving me with a pale green sky, a cool breeze, and aching bones. I closed my eyes and took slow breaths, letting my lungs fill with the air they desired. It tasted different here, not a flavor I could place, but somehow sweeter than home.

I tried to move and it hurt, but I drew on my magic and let the cool wash of water flow through me. I pictured it soothing the pain, and the magic filled me briefly, but my focus was lost when I heard a soft groan beside me. My eyes opened as the magic vanished and I turned to see a half-naked man lying next to me.

I forced myself to sit up and the body beside me moved. I watched him unfold himself from the fetal position, and his groans told me he was in as much pain as I was. That I wasn't alone in my suffering made me feel better.

The man had short, messy black hair that hung in his face. His eyes were a strange solid orange, and instead of small, round, black pupils he had large, white, triangular ones. His skin was a warm caramel tone and he looked human.

We stared at each other for a long moment and I don't think either of us knew what had happened or what to do about it.

"Who are you?" I asked.

Confusion distorted his face, and at first I thought I had fallen into a dimension in which English wasn't known, but as I was about to repeat my question with gestures, he spoke with a soft, accented tone that was familiar and new at the same time.

"I am Tikimicharnikato, of the Suriattas clan. And you?" His voice was quiet and feminine, matching the soft features of his caramel skin.

"I'm Chase, Chase Williams," I replied.

"No clan?" he asked. "Surely you belong to one of the clans of the Underworld."

I shook my head. "I'm not from here. In the world I'm from, I was a part of a group once. They are called the Circle."

"You are from the Earth dimension? That is not possible! Your kind has not been in these worlds for millennia." He crawled away from me in fear.

"I assure you, I'm telling the truth and I mean you no harm."

"How can you mean me no harm? Your kind was built to destroy us."

"I give you my word."

"How? Why? You are bred to kill."

"No. I mean, yes, but things aren't like that anymore, not for me. I'm only here to find someone: a friend. She's a demon too, or a half demon anyways."

His eyes widened. "Your friend is a half demon? Like me?"

I nodded. "I need to find her."

"You give me your word everything you've said is true?"

"I swear. My friend's been kidnapped by hunters, other members of the Circle."

"You're here to save a demon from your own kind?"

"Like I said, things are not as they were."

He stared at me a moment, got to his feet, and offered me his hand. He helped pull me up and I realized he was shorter than me and his clothing – if you could call it that - was ragged at best. He wore no shirt and his bare feet looked dirty and worn. His loose pants were made of a white silky material, held up by a tattered piece of rope.

"Well, Chase Williams, it is good to meet you," he said.

"You too."

"Do you know where they've taken your friend?"

"No Tikima..." I tried to say his name but couldn't. "I'm just going to call you Tiki."

He laughed. "That is very good."

"I don't know where she is. I came through the portal right after them. They should've been right here!"

"Portals do not work like that. If you weren't physically touching them, then they are in a different place. The portal will have taken them to the same dimension, but never the same place. Plus, we collided in the portal; that too will have thrown you off course," he said.

"Collided?"

Tiki nodded. "I'm a dimensional jumper, I move from dimension to dimension as I please. I've never run into anybody else mid-jump before, though. The odds of that happening are astoundingly small."

"This isn't good. Rayna's in danger and I need to find her soon, before anything else happens."

"You will find her, Chase Williams, do not worry. Do you know why they have brought her here?" He spoke with strangely crisp pronunciation and a calm, even tone.

"Rayna's blood was the key to unlocking the portal. She's both a demon and a hunter, a piece of both our worlds."

Tiki's eyes widened. "She is the one you seek, the one from the prophecy? I thought it but a myth!"

"Believe me, it's no myth."

"Then the prophecy has begun. You are right that we must find her soon."

"Am I the only one who doesn't know what this prophecy is?"

"There is a prophecy that speaks of one who belongs to both worlds, one who will cause the beginning of the end."

"The end of what?"

Tiki shrugged. "Prophecies are rarely specific. It could be anything from the end of all our worlds, to the end of an era and the beginning of a new one. Do you know what they have brought her here for? If the portals are open, I would think she is of no use to them anymore."

"One of them plans to invoke Ithreal and..."

"Invoke the god himself? That is an amazing ambition!" he interrupted. I glared at Tiki, who looked genuinely impressed. He cleared his throat and continued. "Although I'm not sure it's possible. If it was, that wouldn't be good for any of us," he said. "We must go at once."

"We? You're going to help me?"

"I must. It has been seen."

"Seen?"

"Krulear spoke of you many years ago. She said I would meet a hunter who would require my help one day. I thought she meant it metaphorically. I didn't expect a true blooded hunter."

"Who's Krulear?"

"Krulear is the seer, the greatest in all of the dimensions. I will you take you to her. She will help," he said.

Tiki led the way and I couldn't help but follow. I wished I didn't have to put my trust in a stranger from another world, but without him, I didn't even know where to start.

We climbed down from the base of the mountain we'd landed on. We were surrounded by a red, rocky expanse that seemed to go on for miles in every direction.

"How are we going to find anything here? This plain stretches on forever."

Tiki laughed. "I'm not sure what your world is like, but in this world, things are rarely as they seem. Just because you cannot see it, does not mean it is not there. Magic conceals," he said.

I stared out over the plain and fresh air moved over my skin. The sky was cloudless and three suns beat down upon us, two yellow and one blue, but the temperature was cool. I pulled at my magic as though I was peeling away layers of glamour.

The land in front of me faded, revealing a lake. The water was calm, and instead of the water being blue, it was purple. The suns didn't reflect off of it and I walked towards it in bewilderment.

I stood at the shore and looked down, but I couldn't see into the water; it was too dark. I crouched lower, but the surface didn't reflect my face, or anything else. The substance was cool, smooth, and rolled off my skin. It felt like water.

"Is it safe to drink?"

Tiki laughed "Of course. It's very, very good."

I cupped my hands, dipped them into the strange liquid and brought it to my lips. It flowed over my tongue and down my throat. It had a taste all its own, the purest and richest water to ever touch my mouth, and as it slid down my throat, I closed my eyes to revel in its flavor.

"It's like nothing I've ever tasted."

"Drakar is known for its rich water. People travel over many dimensions to try it."

"Drakar – that's the name of this world?"

"Yes."

I looked out over the water and took another drink. "So where do we go from here?"

"We go in."

Before I could ask for an explanation, Tiki dove into the water. I waited a few moments for him to resurface, and when he didn't, I followed him down into the purple lake.

The water felt smooth as it slid over my body. I opened my eyes expecting to see nothing but darkness, but the water was oddly clear. I swam deeper and it didn't take long to get to the bottom.

The lake floor was all smooth rock with no plant or animal life. Tiki was treading water next to a strange stone arch embedded in the rock. He gestured towards it, and as I got closer he swam through it and disappeared.

I swam around the arch in bewilderment. He hadn't come through the other side. I put my hand through and it disappeared. I felt warmth on the other side and I put my other hand through the arch and propelled my body through. The cool sensation of water vanished and was replaced by dry warmth.

I didn't so much swim through the portal as walk, stepping onto a stone path on the other side. My skin was dry and I could see the dark purple water on the other side of the archway. I reached out and touched the cool liquid floating in front of me, but when I pulled my hand back it was dry once again. I turned as the familiar tingling sensation moved down my neck.

The tingling came in waves as hoards of Underworlders walked in front of me. We stood at the entrance to a marketplace, filled with pure blood demons roaming everywhere. It was difficult not to stare at creatures with black, blue, green and other colors of skin. Some of the pure bloods towered over me while others came up only to my knees. A few of them had tusks protruding from their lips and others were covered in hair from head to toe. The majority of them did not look human, more like the demons I'd fought in the sanctuary, but those that did look human did not seem to be treated well. Everybody stared at me as though I had a horn growing out my forehead, although if I did, it would've helped me fit in.

"Stay close to me and don't talk to anyone or make eye contact," Tiki said, but his musical tone didn't match his serious expression.

He led me through the market while different creatures stared at me, mostly like I was lunch. Some drew their weapons as I walked by, while others shoved past me with their shoulders. I did my best to ignore their antagonizing efforts and followed Tiki.

"The pure bloods don't like half breeds," he said.

"No kidding. Why do you get to walk around so freely?"

"Most of them have come to know me, some through Krulear, some through...other means. I have their respect."

We passed booth after booth, some selling weapons and others selling objects I didn't recognize. Each stall sold something different, but I didn't stop to admire anything. I had little interest in holding some sort of food that looked like a pineapple but sprouted strange moving tentacles where the stem should be. I'd leave that for the demons.

Tiki turned down an alley between two booths and we came to a small hut sitting by itself. Strands of leaves hung in the doorway and I pushed them to the side as I followed Tiki.

The interior was lit with candles, each with a different colored flame. The mixed glow of colors cast a strange radiance over the room. Skeletons of odd creatures hung from the ceiling. Urns and jars lined the shelves, full of things I'd never seen, some holding glowing viscous fluids and others with living creatures. A rickety table at the end of the room had something strange sitting beside it. Matted hair draped over the table in a blend of brown and gray.

Tiki cleared his throat and the hair rose, revealing a weathered face with small horns protruding from its forehead. It had no eyebrows over solid blood red eyes. Its lips were so thin they almost disappeared, and a smile revealed sharp jagged teeth.

"Tikimicharnikato of the Suriattas Clan, you've brought an outsider to me. Why?" a raspy female voice said.

The creature didn't rise and Tiki moved forward and lowered himself to one knee as he kissed the extended hand she offered.

"It has been too long, Krulear," he said.

She stared at me as she spoke. "That it has, child." The look she gave me was strange, eerie, but not unfriendly.

"This is Chase Williams. He is from a place far from here and in search of his friend. I believe he is the man you told me about many years ago."

Krulear grunted and moved towards me. Her face was flat and had two slits in the center that I took for her nose as she leaned in and sniffed me while running her long nails over my skin. I tried not to move.

"Interesting breed," she said, running a frail hand through my hair. "I have not seen your kind in many millennia, hunter. I saw you in Tikimicharnikato's path many years ago, but I thought my time would have passed by the time you arrived." Her raspy voice reminded me of Grams, but her breath reeked not of cigarettes, but...death.

"Please, Krulear, can you help us?" Tiki asked.

Krulear pulled away from me. "Of course, child. You need help finding this...female, if I'm not mistaken?"

"Indeed."

Krulear grunted again and waddled back to her chair. A long ratty skirt dragged on the dirt floor and an old cloak covered a large hump on her back. Her tangled hair hung to her feet and was laced with colored beads and ribbons. She moved at a turtle's pace, and it looked like the hump caused her pain with each step.

She fell back into her chair, stared at me with her pupil-less eyes and grunted, pointing to the chair across from her. "Come," she demanded.

I sat down and she kept her blood red eyes locked on me. Her wrinkled skin hung loose and the small horns jutting from her forehead were like little white teeth. She stared at me for so long I started to get uncomfortable. I looked at Tiki, but he only gave a reassuring nod.

"Give me your hand," she ordered.

I hesitated before laying my hand on the table. She grabbed my wrist with a speed and strength that shouldn't exist in such a frail body. Her other hand came up with a rusty blade and my discomfort turned to a nervousness. I tried to pull my hand away, but her grip was firm and unrelenting. She turned my wrist until my hand was palm up and her gangly fingers gripped it tightly.

She slid the knife across my hand and I winced, forcing myself to keep my palm open. She moved the rusty blade slowly enough that I felt the skin split and the warm trickle of blood fill my palm. I could only think of the tetanus shot I'd need after this.

Krulear leaned over the table, her lipless mouth hovering above my hand, and a black tongue slipped out from between jagged teeth. The tongue was split multiple times, like a snake's, but with more than one V. She lapped up the blood and slurped it into her mouth. I couldn't keep the disgust off my face.

She released my wrist, leaned back from the table and nearly fell out of her chair. One small black dot appeared in the center of each of her eyes and expanded over the red until jet black orbs stared at me. They flashed white and then back to black several times. Her black tongue slipped out and licked some of the blood smeared around her lips.

"You've a most interesting past, hunter. You don't belong in this world, but you don't belong in yours either," she said. "Your kind has not been here for thousands of years and now you are here, and there are more." She paused and seemed to watch a scene in her head "What is this? A girl of both worlds? This is the one you seek?"

I leaned over the table and I could see my reflection in her flashing orbs. "Yes, Rayna. What do you see?"

An unsettling smile crept over her face. "Interesting," she said. Her long nails tapped the scarred wood surface of the table. "I see many things in your future, hunter, and in hers too." Her nails continued to tap the table before coming to an abrupt stop. "They are far from here, moving towards a cave by Alkalina Lake. There is great power there. They are close, but not there yet." Her eyes moved back and forth. "They are preparing for a ritual. They plan to..." She stopped and a strange look crossed her face. "You are related to this man?"

"He's my father."

"He is not himself."

"What?"

"His aura is his own, but also...not. He does not know what he seeks." I wanted to ask what she meant, but she continued. "Death surrounds you, hunter and..." she stopped again. The flashing in Krulear's eyes slowed and the red began seeping back. Once they were solid again, she looked at Tiki with a hostile expression.

"Leave me. I have seen enough," she said angrily. Whether she was mad or had just seen something she feared I didn't know, but something had unsettled her.

"I can't leave Rayna in their hands," I said.

"Must I repeat myself?" she shouted in voice that was very different from the raspy tone she'd had before.

Tiki's hand came to rest on my shoulder. "We must go," he said.

I looked at him and back to Krulear, but I didn't say anything more. I rose from the chair and turned to leave.

"Take care in your actions, hunter. There will be many who wish you harm. You stand in the way of many wills and they will all try to overcome you. You must remember: you cannot fight fire with fire," she said.

Questions raced through my mind, but her hand went up before I could speak and she waved me away. I turned and walked out of the hut, more confused than ever, despite knowing Rayna's location.

"Well, that was refreshing," I said, trying to rid my mind of the sight of Krulear's jagged teeth.

"Do not take what she said lightly; she is accurate in her readings," Tiki said.

"Is that what that was, a reading? She drank my blood and went all freaky demon on me, only to spout a bunch of randomness."

"You fear that what she said is true. This is acceptable, but do not dismiss her words."

"Fear what? She never actually told me anything."

"What she said will make sense in time."

"She said something about Alkalina Lake. Do you know where that is?"

"Yes, but it is a great distance from here. It will take many days to reach it on foot."

"Can't you teleport us there?"

"I cannot jump from one place to another in a single dimension. I can only move from one dimension to another, and where I end up in that world is not entirely under my control. We must find another means of travel."

Tiki led me back down the alley and further through the market place. After the booths started to thin out, we emerged into an open field.

Green and red blades of grass covered the plain, giving it a festive look. Dirt paths led in several directions, but Tiki chose one and began walking. We went several miles down the road, passing strange plants and animals. Most of the wildlife was similar to things we had on Earth, but each animal had unique characteristics. Birds with two heads fluttered about using multiple pairs of wings, while deer with fangs more fearsome than any tiger's galloped on six legs.

We continued for a few miles before Tiki broke the silence. "Uh oh," he said.

"What?"

A large river flowed before us, with the same dark purple water as the lake. It crashed against the banks and white caps topped the rapids. On the bank was a small village that looked deserted.

As we walked towards the river, I saw a thin wooden bridge held together with ropes swaying above the rapids. To the side of it sat a small, strange creature.

"Trolls," Tiki said.

"Trolls? Like actual trolls?" I wasn't sure I should be surprised. These dimensions were home to thousands of creatures, some of which I knew of from legends and common mythology, and others I'd never known existed. As we got closer to the bridge, the creature pulled out a small, vicious looking axe and moved to block the bridge.

The troll was short, his oddly shaped head only coming up to my waist. His chin jutted to the side instead of forward, and a few large warts and dark black scars marred his light gray skin. His eyes were beady dots that peered up at us from beneath a bushy unibrow and matted hair. A matching moustache quivered above thick pouty lips as his spoke.

"Not without paying the toll." His voice was hoarse and deep, and his eyes held fierce determination. His small hands gripped the thick wooden handle of his axe and he puffed out his broad chest.

"You're kidding me. Not only is this an actual troll, but he wants us to pay him to cross a bridge? How cliché," I said.

The troll huffed under his moustache and it curled up in a sneer as he spoke. "That's right, half breed. No demons of pure blood cross this bridge without paying the toll, let alone filthy half breeds. We should charge you double. You should feel blessed by the gods that we give you the option of paying and we don't rip out your innards and leave you to die."

"Half breed..." I started to say, but Tiki stopped me.

"What is the toll?" Tiki asked.

The troll stared at me and I could see the hatred in his eyes. "For you, let's say fifty quartz," he said, holding out his free hand.

"Fifty quartz? That's outrageous!" Tiki replied.

The troll snorted. "Ha, even you don't feel your life is worth that much. Just goes to show we should rid our worlds of your kind," he said, pointing at us with his axe.

"I do not have this money," Tiki said to me.

I shrugged. "I don't have one quartz, let alone fifty."

"Is there anything else we can offer you that would grant us passage?" Tiki asked.

"No," the troll was quick to reply.

"This is ridiculous, Tiki. How much trouble can one troll cause?" I moved past Tiki and pushed my way past the troll.

In an assortment of quick movements, the troll hit the back of my legs with the back of his axe. I flipped onto my back and the blade of his axe pressed against my throat. His dark beady eyes stared down at me and I heard Tiki's soft voice say "Plenty."

"I am Garsmith, of the Barvish clan, and I will not be disrespected by the likes of you!" the troll shouted, pushing the blade hard against my throat.

Small heads started to peek out of the nearby tents and before long we had a group of warty trolls gathered around us. Each face was different, but they all had the same bushy unibrows, awkwardly shaped heads and beady black eyes.

"Perhaps there is one way we could let you pass without paying in quartz," Garsmith said, drops of his spit showering me as he spoke.

I squinted through the sprinkle. "And what's that?"

"A battle," he said. "Between you two and one of my people."

I tilted my head towards Tiki. "What do you think?"

"The trolls are known to be savage in battle. I'm not sure it's wise. Perhaps we can find another way across."

"Let me rephrase," Garsmith said. "You can do battle and possibly earn yourself safe passage, or you can die for your insults here and now."

I looked back up at Tiki and we both said "Deal."

The troll lifted his axe from my throat and swung it back into its holster. "Then we have an agreement."

I nodded, still lying on my back.

"Well, get up, I haven't got all day," he said.

Funny, I thought, since he was doing nothing but standing by the bridge making sure nobody crossed it, all day was precisely what he had.

I pushed myself to my feet, brushing off the rocks and gravel that clung to my shirt. We followed Garsmith, weaving our way through small tents and huts, each with its own fire burning. Some of the fires warmed pots, cooking things that smelled awful and looked worse. A thick troll, shorter than the rest, hammered away at piece of steel on an anvil. He grunted as we walked by and I had to keep myself from jumping.

We were led to the center of the village, where a large open space was enclosed by wooden railings.

"This is where you battle," the troll said. Garsmith pulled at the latch on one of the wooden railings and pushed a small gate inwards. He nodded at us to get inside. I looked back at Tiki, who shrugged, and before we could decide anything, a press of bodies behind us pushed us through the gate. Garsmith shut the gate and slid the latch back into place.

"Are we fighting you?" I asked.

The troll laughed a hoarse and crackly laugh and the crowd that gathered behind him laughed with him. "No, you are not worthy of my blade, half breed. I have something special for you." He smiled, brought stubby fingers to his mouth and blew a high pitched whistle. When the sound stopped, we waited, and I looked around in the silence.

A thundering sound came from behind the crowd. Something crawled out of a long tent, grunting and snorting, and when the creature rose to its feet I was in awe. It was twice my height, and a long beard hung from its chin to the middle of its chest. Thick gray arms and legs bulged with muscles. Its hands were wide but had the same short, stubby fingers as the other trolls, and somehow its large black eyes still appeared beady below a pronounced brow.

It raised its arms above its head and groaned as it stretched, a deep grumble escaping its lips. The small cloth that covered its groin lifted as it stretched, revealing an organ proportionate to his stature. The *it* that we were fighting was definitely a *he*. I shuddered at the sight and looked at Tiki, whose eyes were wide.

"You will battle Ishmar, my son," Garsmith said, with a fatherly grin stretching from ear to ear.

Ishmar stormed towards us with long strides that thumped against the ground. His eyes were huge and uneven, but he had the same glare as his father as he stepped over the wooden railing and into the makeshift arena.

"Great," I said.

"The rules are as follows: the fight begins when I sound the bell, and does not end until either Ishmar kills you or you kill Ishmar. Those are the rules," Garsmith said.

"One rule?" I said.

"Yep."

"You honestly expect me to believe that if we kill your son, you're going to let us walk out of here?"

Garsmith grunted. "If I thought for a moment that you could win, I would've killed you myself. I've offered you this opportunity only for the entertainment it will bring my people. But should you win, yes, you will be allowed to leave unharmed."

"And cross the bridge without paying the quartz?" I added.

"Yes, yes, of course, and cross the bridge without paying the toll," he said, waving my words away.

"Okay, agreed."

Before Tiki or I had a chance to prepare a strategy, a bell rung and Ishmar thundered towards us. In two steps, he had crossed the ring, and a thick fist swung down at us. We ducked as it flew over our heads and I dove through Ishmar's legs. I came up behind him and Ishmar bent over – giving me a less than pleasant view – and stared at me through his legs. He grunted and turned to face me.

He was raising a clenched fist when Tiki's small form soared through the air until his small caramel arms wrapped around Ishmar's neck. Tiki squeezed the thick gray flesh, but Ishmar was unfazed. The giant troll reached a long arm behind himself, grabbed Tiki and threw him to the ground. Tiki's body hit the dirt so hard it bounced. A groan escaped his lips and I could tell that although he wasn't unconscious, he was hurt.

I pulled both daggers from their sheaths and jumped towards Ishmar. The blades came down and hit the small of his back, but slipped off, the dull gray skin too thick to pierce. Ishmar turned and swung his fist at my face. Suddenly I was airborne. My body broke the railing of the arena and a large piece of splintered wood stabbed through my side.

I fell into a tent, which collapsed around me as the poles snapped. I struggled to stand up among the heavy fabric, the pain in my side sending waves of agony and then adrenaline through me. It was painful to lift my arm, but I pushed through it, managing to untangle myself.

Ishmar stood over Tiki, raining fists down on him as Tiki curled up to protect himself. Anger flared inside me and I pulled the wood from my side. Blood followed it to flow down my leg, but I took a step forward and pulled my magic up.

The fire flowed through my stomach and chest then down my arms. Blue and silver fire burst from both my hands. The flame shot forward in a stream until it hit Ishmar's back and engulfed him. He roared and stopped his flurry of punches. His large gray body turned and I pulled the flame back.

"Not fair, not fair!" Garsmith said.

"Are there rules saying I can't use magic?" Garsmith shook his head and a sullen look washed over his face. "I didn't think so."

As the smoke cleared around Ishmar, I saw his gray skin undamaged by the flame and my stomach clenched with nervousness.

"Haha, that's my boy! Use your fire magic, half breed; his hide is too strong for your trickery." Garsmith laughed and the crowd joined in and began cheering Ishmar on.

Ishmar's fists swung at me in a fury and I did everything I could to block them, but he was too strong. His physical strength was beyond anything I'd ever faced.

My body swelled and bruised as fists smashed my face and torso. When I did manage to duck one of his blows, I followed through with force of my own. I smashed my fist into his stomach and jumped to strike his face, but he didn't react. I was on the verge of exhaustion when Ishmar stopped swinging and lifted me into the air with ease.

The crowd cheered. "Eat him! Eat him! Eat him!" the trolls chanted.

"Bite his head off!" a woman's voice yelled.

Ishmar smiled and lifted me above his head. He pulled me closer to his face, licking his lips, and I struggled against his grip and freed both my arms. I pushed at his hands, trying to break free, but he squeezed the air from my lungs.

I could feel the blood drain from my face and my head lolled to one side as I struggled for breath. I was high enough to see the white caps crashing against the bank of the river and the sight of the water filled me with determination.

I grabbed his wrists with both hands and pulled a different magic up from my soul. I focused as best I could with little air in my lungs and the pain in my side. I thought of that river, the dark purple rapids smashing against each other with force. Water was a relaxing and healing element when it was calm, but when it was angry, it pulled its victims under its wrath. I was going to see how far my magic could stretch untrained.

I focused my power and let it spill from my body. The cool rush of water filled my veins as the magic moved into Ishmar. His black eyes widened in panic and he released me. I wrapped my hands around his thick neck as I fell, letting the magic flow into him. He fell to the ground with a crash and water spilled from his nostrils. His body convulsed and he coughed waves of water as he took his turn to struggle for air.

202

"Ishmar!" Garsmith yelled. I turned my eyes on him and his gray skin paled. "Don't kill him! Please, not my boy," Garsmith begged.

"Do you forfeit?"

"Never!" Garsmith said in a rush of pride.

"Then so be it," I said and I turned my focus back to Ishmar. His stubby fingers pawed at me, trying to bat me from his chest, but I put all my strength into holding on to his throat.

His strength dwindled under my magic. He rolled to his stomach, water pouring from his ears and eyes sockets now. I kept my grip on his neck, straddling his back while he fought to hold himself up on his elbows. A rush of water poured from his mouth and he gasped for air, grabbing at the loose dirt around him.

"Papa!" He managed to cry out in a gurgle, clawing his way towards Garsmith.

Garsmith backed up, his prideful face showing a hint of sadness. I let him see the determination in my face until he finally conceded.

"Alright," Garsmith said.

"Alright what?"

"We forfeit."

"And?"

"You and your friend can leave, unharmed, and cross the bridge. You have my word," he said through gritted teeth.

"Agreed," I said, and released my grip and pulled the magic back inside me. I fell off Ishmar's back and onto the ground, panting to pull air into my own lungs. My swollen body ached as I crawled to Tiki.

Ishmar coughed heavily, expelling a flood of water from his body. His gray skin had turned white, and when he had coughed the last of the water from his lungs, he collapsed. Garsmith rushed to his son's aid and began rubbing his back and soothing him.

Tiki moved slowly and jerkily, black and purple with bruises from the waist up. His nose was pouring bright red blood and his lips had multiple splits. Dried blood and dirt added their colors to his flesh. I collapsed beside him in exhaustion.

"Well, that went well," I said between pants. The magic had taken most of my energy and I was extremely tired and hungry.

"If that is your idea of going well, I do not want to know what you classify as going badly. Ishmar has a strange magic. I could not bring my demon out," Tiki said.

Loud footsteps neared us, but I couldn't be bothered to move. Ishmar cast a large shadow over us, the gray coloring coming back into his skin. Panic ran through me, but his thick arms extended and he offered each of us a hand.

"You are a most worthy opponent," Ishmar said, and bowed his head to me.

"As are you," I said.

"Thank you for sparing me. You are most honorable."

"I wouldn't say that, but thank you."

Ishmar shook his head. "I threatened to end your life, and still you spared me. If that's not honorable, then I do not know the meaning of the word." His voice was gentle, and deeper than any I'd ever heard.

"Thank you, Ishmar."

"You are hurt and tired. Please, come eat and rest with us." I looked at Tiki, who looked to be in too much pain to argue. "I promise you will be safe here," Ishmar added.

"Okay," I said.

Ishmar led us into another open space. Thick logs surrounded a large fire pit. Three trolls worked around a big pot hanging above the fire, stirring whatever was inside. If it hadn't been for their breasts, I wouldn't have known they were female.

"Please sit," Ishmar said.

Tiki and I groaned as we lowered ourselves onto a log.

"You okay?" I asked.

"I will be fine."

"I can help heal you."

"No, no. I have seen what your magic can do."

I laughed and it made me wince again. "Really, I can." I reached out towards him and he tried to pull away from me, but it hurt him too much to move. I placed both my hands on his back and called on my magic. The water flowed up through my soul in a smooth calm wave and out my hands.

Tiki gasped, but quieted as his muscles relaxed. I sent my magic out over his body and imagined that smooth water was rolling over his wounds, washing away the blood and bruises as undamaged caramel skin revealed itself. It took everything I had left.

When I opened my eyes, his bruises were gone, replaced by flawless flesh. His lips had healed and all that remained of his wounds were the stains of dried blood.

"Amazing," he said as I pulled my magic back into me.

All the trolls had stopped and were staring at us, some with awe, others with surprise, and some with anger, which I didn't understand. I didn't know how to react, and I didn't have the energy to move. I hadn't realized how much the magic would take out of me.

I tried to pull up my magic again and heal my own wounds, but I couldn't focus; I needed food and rest. I tried to stand, but black dots swam around me and I had to force my eyelids to stay open.

"Chase?" Tiki said, his voice was distant.

"I'm fine. I just need...." I started, but the light around me dimmed and I fell to the ground. I remembered seeing the dirt approaching, but the darkness swallowed me before I hit it.

Chapter 28

I awoke in somebody's tent and could see the flickering light of a fire through the opening. I tried to move and realized I was in a cot of some kind.

"Chase!" Tiki said. He moved to the side of the bed. "Are you alright?"

I tried to sit up. I was still in pain, but it had receded. "I'm fine. I think. I don't know what happened."

"You blacked out. Your magic, it drains you."

I knew that using your magic took energy, but I'd never seen anybody react like this.

"What time is it?"

"It will be morning soon."

Panic coursed through me and I swung my legs over the edge. "We need to go! We have to get to Rayna."

"I know, but first you must eat."

"We don't have time, Tiki! I've slept for too long."

"You will be of no use to Rayna if you are weak. You must eat. The trolls' chief has offered to take us to Galthor, a man who can help us with travel arrangements. The trolls are a powerful people of many abilities, and you have earned their respect."

"Fine, first we eat, but then we leave."

Only a few trolls remained around the fire and Ishmar was one of them. His attention turned to me as I sat on one of the logs, and he came over immediately with a steaming wooden bowl and matching spoon.

"Here, eat," he said.

"Thanks."

I looked down at the steaming bowl filled with a thin black liquid with strange green lumps. I lifted my gaze to Ishmar and raised a brow.

"It is very good. Eat," he said.

"What is it?" I asked, poking at the lumps with my spoon.

"It is vesorla soup. I caught it myself in the river this morning," he said with a proud smile.

I took a spoonful and examined it. It smelled kind of like old socks, but I needed to eat something. My stomach growled and I slid the spoon into my mouth. After you got past the dirty foot flavor, it wasn't disgusting, and I was grateful. Tiki was right; I wasn't going to save Rayna on an empty stomach.

"Ishmar, why are you so much bigger than the rest of the trolls?" Tiki asked.

Ishmar lowered himself and sat crossed legged in front of us. "I get my size from my mother. She's a giant."

I coughed and choked down the mouthful of food I had. "I'm sorry, did you say a giant?"

Ishmar nodded.

"How do a giant and a troll..." I started. "Never mind. I don't want to know."

"That's why my demon was contained," Tiki said.

"Yes, the giants have strange abilities," Ishmar said. "My mother and father had me at a young age and were not ready for marriage. I split my time between their tribes. Although I may seem oversized here, I am small when I am among my mother's family."

Ishmar didn't speak with grunting and snorting between his words like the other trolls, but his voice was so deep I found it hard to understand at times.

"The friend I'm looking for comes from a similar situation," I said.

"Her mother is a giant and her father is a troll?" Ishmar asked with excitement.

"Not exactly," I said.

Ishmar didn't have time to ask any more questions, as footsteps came up beside us and he jumped to his feet. He lowered himself onto one knee and bowed to the men that arrived.

A short, thick man with a black beard that hung from his strange chin to the ground stood beside me. His small beady eyes watched me with a strange expression as he pulled his ankle length hair into a ponytail. Two more trolls behind him stood motionless, dressed in armor and holding their helmets under their arms. Both had matted black hair twisted into dreadlocks and black scars on their faces.

"Chief Sorent," Tiki said.

"Are you ready?" Sorent asked.

"I think so," he said, looking at me.

I nodded and Sorent stared down at me, an odd look on his face. "So you are the one who almost killed our Ishmar," he stated.

I looked up at him but didn't respond.

"A noble thing you did, boy," he said, followed by a snort. "The trolls owe you great thanks for having spared his life. He is a great warrior among our people, but I suppose not as great as you."

I was left wordless again. I didn't want to say anything to offend him. I was relying on him to get us to Alkalina Lake.

"Regardless," he continued, "he is of great value to my army and I owe you thanks. Your friend Tikimicharnikato of the Suriattas clan has told us you need to get to Alkalina Lake."

"Yes, as soon as possible."

"We cannot take you there ourselves. It is in a land where we are forbidden to travel, but we can take you to Galthor. He can help."

"Galthor is a troll?"

Sorent snorted and grimaced. "Oh for gods' sake, no. He is a filthy goblin, but the best in Drakar to meet your needs. If we leave now, we should get to him by high sun."

"Thank you, Sorent."

Sorent led us back to the bridge. One of his guards went first, the chief second, then the other guard. We followed and Ishmar trailed behind, making the bridge swing with each of his steps. I gripped the rope tightly and was relived to reach solid ground on the other side.

Two of the three suns had started to rise and the sky with decorated with hues of blue and yellow. Chief Sorent led us through the Christmas-colored grass to a path he said would take us straight to Galthor.

"I'm sure we can manage on our own, Chief," I said.

"Nonsense. We will guide you and ensure your safety. It's the least we can do," he replied with a snort.

I didn't think it was an argument I could win so I didn't bother to object. Having a few extra people on our side couldn't hurt.

Chapter 29

The Chief hadn't been kidding when he said the path would take us to Galthor's. We followed it all morning until all three suns were at their peak in the dark green sky. The trail ended at a large field of green, red, and now also blue grass.

A small structure in the middle of the field was surrounded by a large fence. Strange yellow vines with white and red flowers wove themselves through each slat. Inside the enclosure, various creatures were grazing and resting in the shade of strange trees.

Sorent stopped at the edge of the path. "There it is: Galthor's!" he said.

I looked at the old wooden building I assumed was a house, although it was much smaller than any I'd ever seen.

"You're not coming?" I asked.

Sorent grunted and shook his head. "I'm afraid not. The trolls and goblins have a history of war, and although Galthor himself would welcome us, I cannot step onto his land without breaking the treaty."

"Well, thank you. For everything," I said.

He snorted. "This is the least we can do for you, hunter."

I must have looked surprised and Sorent laughed. "Your friend told us about your heritage, but do not worry. You have already proven you are not like the hunters of our legends. We are people of Drakar, and this is not one of Ithreal's worlds. Not all creatures of the Underworlds despise your kind."

I looked at Tiki, who shrugged. "I appreciate your help," I said.

"It was our pleasure, but our debt to you is hardly erased. You spared the life of one of my people, and that is not easily repaid," he said with a snort and a grunt. "Good luck." His guards fell in line around him.

Ishmar smiled and bowed to me before he turned, and the quartet set off back down the path.

Tiki and I started walking toward the old structure, but Sorent called back to us. "Oh, I nearly forgot..." he shouted. "Goblins are strange creatures. You don't want to upset them. Trust me, be polite. You don't want him to get him angry."

"Good to know," I said, and they disappeared behind a hill.

As we neared the house I could see a small figure at the far end of the property, watering some plants along the side of his house and watching us as we approached. Once we neared the gate, he moved straight towards us.

"Remember, be polite," Tiki said, but I didn't have time to ask what happened when a goblin got mad.

Galthor was short, with thick green skin coated in warts and pimples. Two tusks jutted from his lower jaw and square teeth showed brown between plump, dark purple lips. His red eyes looked small and angry.

"Whadya want?" His speech was clipped and his accent sounded vaguely Irish.

"We'd like to speak with Galthor. Please," I said.

"Yeah I'm Galthor. Like I said, whadya want?"

"We need a means of travel to Alkalina Lake. We need to be there as soon as possible and Chief Sorent told us you were the best person to help us with that."

The goblin stared at me for a moment and then looked proud. He put his thumbs through the black suspenders holding up his brown pants and grunted. "I am Galthor, da finest beast trainer in all da dimensions. But I don't do charity work, not even for Sorent, and you don't look like ya 'ave a quartz to ya name." He turned to walk away.

"Perhaps a trade?" Tiki suggested.

"We don't have anything to trade," I whispered.

"We both have something the goblins value more than money."

Galthor moved back towards us. "What could you 'ave dat I would want, 'alf breed?" He scowled.

"Blood," Tiki said.

"Bah, I would die before I drank da blood of a half breed! I wouldn't want dat filth inside of me."

"What about mine?" I said.

The goblin laughed. "If I won't take his dirty blood, why would I take yers? One half breed is no better den anudder. Yer all disgusting creatures and our world's should be rid 'o ya."

"But I'm not a half breed. I'm not even a demon."

Galthor took a step closer and stared up at me. His massive nose moved as he leaned towards me and sniffed. "Ya do smell different. Whadya supposed to be?"

"I'm not from this world. I'm from a world called Earth and I was born a hunter of the Circle of Light. My blood is hunter's blood."

The goblin snorted and laughed, looking at Tiki, who nodded in confirmation. Galthor eyed me up and down again, hunger filling his eyes. "Blood offers are rarely made nowadays. Dere must be sumptin important at Alkalina Lake for ya ta make such an offer."

"Very important."

"Why would I wanna 'elp you anyways? If ya are what ya say ya are, aren't ya supposed to kill my kind?"

"I don't. Not anymore."

The goblin's red eyes watched me and he sniffed me again. "Dere 'asn't been a 'unter 'ere for millennia, 'ow do I know yer da real deal and not anudder mutt?"

"Why does he keep calling you mixed breed and mutt?" I asked Tiki.

Galthor grunted and Tiki answered. "After the great war millennia ago, many females of our kind came back with child. Their descendants are those who look like me."

I arched a brow. "How old are you?"

Tiki ignored me and looked to the goblin. "I may be a mixed breed, Galthor, which I say without shame, but he is not of my kind, I assure you."

"Yer word means nothing to me, dirty creature," he snarled.

"How about a sample?" I offered. "Someone of your intelligence can surely tell if the blood is pure or not."

"Of course I can," he replied, stretching his suspenders with thick green thumbs.

"Then I offer you a sample. Should you feel it's not blood worthy of your services, then we'll leave."

Galthor stared at me intently, as if I was trying to trick him. "You'll leave, just like dat?"

"Yes."

He seemed to consider it before answering. "Deal," he said. He stuck out a huge green hand that didn't suit his tiny body, and I extended my own to shake on it.

I pulled out a dagger and reopened the cut on my palm. When the blood started to pool, I hesitated to give it to him. The thought of another creature drinking my blood gave me the creeps, but the thought of anything happening to Rayna made me push my disgust aside.

Galthor eyed the blood, and a thick green tongue slid over his purple lips as he took in the scent. He grabbed my hand and brought it to his nostrils. He sniffed deeply and his red eyes rolled back in his head. His tongue felt rough like a cat's as it slid across my palm, and he took a few short licks to moisten the skin before taking a short suck from the wound. His tongue pulled away and his small body shuddered.

"I ain't 'ad da pleasure of such blood in tousands of years. I can taste da power, da magic!"

"So we have a deal?"

"Yah, yah, of course." He undid a latch and opened the gate. "Come in, come in."

The goblin led us into his house and Tiki didn't have as much trouble as I did getting through the door. I had to crouch to avoid putting my head through the roof.

To one side of the entrance was a small eating area, and Galthor ordered us to wait there while he retrieved a jar. He'd specified that he wanted a whole jar, which worried me at first, but when he returned with the vessel I was confident I could fill it. It was goblin sized.

I used the blade he gave me to open my cut further and held the jar beneath it. My blood filled it quickly, and Galthor snatched it from my hand as soon as it was full. He gave me a hungry look that made my stomach turn. He put the lid on the jar then took his blade back and licked it. His eyes lit up as the blood touched his tongue.

"So mortal, yet full of magic," he said with a smile.

"Now we've kept up our end of the bargain, it's your turn."

"Oh yes," he said. "Follow me, follow me."

Galthor led us to the back of his home where we found a stable much larger than the house.

"Now, pickin' a creature ain't like going to da market and pickin' fruit. When yer paired with a creature 'o mine, it's a lifetime connection, not a one-time fling. Ya understand?"

I hid my confusion and nodded. I knew blood was a valuable commodity among goblins, but for what little I gave him I thought we'd be renting something, not purchasing a pet for life.

The huge stable was easier for me to move through. It was full of different creatures, some in stalls, others in cages, while some roamed free. The cages held small cats, large cats, and wolf-like creatures. Birds were held in other areas and animals I didn't know the name of were housed in some of the stalls. I started to wonder if we had come to the right place. We needed something big and fast, and there wasn't a creature here I thought would fit the bill.

Galthor pulled a thick rope that hung against the wall. A series of pulleys and cogs turned, and after a few moments all the stall gates and cage doors opened at once.

"So how does this work? Do we just pick one?" I asked.

Galthor gave a snort. "No. You don't just *pick one*," he mimicked.

"So how do we..."

"Da creature will pick you. For now, we wait," Galthor said, taking up a seat on a bale of something resembling hay.

We waited while animals moved towards us. Several came up to catch our scent, sniffing both Tiki and me before turning and walking away. Bird-like creatures hovered around us, and before long each animal had moved back to their respective area.

I sighed in frustration and turned to Galthor "Look, we don't have time…" I was interrupted by a high pitched chirp.

A small budgie-sized creature that I hadn't noticed sat on my shoulder. White feathers covered its body while gold feathers trailed down its spine and made up its tail. Small blue eyes peered at me while the bird stretched out two incredible pairs of long wings.

"Well look at dat. Dats's a rare commodity right dere," Galthor said, waddling in front of us.

"Wow, it's a…tiny bird," I said.

"Ah, don't let her appearance fool ya. Dat dere's a golden torrent, a close relative to da thunderbird and a rarity in any world. I've had dat dere gal for over a century and if I'da known dat would be yer animal, I wouldn't a made dis deal, hardly fair. But a deal's a deal, I s'pose."

I shook my head and looked down at Galthor. "I think you've misunderstood what we're looking for. We need something that can take us to Alkalina Lake, and fast."

Galthor grunted and waved a hand to shoo me away "Bah! I understand ya just fine, ya see. We made a deal and dis is it."

"No, you don't. I need to get to Alkalina Lake and I can't do that with a little thing like this. I don't care how rare it is!" I raised my voice in frustration.

"Chase…" Tiki started.

"Ya saying I'm not 'oldin' up my end of da deal? Ya callin' me a liar?" The goblin's voice was deeper now, his accent thickening with each word.

The animals began to stir. Birds chirped while other creatures growled, turning in their stalls.

"No, I'm just saying I need to get to Alkalina Lake and I can't do that with this tiny creature," I said, trying to be polite.

Tiki grabbed my shoulders and shook his head. I tried to backpedal, but it was too late.

The small goblin's eyes went redder and small purple veins pushed at his skin. I sighed, fearing I'd done the one thing I wasn't supposed to.

The skin on Galthor's face moved like something was alive beneath it. It rippled and the sound of bones breaking sent a chill down my spine. "How dare ya insult me! Yer ignorance angers me." His voice had become a deep growl that belonged to something much larger than the tiny goblin before us.

"Please, I didn't mean to offend you. I'm just running out of time and..." I was interrupted by the crunching of bones as his whole body started to reconstruct itself.

I stepped back and the golden torrent gripped my shoulder. Its small claws dug into my skin as it chirped frantically. Tiki grabbed my shoulder and pulled me back. "We should leave," he said, his voice trembling. The animals in their pens and cages squawked and howled.

"What's going on? What's happening to him?" I said, looking at Tiki.

"That."

The small green man was no longer small. His bones had shifted and his entire body grew. His skin stretched to the point I thought it would rip and muscles bulged from everywhere on his body. Even his warts grew with him. His flat dirty teeth shifted into sharp fangs longer than my fingers.

He grew until my head was somewhere near the middle of his thigh. Saliva poured from his mouth and his tusks had extended. He growled as his body made the final shift and huge red eyes glared down at us.

Tiki pulled at my shirt and this time I didn't hesitate. We walked backwards to the door and both turned and ran. An earth-shattering roar came from behind us and the ground shook as Galthor started after us. He broke through the stable and splinters of wood flew past. We ran along the fence, racing for the gate.

"Now what?" I yelled at Tiki.

He turned to look back at the pursuing goblin. Galthor jumped high in the air and came crashing to the ground. The force made the earth shake and I lost my balance, catching myself in time to watch Tiki tumble to the ground behind me.

I stopped to pull him to his feet. His triangular pupils had expanded in fear and his eyes were almost entirely white. Those few seconds were enough for the goblin to gain on us.

A massive green arm came down and sent us flying. Cold air flowed around me, then I crashed through the fence and tumbled into the field. I didn't have time to think about the pain; I jumped to my feet and searched for Tiki.

He hadn't gone through the fence, but over it, and was rolling further into the field. I ran full tilt towards him and helped him up. We should have run back towards Sorent and the other trolls, but adrenaline was pumping and we weren't thinking. We ran the opposite way, into an open space.

"Is it too late for apologies?" I shouted at Tiki as he tried to keep up. He glared and we both kept moving.

The small bird chirped in my ear, gripping so tightly to my shoulder I felt its claws pierce my skin. "Sorry, I'm a little busy running for my life here. You're supposed to be some impressive little creature; why don't you do something?"

The goblin started to close in on us, and something needed to happen or we were going to be in his reach. "You've got to be good for something!" I yelled at the bird.

It screeched in my ear, loudly enough that it hurt, and pushed off my shoulder.

"Great, now that we're being chased by an angry goblin, it's leaving."

"They told you to be polite!" Tiki yelled.

"Now isn't the best time to say you told me so!"

A booming caw echoed through the sky above us. The bird's silhouette dove and spun towards the ground and I watched in amazement as it changed form into something else...something bigger.

In seconds, it had shifted into a giant version of itself. Four massive wings stretched across the sky as it coasted to the ground. The earth shook as the bird let out a thunderous cry that made my ears ring.

Hearing a different roar, I turned to find the goblin had stopped. Galthor was hunched over, giant green hands covering his ears. The bird let out another bellowing squawk from its enormous beak and I was forced to cover my ears too. Galthor roared in pain and fell to his knees.

We put some more distance between us and the goblin before the bird wheeled down to the ground. Huge talons tore at the earth as it slowed itself.

"I retract my previous statement. That is impressive," I said.

The golden torrent raised its head and puffed out its chest.

Galthor yelled and the ground rattled as he jumped to his feet and moved towards us again. The bird lowered its tail and looked back at me, letting out a soft caw. I turned to Tiki, who gave me his characteristic shrug, and we grabbed at the golden feathers and climbed up.

I settled myself so my legs fell to either side of the creature's neck. Tiki took a spot between the two pairs of wings, and we both gripped handfuls of feathers, holding on for our lives.

The bird took a few strides forward before its wings flapped and we were airborne. The goblin had closed the distance between us and he grabbed the torrent's tail as it lifted us from the ground. The torrent cried out and needles of pain shot through my head at the high pitched sound.

I heard a soft clicking that sounded like nails on a chalk board before there was a flash of light beneath us and the goblin was struck by a bolt of lightning.

Bright white spots clouded my vision, and when they had cleared, Galthor's green skin had turned black. He roared in pain as he lost his grip and fell to the ground. A loud thud followed his impact and a cloud of dirt and dust exploded around him.

The torrent's wings pumped until the ground beneath us looked like a patchwork of terrain: green, red and blue fields of grass, gray mountains, and the odd splash of purple lakes and streams. The air was cold and I had to press my face against its feathers to protect my skin from the sharp wind.

The bird stopped flapping its wings and coasted along in the cloudy green sky. I kept my face buried in its neck and held on tight as we descended towards a large mountain.

A massive gray structure jutted from the ground, surrounded by a dark purple lake that stretched out for miles in every direction. A single strip of land provided access from the lake to the mountain. If that water was Alkalina Lake, then that mountain was where we needed to be. Only one way in and one way out didn't bode well for somebody wanting to attempt a rescue.

The bird dove towards the earth and the mountain grew with each second, but as we neared I could see smoke billowing out the top of it.

"What is that?" I yelled.

"It's a volcano," Tiki replied, and even from right behind me his voice sounded distant in the rush of wind.

We circled the volcano before gliding across the lake. Above the water, you could see no reflections, but it sprayed around us as the torrent's talons grazed the surface. The bird slowed as we neared the far edge of the lake and its giant claws grasped at the earth. When we'd stopped moving, the creature lowered itself to the ground, allowing us to slide down its back.

The golden torrent stared at me, its large blue eyes flashing from the lighting within.

"Thank you. I'm sorry I doubted your talents," I said.

It lowered its head and pushed the top of its beak against my cheek. I reached up and ran my fingers through its incredibly soft feathers, and the huge creature made a very gentle chirping sound.

It pulled its head away and leapt upwards. Its body exploded in feathers, morphing until nothing remained but the small, white and gold bird we'd met. It chirped a few times before finding its place on my shoulder once again. "Well, that was different," I said, as large feathers littered the ground and danced in the cool breeze.

Tiki nodded. "They are rare creatures. I had never seen one myself until now. They've been rumored to be extinct for centuries."

"What did it do to the goblin?"

"Golden torrents are gifted with the ability to create lighting by scraping their talons together. It's a most rare and powerful gift."

"You can say that again."

Tiki arched a brow. "It's a most rare and powerful gift."

I shook my head and smiled. "Thank you," I said. I realized how lucky I was to have, quite literally, run into Tiki. I wouldn't have survived in this world alone.

"For what?"

"For helping me. I won't know whether we're on time or not until I go in there, but if it wasn't for you, I wouldn't be here now."

"You're welcome, Chase Williams, but I know you meant to say *we* won't know until *we* go in there."

"No, Tiki, I didn't. You've come this far with me; I can't let you come in there. It's too dangerous and I've put enough people in danger lately."

"I must aid you in your quest, Chase Williams. I..."

"And you have helped me, Tiki, but I don't want to be the reason you die. It's best we go our separate ways now. You'd never seen a hunter before me; trust me when I say you don't want to meet the one inside."

Tiki laughed and it caught me off guard. "I think you forget your place. I am Tikimicharnikato of the Suriattas clan. I am a half demon and I have fought demons of the purest blood and still, I live to tell of it. I will not part ways with you now for fear of people who may harm me. I have come this far with you, and I will stay. It is part of my destiny to be here. It has been seen." He spoke with such confidence that I could no longer argue.

I hadn't thought of Tiki as a warrior. He was smaller than me, although he appeared to be in good shape. He didn't carry a weapon, and his feminine features and soft caramel skin looked like they'd be out of place in a battle. Still, his bright orange eyes regarded me with great certainty, in himself and his decision.

"Besides, I am a dimension jumper. Just because the portals to Earth are unlocked doesn't mean they are always open," he said. "Do you know how to open a portal?"

He was right; I hadn't thought about that. Nothing had mattered except saving Rayna.

"Alright, Tiki, you win." I said, and seeing the satisfaction on his face was worth taking the risk.

I pulled my sword from its sheath and handed it to him, but he shook his head. "No, I cannot take your weapon."

"But I have more."

"When the time comes, I will not need it." The look in his eyes was chilling. His sweetness was replaced with the fighting spirit of a warrior, and I could see the scars of battle in his eyes. It was impressive and unnerving all at once.

"If you say so."

We didn't pause to come up with a plan. Neither of us knew what to expect once we entered the cave. As far as we could tell, there was only one way in and one way out, so our course of action was simple: go in, save Rayna, and kill anybody who got in our way.

Chapter 30

We walked down the bridge of land towards the cave in silence, except for the sounds of wind and water. My stomach churned, my pulse sped, and sweat gathered on my palms as we neared the entrance. The golden torrent chirped in panic and flew from my shoulder as we crossed the threshold of the cave, winging back out over the lake and disappearing into the sky.

The winding cave was dimly lit with torches lining the walls, and I drew my sword in silence, taking care with each step. We followed the torches to a fork in the path and listened hard, but heard nothing. We came to a silent agreement to split up.

Fear for Tiki washed over me again. All I had was his word he could handle himself. I believed what I could see and trusted what I knew, but Tiki's battle skills didn't fit into either of those categories yet. After all the help he'd given me, I knew I could trust him as a person, but trusting him to handle what we were walking into was a different story. I wished I had Rayna at my back then.

The corridor was dark and the further I went, the tighter the knot in my stomach got. I was going to have to face my father to get Rayna back, and I wasn't prepared for that, physically, magically, or emotionally.

I'd learned my father wasn't everything I had thought he was, that the Circle was involved with creatures they were supposed to be fighting, and that not all demons were my enemies. It had been a hell of a month so far, everything happening so fast it seemed like one long day – or one really bad nightmare.

I froze in an instant when I heard screams, and a loud crash echoed around me. I knew then that even though the cave split into two paths, they met in one area. The route Tiki had taken must have been shorter and he was now in the middle of what should be my fight.

I ran forward, hoping it would be faster than turning around. We were outnumbered and our one advantage, surprise, was gone. I moved with all the grace and speed I could, waves of warm air moving over me as I went further into the volcano. I came around one last corner and slowed. The fighting had stopped. That couldn't be a good thing.

Tiki wouldn't have been able to handle my father and the Dark Brothers, so something was wrong. I tried to catch my breath and crept toward the opening. The corridor I'd followed opened into a huge space and the ceiling was higher than the light of the torches could reach. I peeked around to see Tiki; his face was bloody and the Dark Brothers were chaining his wrists to one of the stone walls.

Rayna's body was laid on a long stone altar in the middle of the cave. If it wasn't for the slight movement of her chest, I'd have thought she was dead. The wounds on her wrists and ankles had healed, but smears of dried blood clung to her pale skin. I was relieved the cuts hadn't been made with silver.

The Brothers moved away from Tiki and stood in front of my father, forming a triangle around the stone altar. On the floor, they'd painted a symbol centered around the altar, and it was identical to the one in Rayna's old house's basement.

Viscous puddles of dark bluish liquid decorated the cave floor and half a dozen large bodies lay motionless around them. I was in awe that Tiki had managed to do that kind of damage in such a short time. If I had gotten here sooner to help, we might have had a chance to win this. I watched the bodies begin to dwindle, glowing a soft orange before turning to ash.

My pulse spiked as I was grabbed from behind and pushed against the cave wall. They twisted my wrist until I was forced to drop my sword. The huge hands lifted me off my feet with ease and carried me into full view of anyone in the cavern.

I looked down at the slate gray flesh holding my arms. The color alone could have identified the enemy as a demon, but the two fingers and one thumb confirmed this assessment.

It carried me across the cave and I saw that the floor dropped off halfway across the room. The demon held me over the edge of the drop. The red and orange lava below me glowed and roiled. Black smoke rose and wrapped around me, making it hard to breathe.

"No." Riley's voice came from behind us.

The demon grunted and turned, carrying me towards the altar.

"I'm so happy you thought to join us, son. I was disappointed to think we'd left you behind. It will be much more pleasant to share this experience with you," Riley said.

"I'm here for Rayna, not to help you with your twisted plans."

Riley laughed, and the deep bellow echoed throughout the cave. He gestured and the demon released me.

I turned to see a creature not much taller than I. A single blue eye in the center of a large oval head stared at me. A huge furry eyebrow framed the eye and a bald scalp reflected the light from the torches. The cyclops' skin was rough looking, as though it was chiseled from stone. His lower jaw stuck out, his underbite was an orthodontist's worst nightmare, and two sharp gray teeth stuck out over his upper lip. His wide chest and stomach were bare, muscled and veiny. Thankfully, he was covered from the waist down with an oversized loincloth. I absorbed all of him and did the one thing I could think of in that moment: I hit him.

My fist slammed into his jaw and the cyclops grunted, but faced me unfazed. My hand stung and I instantly regretted hitting him. He didn't strike me back, only turned and stared at me with a furrowed brow and confused look.

My father's laugh echoed around me. "Please, Chase. This isn't home. These are pure blood demons, not the cross breeds you so easily associate yourself with."

"Says the man who's surrounded himself with them."

"Indeed I have, but the difference is I use them to further what's best for us. You go jumping through portals and traveling foreign lands on a quest not to save many, but only one, single, filthy half breed: one whose purpose since before her birth has been to unlock the doors to the worlds we've been denied."

"That half breed is my friend, and I won't let you hurt her."

"You've always been a poor judge of character, Chase. She is a necessary sacrifice for the greater good. Once this is over and you see what we can accomplish, you will understand."

"I can't let you use her."

"You don't have a choice."

"We always have choices." I took two quick steps and lunged at him. I soared over Rayna's limp body, pulled a single dagger from its sheath and held it steady, aimed at my father's throat. In that instant, my doubts were gone and I knew I could kill him.

I turned the blade as it neared his flesh, watching in slow motion as the tip pushed against his throat. The blade had nearly split his skin when magic engulfed me and I stopped moving.

I floated over Rayna's body and my father had his head tilted back. The blade had pierced his neck, but caused no worse an injury than you could get shaving. A tiny bubble of blood formed on the tip of my blade and Riley's eyes stared at me. For a moment, fear flickered through them.

The Dark Brothers had their arms extended. Their magic wrapped around me and kept me airborne. I sighed in disappointment.

Riley stepped back from my blade and brought a finger to his neck, touching the cut. The smile had been replaced with a furious expression.

"I'd hoped we'd move past this, son, but I see we're going to have to do this the hard way." He nodded to the Brothers, and at a flick of their wrists I was moving through the air. The only thing that stopped my body was the wall, and rock and dirt crumbled around me as I fell to the ground. By the time I could see, metal clasps attached to chains were being locked around my wrists.

Riley dabbed at his cut until he was satisfied the bleeding had stopped. He walked towards me and stopped just out of reach. He was an arrogant man, and the fact that he had left that space told me he was afraid of what I could do.

"What a waste of talent." He sighed. "You aren't willing to change your mind, are you?"

"Not a chance."

"I can respect that, defiance until the last. You are more my son than I knew."

Shock filled me. My father had never given me a compliment before. It was unfortunate that this was the context of his praise.

"Thanks?"

"It is for this reason alone I shall let you be the first to see the power I will hold. For you, like I, will not stop until we've won or died trying. I will give you that peace."

All the emotion I'd felt following his ill-timed compliment vanished, leaving me empty.

"Now, let's hope we're done with interruptions," Riley said. "Send more down the corridors; I want no more disturbances."

A cyclops grunted and two more moved down the corridor and out of sight.

Riley moved to the altar, bowed his head and extended his arms towards the Brothers. They mirrored his actions and reformed the triangle, chanting in the same strange language as back on Earth, but the ritual was different now.

They weren't trying to open a portal to another dimension, but trying to raise Ithreal, the god that created the Underworlds. The despair of failure tugged at me. Was this it? My thoughts were interrupted as the chanting stopped. The Dark Brothers brought their blades to Rayna's feet and Riley brought his blade to her neck.

"Riley, don't do this!" I shouted. I pulled at my chains, but they wouldn't budge. "Dad!" I yelled again. Fear and anger stirred inside me and there was one thing left I could do: call upon my powers.

I didn't wait for the magic to fill me up and course through my body. It didn't move through my hands and flow from my fingers. I ripped it from my soul and let it explode over me.

The metal around my wrists started to smoke. The steel softened and molten drops trickled slowly down my arm. I didn't let the pain stop me. I tugged on the chains, pulling at the softening metal, and as I pulled harder it started to stretch. I wrenched my wrists free of the hot metal and the broken clasps clanked as they hit the stone floor.

The sound alerted the demons and the cyclopes charged, but I didn't stop. I burst between the first two demons and moved towards the altar. I pushed the fire out my hands and released bright blue and silver flames in a stream, but I was too late.

All three men pulled their blades across Rayna's skin and blood flowed from her wounds and onto the stone floor.

The blood exploded as it hit the symbol and a barrier of magic came up around them all. Two of the cyclopes ran towards me, each with a fist raised. They made contact with either side of my face and my head snapped back as I dropped to the floor.

I didn't stop to feel the pain. I thrust the fire from my hands and let it rush over them. They screamed and I could see blisters bursting on their faces. I pulled the magic back and watched blue ooze drip from their bodies as they tried to repair themselves.

I rose to my feet and pulled the single dagger I had left from its sheath. I leapt and stuck it in the neck of one demon and let it slide through to the front. Blue blood sprayed in every direction and poured down his chest. The cyclops dropped to its knees and collapsed on the floor. I reached down and pulled the blade through the back of its neck and watched it explode.

The other came from behind me and picked me up. Gray-blue hands tossed me against the wall with ease. I felt the pain only faintly through the adrenaline. I dropped the dagger and pushed my magic through my hands. It hurt more, tearing it out rather than letting it flow naturally, but I didn't care.

Balls of flame rolled towards him and melted his skin. The cyclops screamed and I pushed harder, ignoring the burning along my own skin. Once the demonic screaming stopped, I let the magic recede and found the demon splayed on the floor in a pool of blue blood. His skin bubbled before his death rained down ashes over the sticky stone floor.

Two other cyclopes had approached and were on all fours whimpering, having been caught in the backlash of my flame. One had blue blood dripping from his face where the heat had burned away his flesh. The other's skin was smoking and hanging loose from his body.

I picked up the dagger and brought it down on the back of one's neck. I pushed down with all my weight, letting the blade snap his spine and slide with ease through the front of his throat. He screamed through gritted teeth and clawed at the ground until his head fell from his shoulders.

I could feel the heat of the last one's skin as I wrapped my arm around his head. I squeezed it tight against my body and twisted until I heard the unpleasant snap of his spine. I let his body fall to the ground in a lump of smoking flesh.

I went to Tiki and grabbed the clasps around his wrists. Strength I'd never known snapped the metal cuffs with ease. His orange eyes were wide and his jaw hung slack. More cyclopes flooded in from the tunnels and he decided they were his job. I picked up my blade and went running full tilt for the altar.

A circle of blue light sprung up around Rayna and reached up into the darkness. The Brothers stepped away from the circle and handed Riley a large chalice. He circled Rayna and filled it with blood from each of her wounds.

I froze as the light surrounding Rayna vanished and all the torches went out.

I couldn't see anything in the pitch black, but Riley chanted and I inched closer, following his voice. When I thought I was getting close, the torches burst into flame again.

When my eyes readjusted to the light, I could see my father with the chalice in hand, kneeling at Rayna's feet. I stepped over the threshold of the symbol and the Brothers and my father looked up in shock.

"Maybe my magic can't penetrate the circle, but I sure as hell can."

I leapt forward and the Brothers reached out to stop me, but they were too late. I let my shoulder smash into my father as he brought the cup to his lips. He jerked and fell to the ground, the chalice rolling from his hand, spilling Rayna's blood.

The cave rumbled as the blood hit the floor, and I wrapped my arms around Riley as we fell, but he turned and used my momentum against me. He thrust me to the side and I went head over heels, landing on my back. I jumped to my feet, but he was too fast. His hands hit my chest and sent me airborne again.

"Enough!" he screamed, a fire in his eyes I'd never seen before.

I hit the floor and rolled to my feet, preparing for another hit, but it didn't come.

"Hold him," he commanded as he picked up the chalice.

He returned to Rayna's wounds that now dripped instead of flowing freely. He put the chalice back against each wound, squeezing at her flesh to force her blood out.

I tried to move, but the Brothers had hung a wall of magic in front of me. I was stuck behind an invisible barrier as my father forced Rayna's blood from her wounds. He tilted the chalice back and brought it to his lips.

Blood dripped from his chin and I screamed involuntarily. Seeing my father's success and Rayna's body cold, pale, and drained filled me with a pain I couldn't describe. I pounded against the barrier with my fists, and when that was unsuccessful, I ripped the flames from inside me, but the wall absorbed my magic. It was no use.

The Brothers stared at me with expressionless faces. I wanted to burn the pale flesh from their skin and watch them cough up the water I'd flood their bodies with. Anger swirled inside me as images of their deaths filled my mind.

In a blur, the Brothers were lifted into the air and soared up into the darkness. They crashed to the ground and I looked at my hands. Had I done that?

Relief washed through me as the giant dark form of Marcus emerged from one corridor. He walked towards Riley, looking battle-ready.

"Ah, my dear brother," Riley said, stepping to the side to block Rayna's body. He wiped the blood from his lips and smiled, his perfect white teeth stained red.

"You stay where you are," Marcus said, extending an arm.

Riley tried to move and couldn't, but a strange smile crossed his face. "Your powers are no match for mine, brother. They weren't before, and they certainly aren't now." Riley waved his hand and a wall of flame shot up in front of him. The magic holding him collapsed as the flame vanished and Riley stepped forward. "This is but the first step in the journey, my brother, a taste of what Ithreal has to offer. Imagine what I'll be capable of when I have the full potential of his power inside me." Riley's voice was a darker version of the one I knew so well.

"Riley, you must stop this! You are delusional if you believe that you can control the power of a god," Marcus said.

"I have no delusions. Join me, brother. Stand by my side like you once did, and you too will reap the rewards of this power."

"I took an oath to protect the innocent and I plan to keep it."

"I took that same oath, but you have been protecting the enemy while I've made progress. With the power of Ithreal inside me, I will be able to control demons. Don't you see? What I'm doing will protect all of us."

"It's not that simple," Marcus said.

"Oh but it is, brother, you will see. She was but a small sacrifice for a better world," Riley said, stepping aside to reveal Rayna's body.

Marcus's back was to me, so I couldn't see his face, but I think that was for the best. His power surged and the barrier in front of me wavered. I could feel cracks in the magic.

Marcus raised his hands and Riley's body lifted off the ground for a moment. An angry scream escaped Marcus and a sinister smile warped Riley's lips. My father closed his eyes and started chanting again.

Despite Marcus's effort, Riley's body remained still, and I felt Marcus's magic break as a new power emerged. The Dark Brothers moved to either side of Marcus, but his magic claimed them. The warlocks were lifted off the ground again and sent crashing against the cave wall. The impact forced the barrier in front of me to crack again before collapsing.

A dark blue glow surrounded Riley as he chanted, arms extended. As I neared him, the blue light turned red, and then green, swirling around him in a whirlwind. Each time the color changed, I felt a new wave of magic pulsate through the cave.

The ground shook beneath my feet and bits of rock fell from the ceiling. It started to crack and Riley jerked and began spinning in the air. He screamed as he spun higher into the darkness. His body had disappeared into the shadows when a blast of multicolored light forced me to turn away.

When it faded, I could see my father's body gliding down from the darkness, a set of black shadowed wings extended behind him. He landed with ease, the wings vanishing like smoke. He knelt and whispered a few soft words before looking up at me.

His pale blue eyes were gone, filled with black, and power emanated from his body. An alien smile crossed his lips. "Come to me, my son," he said.

His magic wrapped around me and jerked me forward. I stopped only a few feet away from him and gripped my dagger so tightly I thought my knuckles might burst. Anger, sadness and fear all rushed through my veins.

Riley's smile didn't fade as I neared, and he opened his arms as though he might accept me into a fatherly embrace. I moved with a speed I'd never reached before and drove the dagger into his chest. He made no effort to stop me, and the blade slid into his flesh with ease. Riley watched the blade with the smile still on his lips, and when I'd pushed it in as far as I could, I twisted the blade. Red blood streaked with black leaked from the hole in his chest and laughter bubbled from his lips.

He grabbed my wrist and twisted until I dropped the dagger. His hands moved too quickly for my eyes to follow and before I could move, he'd grabbed the falling blade and pushed it into my stomach.

A gasp escaped my lips. He drove the blade in to the hilt and pulled it up from my stomach to my ribs. He released the blade and laughed, watching the fear in my eyes. His laughter stopped abruptly and he shoved me backwards.

I cried out in pain and felt my ribs strain as I hit the ground and slid across the stone floor. The back of my shirt tore and shards of rocks gave me friction burns, which paled in comparison to the agony in my belly.

Two perfect handprints were burned into the front of my shirt, revealing matching red and black blisters that seeped fluid as my body struggled to repair itself. The knife was still deep in my stomach and I couldn't help but hyperventilate in panic when I saw the wound.

I sucked in air and crawled, trying to get away from Riley and at the same time keep myself calm. I didn't want to go into shock. I was too scared to pull the knife out, and I was losing blood at a rapid rate. I struggled to my knees and ripped power from within me and threw it at Riley.

The silver and blue flames shot from my hand and engulfed him. My fire wrapped around his body, but he didn't make a sound. I put all my focus into the heat, picturing his flesh melting off his body.

Riley stepped through the flames, wrapped in the black shadowy wings that hovered inches from his body, shielding him. He waved them away and I saw the same spine-chilling smile still glued to his face. "So you've received your element, son. Congratulations. But do you know how to use it?"

Dark red flame swirled around him then flowed towards me. My own blue flames mixed with his, but my magic succumbed to his and I started to feel the scorching heat. I curled in a ball, waiting for the wave of flame to scald my skin, but it never came.

The heat disappeared and a cool mist of water showered me. I uncurled myself to see my mother standing above me, a wall of smoke billowing between her and my father.

My mother's warm hazel eyes held a new fierceness and the black that filled my father's eyes vanished at the sight of her. Now they were the gentle blue I'd known when I was young.

"Tessa..." he said.

His flames vanished and my mother pulled her magic back. She stared at my father with an intensity I'd never seen in her eyes: pure rage.

"You will not harm my son," she said.

"He has my element, Tessa. He is our son."

"He hasn't been our son for years." My mother spat the words at him. "And what have you done?" she said in a panicked

232

voice when she saw my wounds. She leaned down and put her hand against my stomach, and soon her small pale hand was covered in my blood. Her magic flowed into me stronger than ever, and the skin almost instantly closed in around the blade.

"Are you okay Chase?" she asked.

My skin still smoked as it knitted itself closed over Riley's handprints and I nodded. "I'll be...fine."

"This is going to hurt, honey." She wrapped her hands around the hilt of the blade and pulled it out before I could respond. I pressed my lips together to muffle my scream and waited for the blood to pour from the wound, but it never came. All I felt was cool, moving water, and in seconds the wound was gone.

"I was simply defending myself," Riley said.

"You are a horrible man, Riley Williams. You don't deserve to be called a hunter," Mom said.

"How dare you say such things!" Riley's voice grew darker and deeper with each word.

"I say them because they're true. You disowned your own son and family. You cast us away like we were nothing and here you are, trying to invoke Ithreal, the creator of the creatures you've sworn to kill? You think you can harness this power, but having had only a taste of it you've tried to kill your own son! You're an insult to the Circle, and a disgrace to the gods!"

Rumbling echoed through the cave and chunks of rock fell around us. Marcus and the Dark Brothers were doing battle behind us. The Brothers each had a sword and circled Marcus, who had so far been successful in deflecting their attacks.

"Tessa, Tessa, Tessa," Riley said. His pupils again grew larger until nothing but darkness filled them. "I disowned you because you disobeyed me. You challenged my ideals, therefore challenging what was best for the Circle. I've done what needed to be done and made the necessary sacrifices. If you and Chase join me, we can be a family again."

"You stopped being a father and a husband long before we were exiled."

Riley sighed. "I'd hoped we could get past this, Tessa. As I told Chase, this is all for the greater good. But if you are not with me, then you are against me."

"We are against you," Tessa replied.

"I love you Tessa, with all my heart. You and Chase will always be special to me, but I cannot stop doing what I know will better our kind."

"You don't have to stop. I will stop you."

My mother's magic exploded and a tidal wave made of fury engulfed my father. Water streamed from his nose and poured from his mouth. He fell to his knees, choking and drowning.

I felt just an ounce of sadness watching his face and eyes, black as they were, fill with panic and fear. He clawed at the stone floor and my mother didn't pause her torrent of power. He choked on wave after wave and his dark eyes shot to me. The look he gave me made my stomach clench and any sorrow I felt vanished.

A column of power came down from the darkness above us and surrounded him. I could almost see his magic moving under his skin before it exploded from his body.

"Go help Marcus," my mother said.

I started to argue, but the look on her face stopped me. I jumped to my feet and ran towards the Brothers, who were closing in on Marcus.

I leapt at Drake from behind and brought my dagger down into his shoulder, letting it sink deep. I pulled the blade down, cutting through skin and muscle from his shoulder to the middle of his back. He screamed and turned, and I lost my grip on the knife. The warlock pushed me back without a touch, then was on top of me, his hands squeezing the air from my throat. His solid black eyes poured hatred into me, while my blade was still stuck in his back.

I could feel my airway being crushed while his death magic filled me. Pain in my chest came to rest around my heart while he pulled at all my organs and my body grew weak. I clawed at his hands, but his power was too strong. I reached as far as I could around him and my fingers groped at the handle of the blade.

Unconsciousness tugged at me, but I gave one final effort and managed to grip the dagger and pull it downwards. The magic around me collapsed as he screamed and fell backwards, dislodging my blade. He writhed in pain and I took a few breaths as my body found its rhythm again. I picked up the knife, raised it above my head and smashed it through his chest, then lifted and brought it down again into his stomach. I was bringing it up a third time when Marcus's voice called to me.

"Chase!" I looked up to see that he had Darius on his knees and was pressing a blade against his throat. "You need to get Rayna and get out before this place falls apart," he said. I looked down at the demon who gasped for breath beneath me. "Now!" Marcus demanded.

I headed for the altar, leaving Drake in a puddle of his own blood. As I neared, I watched Riley regaining his footing. Fire leapt from his hand and hit my mother, knocking her to the ground. Her magic dissipated and Riley coughed the last of the water out of his lungs.

I changed direction and moved straight for him. My silvery spheres of flame soared through the air, connected with my father's chest and knocked him to the ground. The shadowy wings appeared and deflected the rest of my fiery assault.

My mother recovered and rose to her feet. Her magic surrounded her again and water shot from her hands towards Riley. He lay on his back, his own magic flaring around him. Black wings flapped once and in an instant he was on his feet. Streams of red flame shot from his hand and met my mother's onslaught. Their elements pushed against each other, their strength perfectly matched.

I kept moving towards him, hoping my mother's magic was enough to distract him. I felt the fire grow inside me, but as it was leaving my hands, a dark shadow shot out and struck me to the ground.

"You will not interfere, boy," Riley's dark voice growled. The wing swept along the floor and sent my body skidding across the concrete.

I collided with the altar and the cave shook. The floor cracked and black smoke wafted up from the web of crevices.

"Get Rayna and go," my mother commanded.

I crawled to my feet to see Riley's fire had not yet overwhelmed my mother, but he seemed to be gaining ground. Smoke oozed from the wings and merged with Riley's flames, turning them black. It crept over my mother's waterspout and turned it dark, murky gray.

"I can help you!" I protested.

"Rayna is more important. Now go!" I knew it wasn't up for discussion. I watched her a moment longer, the warm color of her hazel eyes being obscured by steam as Riley's magic crept closer. "Go..."

I didn't hesitate again and went to Rayna, limp on the stone table. Her wounds had stopped bleeding, but I didn't know if it was because her blood had clotted, or because she didn't have any left.

Her flesh was cold to the touch, and her skin's usual milky white color had been replaced by a cold grayish blue tone. I placed a finger on her neck and could feel her pulse beating weakly, but she wasn't breathing.

Tiki was standing over her, trying to keep her safe from falling rocks. I heard a loud crash as the cave floor cracked again beneath us and looked back to the others.

Darius had broken free of Marcus's hold, but Marcus was still swinging his sword and forcing him back to the edge of the cave. Drake lay on the ground, writhing with what little bit of life remained, the puddle of blood around him expanding. Mom still had her arms out and the streams of water that spurted from her hands met Riley's fire.

"Go!" she screamed a final time as the black flame nearly reached her fingertips. I didn't argue and slipped Rayna into my arms.

The cavern shook again and this time the falling rocks were boulders. Dark smoke billowed from the hole in the cave floor and the cracks in the stone walls. An orange glow grew brighter as lava crept up and started to shine through the floor.

Sweat dripped from my face as I ran towards the corridor. The ground split beneath us and I took a step back to keep my balance. The floor collapsed in front of me and disappeared into a pit of molten rock beneath. Panic raced through me; the surface we stood on was going to be swallowed.

I ran towards the second tunnel with all the speed I could muster. I dodged the boulders as they crashed around us and held Rayna closer, trying to shield her, and Tiki followed close behind. We saw Darius regaining ground and pushing Marcus back with blasts of dark magic. I prayed for the other corridor not to collapse as we ran through a shower of dust and rocks. I had to sidestep several puddles of lava. I let my magic push me harder and faster than I knew I should be able to go, and relief washed over me at the sight of the cave opening.

Cold, fresh air washed over my face and tasted sweet as I drew it into lungs. The lake came into sight and then the shore, giving me hope. The water was rougher than before, and it rippled with small waves clapping together. The suns had vanished from the green sky that was now almost black with threatening clouds that hung above the volcano. Earth exploded as lightning struck the ground. It wasn't just the cave shaking – it was the whole island.

We ran down the aisle of land into the open plain and I collapsed to the shaking ground. Thick steam and periodic explosions of ash pumped from the top of the volcano and more dirt exploded around us as lightning struck.

I set Rayna on the ground and laid my hands on her, drawing on my magic as I had done in the condo. Thoughts of healing rivers that ran through my imagination, and I closed her wounds in my mind, letting the water wash away her scars. I could feel my power filling her body and I had hope, but she still wasn't breathing. I focused my magic until her wounds began to close, but her skin was icy to the touch.

"Don't you die on me," I whispered. The thought of her not being with me made my heart ache and gave me an extra rush of adrenaline. I used that energy, shaking with emotion.

Tiki tried to place a hand on my shoulder, but the moment he touched me he gasped and pulled it back, clutching it in his other hand as though I'd burned him.

"Come on!" I yelled, but it was no use.

I pulled my hands away from Rayna as tears found their way out of my eyes. I couldn't give her lungs the breath of life they needed. Tears fell from my cheeks and rolled over her body.

I watched the world around me crumble: the violent volcano, the angry rapids, and the thundering clouds that shot bursts of light into the earth. Tiki was cut, bruised, and on the edge of exhaustion. I pictured my mother and the way the light in her eyes had faded as my father's dark magic crept over her. I looked at Rayna. Even in the state she was in, I could see her beauty, remember her laugh, and wish I'd never said an angry word to her.

I screamed at the stormy sky and cursed the gods. I reached towards the lake and released my magic. The lake responded with a power of its own and pushed back. Thunder rumbled and a flash of lightning flickered down from the clouds and struck my chest. Everything slowed and the surge of electricity crackled through my veins.

I pulled all the power I could from the lake and merged it with the energy of the lighting. I dropped my hands to rest on Rayna and let the blend fill her. I didn't know what I was doing or how I was doing it, but I willed her to breathe.

Drops of violet rain began to fall on us, washing the blood and dirt from our skin. Streaks of black rolled down my chest where the lightning had charred me. Power seared through my body, changing my senses and bringing everything to life in a new way.

I could hear blades of grass rustling against one another. The wind carried a sweeter taste than before, and I could feel the heat of the lava brewing inside the volcano. The waves crashed against the shore and the moisture that hung on the air danced along my skin with an electric current.

A final tear slid down my face and onto Rayna's body before the power was gone and I collapsed over top of her.

There seemed to be an eternity between that moment and the next, but when the strange sensation ended, I felt Rayna's chest rise. I pulled myself off of her to watch her ribcage rise and fall again, and I put two fingers to her neck to find a strengthening pulse. Her skin's color slowly returned to the milky white I remembered, and it seemed to be getting warmer.

I felt the weight of a mountain leave my shoulders as her breathing became consistent. But the ground shook again and rocks rolled down the side of the volcano, splashing into the already violent water. The weight returned when I thought of my mother and Marcus still in danger.

"I need to go back," I said.

"You cannot. They told us to get out while we could," Tiki said.

I ignored him and ran back towards the land bridge, but Tiki moved with speed I hadn't seen him use and stood in my way.

"I can't leave them in there!" I shouted. I tried to push past him, but Tiki wouldn't budge.

"Chase Williams, do not let their sacrifice be in vain," he said and I stopped, regarding him with loathing. I knew he was right, but I didn't want to accept that Mom and Marcus were forfeiting their lives for us.

The top of the volcano began to cave in. The mouth of the cave was beginning to shatter and I watched uneasily as the mountain consumed itself. Joy filled me when I saw a figure appear in the cave opening.

Dust and smoke billowed around them and I couldn't see who it was, but for that one moment I was happy to see anything promising. I ran towards the figure, but when I got closer I collapsed to my knees.

Marcus's skin was blacker than midnight, covered in ash. Patches of raw skin were exposed, and fresh burns coated his arms and tatters of his shirt stuck to him. I could see vicious old burn scars on his chest and back, and for the first time I saw a strong emotion on his face: sorrow.

He carried a limp figure in his arms, and I felt my stomach twist as they came closer. My world started to spin, Marcus moving in slow motion towards me.

A loud crash shook the ground as the cave mouth collapsed behind him, releasing dust and ash. I tried to stand, but I couldn't get off my knees. I felt like I was steel and the earth was a magnet, unrelenting in its hold on me. Tears ran down my face like waterfalls and the spinning stopped – there was no sound, no feeling, in that moment. I didn't hear myself screaming and I didn't feel Tiki trying to wrap his arms around me and calm me down. Marcus was in front of me. He knelt slowly and laid my mother on the ground in front of me.

The world rushed back as I put my hands over her still smoking body. Spots of her flesh were burnt black while others were bright red. I pushed my water magic into her as she had done so many times for me. Her skin was scalding to the touch and I fought not to pull away.

"It's no use, Chase, she's gone," Marcus said.

It was a good thing looks couldn't kill, or he would have been on the ground too. "No, I can bring her back," I insisted.

No matter how hard I pushed my magic, it was no use. I couldn't get the faintest of breaths or the softest of heartbeats.

"Come on!" I screamed. I tried to pull energy from the elements around us. "I know I can do this! I did it for Rayna," I yelled at no one and everyone. I tried until Mom's skin was icy and colorless. My mother was dead, and my own father had killed her.

I stared at her body until I had no more tears left. My stomach felt hollow and guilt washed over me. I was supposed to protect her. I was the reason she died.

I wiped the remaining droplets from my face and finally rose to my feet. I turned to Marcus and let him see all the anger and hate in my eyes.

"Where is he?"

Marcus shook his head, his face covered in ashes, blood, and grief. "He was still inside, son."

"I'm not your son." I could see my anger hurt him, but in that moment I didn't care. "Are you sure they didn't get out?"

Marcus watched me for a moment. "Drake was unconscious when I left, and Darius was near death. But they are powerful warlocks, so I cannot be sure."

"And Riley?"

"I managed to distract him long enough to get your mother and myself out. I nearly met the same fate as she."

"Well there's only one way in and one way out, right? He has to be inside." I was going back in to make sure he died tonight.

Marcus's hands pulled at me but I brushed them away. "I have to do this," I demanded.

The volcano exploded and rocks and lava shot out of its mouth, raining down into the lake. Fountains of purple water shot into the air and I had to jump back. Waves of red and orange lava seeped from the top of the crumbled volcano and Marcus's hands succeeded in holding me back.

"I can't let you go, Chase," he said.

I tried to convince myself that the man who killed my mother was dead, caught by the lava that filled the volcano. But I couldn't believe it until I saw his body for myself. Yet if he had still been in there, his body would be gone, lost in the river of fire, and I would never know for certain.

I hadn't ever thought of a life without my mother, the woman who stood by me through everything. We were exiled together; we survived the Underworld's attempts on our lives together. She couldn't be gone.

I heard chirping as the golden torrent soared down through the now dark sky. Smoke hung in the air above us while a rain of ash sprinkled the ground. The torrent glided towards me and found my shoulder. It rubbed its head against my cheek and somehow my eyes found more tears to let fall.

Gazing at my mother's body, I felt my sadness replaced with anger, which turned into regret, and then I felt nothing. All emotions had dissipated and I was shutting myself away from the truth.

Marcus pulled me against his chest and wrapped his arms around me. I realized I was shaking, and I couldn't help but put my arms around him too.

"What now?" I said, through gasps and sobs.

"We go home," he said in a voice full of sadness.

"I don't have a home. She was my home."

"You will always have a home with us," Marcus replied.

I wanted to push away from his embrace but I couldn't find the strength. My whole life had been destroyed in hours. I let him hold me because I wasn't sure I could stand on my own.

I stayed there while the volcano erupted again, more violently than before. When I was sure I could stand without help, I pulled away and turned to Tiki.

"Can you get us home?" I asked, my voice just above a whisper.

"If the door is unlocked, I can go through it."

"I think it's safe to say it's open."

I slipped my arms under my mother's body and picked her up. I looked down at her limp form and cradled her in my arms, feeling like somebody had pulled my insides out. I leaned over and kissed her cold forehead.

Rayna twitched and my eyes went to her. Her body jerked up and her bright green cat eyes opened, then morphed into a strange mixture of gold and blue. "Riley and the Brothers aren't dead," she said.

"What?" I said, stumbling as her words nearly brought me to my knees again. My pulse raced in my throat and my stomach turned.

Marcus knelt beside her and put a hand on her shoulder. "Rayna?"

Rayna shook her head, almost robotically. "Riley and the Brothers live. They've completed the first step of the invocation and have moved on from this world."

"Where are they?" I asked. Rayna turned her strange eyes on me but stayed silent. "Rayna, where?" I yelled.

The blue and gold that filled her eyes dissipated and her eyelids fell. Her body went limp and Marcus caught her as she collapsed.

"What the hell was that?" I said.

"I believe that was a type of vision."

"Since when does Rayna get visions?"

"She doesn't," Marcus said.

Marcus took Rayna up in his arms. She seemed to be breathing evenly and her wounds were gone, but her body was limp and she was unconscious. The volcano continued to explode, and Marcus turned to me. "We need to leave."

Tiki stepped forward. "We must all be touching. If anyone breaks contact, there is no way of knowing where they will end up."

Marcus and I linked arms and Tiki gripped our shoulders.

"Is there any way to know where we'll end up?" I asked.

"No guarantee, but if there was a portal opened recently on Earth, I should be able to draw on its energy and reopen it. It's easier than opening a new portal. Are you ready?"

I adjusted my hold on my mother's body, and Marcus and I nodded.

"Okay, I will count down from five," Tiki said.

"Five." The volcano pumped a darker smoke now. Waves of lava poured over the lip of its mouth and rolled down the sides in a heavy flow of liquid fire.

"Four." Ashes shot from the top of the volcano and filled the black sky, trickling down over us in a gray snowfall.

"Three." The lava reached the bottom of the mountain and slid into the lake. The purple water began to steam.

"Two." The lake turned from dark to light purple and bubbles formed on the surface as the water boiled.

"One." The light purple faded, overridden by orange and red. The volcano rumbled and streams of liquid fire rained from above as a dark circle opened beneath our feet. The ground gave way and swallowed us. We disappeared into the portal and were gone.

Epilogue

When we came through the portal, we were in Rayna's old basement again. We took our time climbing the stairs, and when we got outside we piled into the Jeep. I could see the amazement on Tiki's face at everything around him, but he refrained from asking any questions.

It was several days before Rayna woke up. Her wounds were healed and she thanked the gods that the warlocks hadn't used silver. She was disoriented at first, and when she asked about Tessa I had to leave the room. I was thankful that Rayna was alive, but I couldn't be happy about anything yet. I knew I had to be strong, for everybody, but all I wanted was to be alone.

Tiki had decided to stay with us. He found our world fascinating, and spent most of his time in the library. Most of us left him alone to read and learn about this strange new world, except for Willy. He had been coming by daily, if he'd even left the night before.

Willy had taken a liking to Tiki, and Tiki seemed to do the same, or he was just too polite to say anything. Willy helped Tiki understand what it was like to be a half demon on Earth.

I'd learned that after I went through the portal, Marcus had arrived and requested Willy's help, and so Willy called Grams. She was strong enough to reopen the portal. Vincent had refused to come help, even for Rayna. He claimed the sunlight in the other world would kill him. Vincent's actions didn't surprise me, but fact that Grams was willing to help did. We had her to thank for being alive – at least most of us.

The unusual little bird that had managed to make its way home with us had been given the name Rai, courtesy of Tiki, for her ability to create lightning. She almost never left my shoulder, which was a combination of cute and annoying.

I spent most of the few weeks following our return wondering about all the different ways everything could have turned out had I done things differently. But I knew I could wonder all I wanted and it still wouldn't bring my mother back.

We didn't see a trace of Riley or the Dark Brothers. We had yet to confirm whether they had gotten out of the cave alive by some means. Part of me hoped Rayna's vision was right, that my father was alive, so I could have the satisfaction of killing him myself. The other part hoped she had been wrong and this fight was over for good.

I knew if Riley was alive, I would get my revenge. I knew it wasn't what my mother would want, but my ego told me I had to do it: for Rayna, Mom, and even Marcus, who I knew was hurting. He hid the pain well, but I knew him well enough now to see beyond the mask. He and Tessa had a deeper relationship than they had let on, and I knew I wasn't the only one feeling the loss.

With the portals open, the war that had ended thousands of years ago should've been starting again. Our world should've been overrun with pure blood demons, but it wasn't. That was unnerving in and of itself, and gave me an eerie feeling.

Marcus contacted the other exiled and rogue hunters, in part to share the bad news, and in part to ask for help. If pure blood demons started walking the streets, we were going to need it.

Today is my birthday and I can't bear to leave my room. Marcus and Rayna both wished me a happy birthday, but understood that I'm not in the mood to celebrate. Willy brought a small package up to my room that had been delivered to the condo, a small brown box that I opened in private. Inside was a pair of daggers made of pure silver, right down to the handles. Each was engraved with an eagle, accented in yellow gold with red gems for the eyes. The weapons were beautiful, sharp, with perfect weight and balance.

With them came a small white envelope, containing a single piece of paper. I unfolded it and my heart stopped.

Chase,

Happy Birthday! I know our life has been turned upside down lately, but I want you to know, no matter what you do to get out of it, I'm still going to make you celebrate your big day. Eighteen years ago you came into this world and into my life. I've loved you more every day since, and I want you know that.

You have a tough time understanding this, but our exile from the Circle was the best thing for us. It gives us a chance to live real lives that don't involve killing every single day. Things are tough now, between paying the bills and surviving the Underworld's attacks, but I want you to enjoy your youth. It won't last forever. Make friends, go to parties, do things normal guys do. One day, you might even wake up and realize all the other troubles are behind you.

You're skeptical about everything that is happening right now and I understand that, but you must try to be open to Marcus and Rayna. They are good people who have welcomed us into their lives and we need to be thankful for them. Who knows, after a while you may even realize that you and Rayna have some things in common.

Lastly, I want you to do something for me. I want you to push your doubts away and enjoy this day. It's true you had one hell of a birthday three years ago, but that doesn't mean they all have to remind you of that. They don't have to be full of sadness and anger. They can be full of happiness and gratitude to be alive and in good company. Do this for me, just for today.

I hope you have an amazing birthday and never forget how much I love you. Congrats on the big 18! I love you and I'm proud to have you as my son. And don't forget, no matter what happens, I will always be there for you. You and me, always.

Love,
Mom

Tears welled up in my eyes and streamed down my face. When I had started reading the letter, my sorrow came from missing her, but by the time I'd finished, I was shaking, and the sadness had been replaced by rage at Riley. Some of the ink had been smeared by tears, and I carefully wiped them away, not wanting to ruin the last thing my mother would ever give me.

She was the one person who believed in me. When the whole world seemed to be against us, she kept us strong. If Riley is alive, he'll pay for the pain he caused and for the life he took. Something in my gut tells me he's out there somewhere, and that's why we haven't seen the pure blood demons yet. He's holding them off for some reason, and I'll find out why.

I will defend this family: Marcus, Rayna, Willy, Tiki and any others who need us, whether they be hunters, demons, or the oblivious mundane humans. I was chosen to carry the mark of the gods. I will stand up and be what the spirit named me: their protector.

######

About The Author

Matthew is a proud father, husband, and pet owner. Exiled is his debut novel and the first in the Protector Series. He's an avid coffee drinker, music lover, movie buff, and cereal enthusiast, who lives in Red Deer, Alberta with his wife, and two daughters.

~~~~~~

Connect with Matthew

Stay up to date on future books, writing, and life:

Website: http://www.matthew-merrick.blogspot.com

Turn the page for a sample of SHIFT, Book 2 in The Protector series by M.R. Merrick

Chapter 1

My eyes tore open to the sound of screaming. The drywall rattled and Rayna's voice raged through the wall. My pulse jumped as panic set in and I leapt from my bed moving straight for the door.

I ran through the archway, pants tangling on my legs as I tried to pull them up. Marcus, Willy, and Tiki were halfway down the hall, their faces owned by fear.

Marcus reached the door before me, turned the silver handle, and pushed through. The door creaked and the smell of blood, sweat, and something else seeped from the darkness. Marcus flicked on the light and I saw what I already feared.

Rayna was on her hands and knees. Sweat ran down her face in streams, and her eyes moved to us. A deep growl that belonged to something far more ferocious snarled from her lips.

Marcus and I moved to either side of her, leaving Willy and Tiki to guard the door. This was her beast's third attempt at a shift this week. I wasn't chasing a half-naked Rayna down the street. Not again.

The hardwood floor was cold and stuck to my bare feet, and bright green cat eyes followed as I sidestepped around her. Another growl rumbled deep in her throat. A warning.

Rayna bent at the elbows and lowered herself to the ground. Her back end lifted in the air and her body moved with unnatural grace, her eyes consuming my every move. The muscles in her arms flexed as she prepared to pounce. She leaned forward, but her body bucked and twisted at an awkward angle. She collapsed to the ground and Rayna's voice cried out, but even that didn't override the sound of bones crunching.

Alien muscles moved beneath her skin as her body distorted from one angle to another. Something was pushing from the inside. A monster trying to claw its way out. Clear fluid burst as her skin split, and the hint of something primal spilled out over her arms. Her green feline gaze flashed back to me, but it wasn't the beast looking through; it was Rayna. Her eyes pleaded with me to make it stop, but we both knew I couldn't.

"Calm yourself, Rayna. You need to take control of the shift," Marcus said. His massive midnight torso was bare, revealing a smooth and muscled chest that disappeared into baggy, gray sweats. The light reflected off his shaven head, and a small patch of neatly trimmed hair grew under his lower lip. His dark brown eyes were calm but I could see the worry behind them.

Rayna whimpered and her eyes rolled back in her head, revealing nothing but thick bloodshot veins. More blood and fluid burst from her stomach, flying through the air and raining over us. Black fur pushed through the slits in her arms and stomach, and stood on edge. Veins pushed against her skin, changing from blue to black. Her vibrant, pale flesh glistened with sweat as thick, black veins creased around her eyes and spread across her face.

Rayna gasped as her fingers snapped and shifted. Her nails bled as claws tried to break through her human shell. Bones ground against one another until she screamed, and long, black talons burst through her fingertips. The beast reclaimed her eyes. I knew Rayna well enough to know when it was her looking at me. Right now, it wasn't.

Her skin stretched and rippled. The demon inside was pushing her body into another impossible position and Rayna screamed. She started panting heavily and her teeth shattered as fangs tore through her gums.

"Fight it, Rayna. You can do this," Marcus said.

Her limbs snapped and twisted, the sound alone making me wince with anticipated pain. Tears fell from Rayna's eyes as she fought the beast. She stared up at me as she tried to reclaim her body, but the monster inside was too strong.

I wanted to speak. I wanted to encourage her, but I couldn't find the words. I stepped forward and reached towards her, but with unparalleled speed, black claws tore across my arm and blood spurted from the wound. I screamed through gritted teeth and pulled my arm back, grasping it with my free hand and trying to stop the gush of blood.

Rayna stretched her back and rolled onto all fours. Her eyes flickered and the beast stared at me, pulling back its lips to reveal long fangs that took over both the top and bottom jaw. She paced from side to side and Rayna's bra strap hung on for dear life. Black pajama pants split down the sides as new muscles bulged from her legs. Dark fur and fierce claws owned her still human shaped feet, and tapped along the floor as she moved. Rayna arched her back and black fur exploded from her spine. Blood and fluid soared across the room, and made a splat as it hit Tiki, Willy, and the walls around them.

Rayna's near human hands crept onto the bed. Long, black claws ripped into the blankets as she pulled herself up. With each pull forward, feathers and cotton spilled into the air, talons tearing into the bedding with ease.

I tried to step back, but I hit the wall, unable to move as the beast closed in.

"Be calm, Chase. The beast can smell your fear. It will only make it more aggressive," Marcus said.

"Really? Thanks for the update," I said sarcastically. Blood rolled off my wrist in thick streams and a burning sensation covered my arm. I closed my eyes, reached inside, and pulled the magic up from that place in my soul.

The elemental power rose to the surface in a gentle wash. I imagined a cool rain falling over me, drops of water that would wash away the pain rushing through my arm. I pictured the bleeding coming to a stop and new skin pulling itself over the wounds.

I used that same power to help push away my fear. The water battled the storm of emotions roaring through me and brought with it the calm. Fear faded beneath the imagery of cold drops against my skin, and my muscles relaxed. My breathing steadied and my eyelids lifted, only to gaze into the green cat eyes before me. Rayna was on the edge of the bed and only an arm's length away.

The skin of my arm pulled itself shut and the final drop of blood hit the floor. My water element closed the wounds, but I didn't have enough control to pull it back and it spilled out into the room.

"Chase..." Marcus started, but it was too late.

My element emanated off of me, pushing against the monster like an invisible hand. The magic rolled over Rayna's skin and moved through the beast's fur, reaching down into her soul.

Rayna regained her composure as the magic coaxed the monster back, allowing her to regain control of her body. The beast in her eyes faded and I had a moment's hope, but in a jerk of awkward movements, her body shuddered and she was gone.

Bones crunched and Rayna's arms snapped, reversing which way they bent. She tumbled off the bed and clawed at the floor near my feet. Muscles flexed and strained, scarring the hardwood. Splinters slid underneath her nails, causing her fingers to bleed.

"Please..." Rayna gasped. She slurred her words as fangs jutted from red gums raw with pain. She winced in agony and her eyes pleaded, letting a single tear trickle down her cheek.

"How do we stop it, Marcus?"

Marcus shook his head. "We can't. *She* has to fight it."

"We have to do something. It's killing her."

"This is the only way I know..."

I looked at Tiki and worry owned his face. White, triangular pupils expanded over solid, orange eyes, and he flinched at the sound of Rayna's bones grinding together. His frame filled the doorway, muscles flexing beneath the caramel flesh of his shirtless body. Messy, black hair hung in his eyes and he continually brushed it away.

Willy's face was pale for an instant, quickly changing to match the bright red paint on Rayna's walls. His chameleon skin flickered back and forth between colors as panic filled his eyes. Blood and clear fluid dripped from his face, but he didn't seem to notice. He was frozen in fear, watching his friend's body break and change before him. This was the first shift Willy had been here for. I didn't think he was quite ready for it.

Frustration won me over and I dropped to the floor, hoping the claws didn't strike me again. I laid my hands over Rayna's body and called my magic back.

"Chase, don't. You could do more damage than good," Marcus said.

I shot dark blue eyes to Marcus. "You know as well as I do, nothing I can do is worse than this, so back off!" I didn't expect for it to come across so harsh, but I didn't have time to worry about his feelings. I wasn't about to lose someone else.

The invisible hand inside me wrapped around the cool rush of my element and tugged it back to the surface. I pulled the wash of water from my soul and let it fill my body. The magic shuddered and the liquid moved under my skin as power prickled through me, making the hairs on the back of my neck stand on end.

"Chase, don't," Marcus said.

"I'm trying!" I yelled, quickly reeling my anger back and letting the element calm me. "It's a lot more than any of us have done for her so far."

Water was a healing and calming element, but it could be as deadly as any other. Marcus was right to be worried; my control was weak at best, but I couldn't watch this. Not again.

Magic ran up my body, into my shoulders, and down my arms in a wave of power. My fingertips tingled as it left me and flowed into Rayna's body.

I focused on calming Rayna. I didn't want to hurt her, and I wasn't sure healing the wounds would help. I focused my energy and hoped if I put enough power into sedating the beast, Rayna could regain control.

The moment my magic filled her, Rayna's earth element pushed back against me, trying to intertwine with mine. It was Rayna's way of reaching out to me.

Our elements met and wrapped themselves in each other, coursing from her body to mine in a circuit of power. Our bodies were one in that moment, our elements just an extension of ourselves. My magic moved through her, dancing beneath her skin as it fed off her power.

I imagined a small creek moving over stones, wearing the rough edges down until they were smooth. That gentle flow of water would push the beast back and carry Rayna to shore.

The beast retreated as the magic splashed through. Feeling the monster's resistance, I forced it back, letting the energy thrust it into a corner until it surrendered. I waited until I was sure it was gone before I turned my focus to her injuries.

I pictured Rayna's bones reforming, the claws and fangs receding, and the cool trickle of water filling her senses to mask the pain.

Rayna gasped as the cold element rushed into her body. She tensed at first, unnatural muscles flexing beneath her flesh, before she collapsed in a wave of exhaustion. She hit the floor and I pushed harder. I had kept the beast back for the moment, but now I needed to make sure it stayed away, at least for tonight.

Her breathing slowed and Rayna's eyes glossed over. Her bones cracked and shifted back into place, and soft cries whispered through her lips. Long talons slid back beneath her pale skin, and the fangs withdrew into her gums. The tears that filled her eyes leaked down the sides of her face. They merged with the blood that covered her skin and caused a pink liquid to disappear into her hair. The red highlights in her black hair stuck to her face, and the moonlight that shone through the windows reflected off her body, revealing a layer of sweat.

It took all I had to pull the magic back. It receded slowly and I tucked it away inside of me. Rayna stared up from the torn hardwood floor. Her tearing eyes showed the pain she'd been in. I brought my hand to her forehead and ran it down her cheek, trying to reassure her she was safe. She released a breath and her eyes fluttered closed.

Her skin was cool to the touch, which was good. When her body tried to shift, her temperature spiked to incredible heights. Heights the human body shouldn't have been able to withstand, but Rayna wasn't human. She was a demon and a hunter. A witch, yet...something more. The temperature drop meant she'd beat the change this time, but I was more concerned about next time.

I pulled my hand away and her eyes didn't open. Her chest rose and fell with deep breaths, her body giving into its demand for rest. I slipped one arm under her neck and the other under her legs, scooping her into my arms. Her body fell limp as I lifted her from the damaged floor, blood and sweat still dripping from her skin.

I moved past the others. Marcus looked sad. Rayna was practically his daughter and watching her go through this was painful for all of us, but I think it struck another chord with him.

I walked to the only spare bedroom we had left. Willy and Tiki were always here now and we were quickly running out of rooms. I laid Rayna in the bed as gently as I could and pulled the covers up over her. Her clothes were in tattered shreds and she was covered in blood and goo, but she finally looked at peace.

Nobody had gotten much sleep the last three nights, but it had been the hardest on Rayna. None of us knew much about shifters, except how to kill them. After watching what she was going though, I think we'd all gathered a new respect and a desire to learn more.

I closed the door and saw the last glimpse of Tiki before he slipped into his room. For reasons I didn't understand, Tiki had sworn an oath to me. He guided me through Drakar, and without him, I would never have been able to save Rayna. I might not have understood his loyalty, but I was grateful for it.

Willy had disappeared. For a demon, he didn't have much of a stomach for stuff like this, but then again, Willy wasn't like most demons.

Marcus stood in the hallway, his dark brown eyes unmoving, and as usual I couldn't read his expression.

My eyes fell to the floor. "Look, I'm sorry I—"

Marcus' hand came up. "What you did in there was quick thinking."

I looked up in surprise.

"This was the worst change she's ever gone through."
Marcus ran a large hand over his cleanly shaven head. "She's
never shifted that far before. You might've just saved her life."

I looked back to the floor and guilt tugged at me. I shouldn't
have spoken to him like I did, but I'd lost my temper. Again. That
was something that happened more often lately.

"Are you sure she can't shift? It looked like she was going all
the way this time."

"I was...I'm not so sure anymore. For now, as always, we're
treating this like she's a hunter and the shift will kill her. Whether
or not that's the case, I don't know, but we don't have the liberty
of experimenting."

"I'm not suggesting we risk her life and see what happens.
I'm saying maybe we should look into it. No hunter could've made
it that far into the change. They'd be dead. Something's different
here."

Marcus sighed. "I know...I'll look into it." He turned and
walked down the hall. His massive black form disappeared into
the shadows and the white door closed, leaving the latch to click
into place.

The cold hardwood felt strange against my feet as silence
engulfed the condo. The moon outside shone faintly and shadows
wrapped themselves around me. I went to my bedroom and
flicked on the lamp.

This room was nicer than my previous one. The wood floors
glistened and the walls were a warm mocha color. The dark
brown dresser was clean, smooth wood. Not scarred and faded
like my old one. My bed was a mattress, on a box spring, on a
frame. Not a weathered sponge on a stained carpet. I even had a
night table with a lamp. Compared to my old room, I might as well
be at the Hilton.

I fell on the bed and stared up at the perfect ceiling. It was
missing the cracks and nicotine stains of the apartment, and I still
hadn't gotten used to it.

The silence followed and I felt its presence linger against me.
It was nights like these that I missed my neighbors. They swore,
they screamed, and they smashed things against the walls, but

after three years it had become my lullaby. I'd give anything to have that apartment back, and the life that belonged there. The life I had with Mom.

I opened up the wooden case that sat on my nightstand and stared at the two daggers inside. Beneath the blades lay the folded up note that came with them, and just looking at the polished silver made me sad. It was the last gift and the last note my mother would ever give me.

Chills shuddered through me at the thought of her and goose bumps rode up my body. Rai fluttered in through the door and found her way to my shoulder. She puffed out her chest and white feathers ruffled themselves. The gold that lined her spine and tail sparkled under the lamp, and lightning crackled in her eyes. Rai stretched and her white feathers were soft as she moved both pairs of wings against my face.

"Hey girl," I said.

Rai tweeted softly in my ear, nipping at it before flying to the open cage on the dresser.

I lay back down, and as my eyelids fell, I could see Mom's face. There she was, smiling at me. Warm hazel eyes swallowed me and instantly I felt better. Soft brown hair fluttered in front of her face, bending to the will of the wind that moved around us, and still she smiled.

It warmed me from the inside out and tears welled beneath my eyelids, but I didn't dare open them. I wouldn't lose this image just to release the tears that fought to be free. But as quickly as it came, Mom's expression changed, and the warmth was stolen from me.

The gentle smile that held me so often disappeared, and fear took over. Her skin turned a sickly green, and a bright orange light reflected off her eyes before flames engulfed her.

My eyes shot open and I jerked myself upwards. The tears I desperately fought to keep back broke free and fell over my face. Her voice rang in my ears, screaming my name and begging for me not to leave her.

I shook my head to escape the sound and it shattered around me.

Silence rushed back into the room and I took a deep breath, trying to clear my head. That image sent waves of panic and fear through my body, jolting awake any part of me that wanted to sleep. I wasn't going back to bed. Not tonight.

Made in the USA
San Bernardino, CA
11 February 2013